Out of Limbo

Mary Florence

Pen Press

First published in Great Britain by Pen Press

All paper used in the printing of this book has been made from wood grown in managed, sustainable forests.

ISBN13: 978-1-78003-699-1

Printed and bound in the UK
Pen Press is an imprint of
Indepenpress Publishing Limited
25 Eastern Place
Brighton
BN2 1GJ

A catalogue record of this book is available from
the British Library

Cover design by Jacqueline Abromeit

Out of Limbo

Chapter One

The sound of the heavy bombers droned overhead; a noise like thunder could be heard every time their bombs exploded. The ground shook and the smell of burning wood drifted into the Anderson shelter where the Brownlows sat huddled together on one side of the six foot square shelter, while the two lodgers (billeted on them after their son had been called up for the navy) sat on the bunk opposite. A nightlight burns in a saucer placed on top of a small cupboard where their emergency-stores are kept. They had been in the shelter for some hours and the tension increased as the raid intensified. Mr Brownlow sat nearest to the door with Nelly, his wife, next to him. He looked up at the roof many times as if he could see through the metal ceiling and the two feet of earth on top. As he sat he rubbed his jaw with his thumb, a sure sign he was worried, their daughter Alice had propped herself up with pillows and was trying to sleep.

"Those bombs are very close tonight," he said.

"Yes, I'm afraid there will be many more homeless by the morning," answered Martin, the younger of the two lodgers from the nearby factory. They were both nice, quiet men but Nelly and Joe objected to having to share their home with strangers and hadn't made them welcome at all. Now that their son was in uniform, it was Joe's opinion that every young male should be in the forces, and those who weren't were cowards. With five adults crowded into the small shelter, the atmosphere became claustrophobic and Nelly began to wheeze, her breathing becoming more difficult.

"We're going to die, we're going to die," she sobbed. "We'll be buried alive, do you hear?" Then she started to scream and became hysterical. Joe just sat; immobilised with fear, not knowing what to do. Ra, the other lodger, held Nelly by the shoulders and tried to reassure her, but she became worse. The lodger then raised his hand and brought it sharply across Nelly's face. She was stunned by the blow, then started to weep softly. Ra thrust her into Joe's care and left the shelter, heading out into the night.

The air raid continued: fire engines could be heard racing along the main road nearby. There was the sound of glass breaking as masonry fell, and the ground seemed to vibrate. Alice Brownlow felt sorry for her mother but could do nothing to help her father, who was now cradling his wife in his arms as she continued to weep. Martin had tried to apologise for Ra's behaviour, but Joe had made life as uncomfortable as possible for both of them during the few weeks they had been living there. Martin was obviously embarrassed and said he didn't know what had come over Ra to make him do such a thing, but Alice explained that it was first aid treatment in cases where a person was beyond control with hysterics.

It was about twenty minutes later when they heard the crunch of footsteps on the cinder path leading to the shelter. The door was opened and carefully closed, and Ra appeared carrying a tray of mugs, milk and a pot of tea. He smiled at Mrs Brownlow who was now fully composed and handed her a cup of tea and two tablets.

"Take these; they will help you feel better."

"What are they?" she asked.

"Just some tablets my wife gave me; they are quite safe. My wife is a doctor."

This was the first time he had mentioned his wife. Until then it had been assumed he was single.

"Thank you," said Nelly, accepting the tea. "We didn't know you had a wife; have you been married long?"

"Five years tomorrow, actually."

"Got any family?" joined in Joe, not liking to be left out.

"No, thank God."

"Ugh," grunted Joe, "That's a queer way to be talking. What you get married for then?"

Ra shrugged his shoulders and said no more.

Soon after, the all-clear sounded and they all breathed a sigh of relief and returned to the house Alice looked at her watch: it was just half passed five in the morning; too late to go to sleep now but there was enough time to fill a hot water bottle and have a rest on the settee, covered with warm blanket. She mustn't be late for work – an air raid lasting most of the night wasn't an acceptable excuse.

After that night in the shelter, tensions in the Brownlows' household lessened and conversation with Ra and Martin became easier. Martin (who *was* single) and Alice became good friends; they went to the cinema together and sometimes to the Saturday dance. Occasionally Ra came too, but most of his free time was spent reading. When asked about his wife and why she never wrote to him he became evasive, stammering something about his letters going to the factory. Joe and Nelly were sure the marriage was a failure, and that his wife had perhaps run off with someone else.

Some time later, Ra was sent on a course to do with his work. Martin didn't know anything about it but thought it may be to do with some new method they were trying out at the factory where the components came from. It was fun for Alice having Martin to escort her to dances: she could enjoy herself and dance with many partners without the kiss and struggle at the end of the evening. If she liked a boy they went outside at the interval for a while, but she was back in time to go home with Martin, who was fortunately courting a girl in his hometown and so wasn't tempted to take anyone else home. He was like a brother to Alice.

Soon Ra had been away on his course for over six weeks, and in all that time he hadn't written to anyone. Alice thought he would have sent a postcard, but no one had heard a word from him.

In the first week in October, Martin managed to get two tickets for the Carl Rosa Opera production of *La Traviata*. It was the first time Alice had attended any musical performance and it was a wonderful experience. When everyone started to clap she asked Martin why this was, and he explained that it was to welcome the leader of the orchestra who had just taken his place amongst the musicians. Then the conductor climbed onto the rostrum, to even greater applause. As he raised his baton, the lights dimmed and the beautiful haunting strains of the overture began. Alice would always remember that evening – the story was very sad, with the heroine dying of consumption in the last act, but the splendour of the stage settings and the lovely gowns worn by the cast made her forget about the factory and the war, and she even stopped worrying about her brother Michael aboard the *Ark Royal* somewhere in the North Sea.

"How about supper out?" asked Martin afterwards.

"OK by me," Alice replied as they took their places in the queue at the fish shop.

When they arrived home that evening, Ra had returned from his course, looking very brown. Martin and Alice welcomed him and chided him for not writing, and Martin commented on his brown skin.

"You've obviously had good weather; where have you been? The south of France?" asked Martin.

Ra smiled. "Not quite, but the weather was kind."

"Kind," Alice said. "Wish I could go brown like that."

"What was the course about?" asked Joe.

"Did you spend some time with your wife?" asked Nelly.

Ra looked embarrassed. It was obvious he didn't want to talk about his marriage, and Alice had noticed before how he became somewhat vague whenever his wife was mentioned, as if he couldn't bear to talk about her to anyone.

4

"Yes, I saw my wife for a little while, but as you will appreciate, with her being a doctor she doesn't have much free time to spend with her family, especially in wartime."

"Does she work in a hospital?" Alice asked, knowing that if she didn't her parents would.

"Well…" He hesitated. "I suppose it's a kind of clinic, really."

"And where is this 'kind of clinic'?" asked Joe sarcastically.

"In the country."

"Is it for consumptives then?" Really Joe was going too far – talk about being grilled by the Gestapo.

"No, they are mostly bullet wounds and other war injuries." He picked up his suitcase, and begging to be excused, went from the room and up the stairs.

"Uhm, not very communicative is he? Did you notice he never once mentioned his course? Funny thing, that – none of the others get to go on courses," said Joe. "You don't, do you?" he continued, addressing himself to Martin.

"Mr Brownlow, I am only a few months out of my apprenticeship. Ra is very senior to me, and I shouldn't tell you this but I know he does special work and sometimes goes to meetings in London."

This stopped Joe in his tracks. He was always putting the lodgers down; making them out to be cowards who obtained safe jobs just to get out of joining the services. It went against all his impressions of them to think that one was actually doing really important work.

"He's got nice and brown though," Alice added wistfully.

"I think he must have been in Cornwall; it's the only place in England where you could get so brown, especially at this time of year," said Martin.

The Gainsborough dance hall was on the upper floor of a Georgian building in Alexander Crescent. Along one side of the hall were the original Georgian casement windows reaching ten feet from the floor. These were now covered with blackout boards but still had their original drapes, which when new, must have been very grand indeed. The eight-piece band were on a raised platform just below the minstrels' gallery at the far end of the hall. Alice and her friends were able to get a table near to the bandstand, and reserved chairs by draping their cardigans along the backs. Daisy, Alice's pal, pulled Ra to his feet and led him onto the dance floor. The band was playing an old Ivy Benson favourite, *She's My Lovely*. Martin nodded to Alice and they joined the dancers. The floor was crowded; there were only a few people sitting out, and a handful of servicemen standing at the bar in the anteroom.

After the interval some more people joined their party and they continued dancing, changing partners all the time. It was nearly half past eleven when Alice exclaimed to Ra, "I persuaded you to come with us, but up to now we haven't had a dance together."

"Sorry, but I thought I'd better get some practise in first so I don't tread on your toes. How about this one?"

Alice stood up and Ra led her onto the dance floor. It was a waltz; he proved to be a very good dancer and in his arms she danced better than she had ever danced before.

"Why, you're an expert!" she declared.

"Not quite the expert, it just happens I have a very good partner," answered Ra.

When the dance finished they stayed on the dance floor and waited for the music to begin again. This time they played a quickstep and the pair danced and danced, then when the music stopped Ra took Alice to the bar and bought her a cool drink. He had just handed her a glass of orange juice when one of the young RAF officers who had been propping up the bar all evening came over to them and slapped Ra on the shoulder.

"Raoul, glad to see you made it back OK." Then, looking at Alice, he said, "How about introducing me to your charming companion?"

"Oh yes, of course," stammered Ra. "This is Alice, my landlady's daughter; Alice, this is Kevin, he very kindly gave me a lift when I went on my course." They shook hands and

Kevin asked Alice to take pity on a lonely bachelor. She would have loved to refuse for she wanted to continue dancing with Ra, but couldn't be rude and so accepted his hand and they moved onto the dance floor.

"I'm sorry," he said as he stepped on her foot, "I shouldn't have asked you to dance when I've had so much to drink. I noticed you earlier in the evening; I wanted to talk to you then but I didn't have the nerve. Do you think we might meet tomorrow evening, please?"

Alice guided him from the floor to where there were two empty chairs. "We'll have to see. Perhaps when you are sober you'll have forgotten all about me," she replied.

Alice had arranged to meet Kevin at six o'clock the next evening, near to the entrance of the dance hall as she felt that as he had been there already he would be able to find his way without any problems. She got there at two minutes to the hour, but there was no sign of anyone in a blue uniform so she waited and waited, and at half past six decided she had been right in her first assumption that when he was sober he would forget all about the dance and whom he had met there. Alice turned towards the main street and started to walk away, scolding herself for being such a fool. She had almost reached the corner of Palmerston Road when she heard someone running behind her.

"Oh thank goodness I've caught you, I'm so sorry I'm late," said Kevin. "We had to fly this morning and I didn't get back until after four. Please will you forgive me?"

Of course she forgave him; it wasn't his fault and he could easily not have bothered to come at all. They went to a little café and ate cheese omelette and chips and drank awful gritty coffee, but it was a wonderful evening. Kevin had nice brown eyes that shone with excitement when he talked about flying. He talked and talked, and Alice listened, enthralled; he had such a lovely voice. He told her about his brother Laurence, who was also a pilot but with the heavy Lancaster bombers. He described the dogfights he had been in. He was so good at relating these stories she felt she'd actually been flying with him. Kevin tried to explain to her what it was like to fly – he adored it, especially at night, he said, when the earth was blackened out and the sky was infinite in its dark density with only the dazzling silver of the twinkling stars. And when there was a moon, it was even more exquisite with the rivers below shining like silver ribbons. Once over France he had cut his engine and glided for a while, and the peace was unimaginable. He had envied the German pilots, for many of them had trained in gliders before the war, later graduating into powered machines.

That night was the first of many. Every night when he wasn't on duty Kevin would cycle the eight miles from the airfield to be with Alice. Often Alice had to work late in the factory, but as it took Kevin an hour to make the journey he usually arrived at the factory as she was leaving.

Soon Kevin and Alice had been going out together for three weeks. The more time they were together, the more they longed for each other, and they had quickly fallen in love. Kevin was always so kind and understanding and so full of fun; he got on well with all of her friends whom he met when they went dancing, and Ra and Martin were always pleased to see him. Once when Alice was late leaving the factory, she found Ra in deep conversation with Kevin and their faces were so serious that she thought there must be some bad news, but when asked, Kevin, laughed and said it was nothing; just Raoul with his funny ways.

"Why do you always call him Raoul?" she asked.

"Because that is his name. I know you always call him Ra, but when I first met him he said his name was Raoul," answered Kevin.

"Well when he first came to be billeted on us, he said to call him Ra. Anyway, Raoul sounds French to me."

"That's because he is French – well, his mother is. His father is a Channel Islander; they live on Jersey. Raoul managed to escape just before the Germans landed."

"Oh you do surprise me, I thought you scarcely knew him. Next you will be telling me you are related," Alice teased.

"Does it matter? It was a long lift I gave him, and he felt like talking. Now can we just forget about him, PLEASE?!" Then Kevin put his arm around Alice and gave her a hug. She was sorry she had been so bitchy – it didn't matter really what Ra or Raoul chose to call himself.

On the 31st October 1941 Kevin's station held a Halloween dance. Fancy dress was the order of the night, and Kevin and Alice went as Harlequin and Columbine. Some people dressed as wizards and witches, while others chose the more colourful characters from history. It was a wonderful evening. The officers' mess had been decorated to resemble a witches' cave, with cobwebs made from fine string and dyed black hanging across the ceiling and down the walls, some with furry spiders climbing through them. There were finer threads hanging from the ceiling, and these brushed across their faces as they danced. Around the walls of the dining room, which had been cleared of tables to make room for the dancing, were large black cauldrons made from cardboard, and also some bats and owls and coarsely-fashioned broomsticks. By the bandstand was a tall tripod from which was suspended a real cauldron, and below it was a fire made from orange and red crepe paper. Inside the bar area, a full-sized model of a witch on her broomstick floated in the air.

This was a new world to Alice and her friends. Everyone was intent on having a good time, and they danced with each other and with some of their friends, but after the superb buffet supper, Kevin wanted Alice all to himself, so for the rest of the evening they stayed together.

"Let's go for a walk," Kevin suggested.

"What time will our bus leave?" Alice asked. The RAF station had organised transport to take the ladies back into town after the dance.

"Not for an hour yet, don't worry. I'll get you back in time."

They walked, hand in hand, out of the mess and along the peri-track which circled the runways. It was out of bounds, but the night was dark and they weren't likely to bump into anyone. When they neared the big hangar Kevin pulled Alice to him and they embraced.

"Alice, you know I love you. Will you marry me?" he whispered in her ear. Alice had known for a while that Kevin was fond of her – well, more than that – and she loved him too, but what would her mother say?

"I love you too, Kevin."

"Does that mean yes?"

"I'm only seventeen. Mum would never let me marry before I'm twenty-one."

"How do you know that? Have you asked her?"

"No, of course not."

"Well ask her tomorrow, because I want to marry you NOW, while I've got the chance."

As they walked back to the mess and the waiting bus, they passed some of the planes. Now her eyes were accustomed to the dark, she could see that many of them bore scars of battle.

"Which one is yours?" Alice asked.

"It's not here at the moment; she is having a new fuel tank fitted."

On the bus back to town, Alice sat next to Daisy. They were all exhilarated with the dance, and living quiet provincial lives as they did, they had never seen such a magnificent buffet. There had been lots of fancy savouries, with ham, shrimps, chicken and eggs galore – a wonderful feast, when civilians were only allocated one egg per ration book per week. In the centre of the table had been a boar's head with an apple clamped in his mouth. On either side of this was a whole fresh salmon, garnished to make it look as if it had come straight from the river, along with large hams baked in honey and cloves. On the other side of the boar's head had been a roast turkey and a whole side of beef. It had made the girls wonder just whose rations they were eating. When Alice mentioned this to Kevin he had laughed and said to eat up and shut up, and that it was best not to ask questions. When the bus stopped near to the church all the girls got off, saying goodnight to the other girls. Daisy and Alice walked part of the way home together, and it was then that Alice told Daisy that Kevin had proposed marriage to her.

"Well, you are a dark horse – a man you're crazy about asks you to marry him and you keep quiet about it for the whole of the bus journey?"

"Yes, that is precisely why I didn't say anything while we were with the others: I knew you would broadcast it and I don't want that."

"But you did say yes?" asked Daisy.

"No – that is, I said my mother wouldn't want me to marry yet."

"Well, there's always one way to make her change her mind," Daisy said with a laugh.

The girls had to work overtime, following a demand for more parachutes, and coming out of the factory Alice looked around to see if Kevin was waiting for her, but each day she was disappointed. She still hadn't told her parents about Kevin's proposal. They had no cause to object to him; he was a very polite, well brought up young man, but she knew her parents would object, if only on principle. Once she had asked her mother if she could invite Kevin to Sunday tea, as he had taken her out for so many meals.

"That's not my fault," she had said. "The food was here for you; you didn't have to eat out."

"Well, can he come to tea the next time he visits us?"

"No, I'm not giving your father's rations to a stranger."

"But Mum, he wouldn't be a stranger if we were to be married; he would be like a second son to you."

Alice's mother looked up with a start. "Never, do you hear me? Never, and don't you dare let me hear you talking such nonsense again. Married indeed – why, you are hardly out of the cradle, and you know nothing about him."

11

"I do, I do. I know all about him, he's told me, and I love him," Alice told her vehemently.

On November 14th 1941, Michael's ship, the *Ark Royal*, was sunk just off the coast of Malta. Only one man died, but many were injured, including Michael. The telegram came just an hour before Kevin arrived. Kevin saw at once that Alice was upset and put his arms around her as she cried all her pent-up emotions away.

When she was calmer Kevin said, "I'm very sorry, luv. Cheer up, things could be a lot worse – they can treat an injury but there's no cure for death. You'll see, they'll soon be flying them home, once they're fit to travel."

Joe Brownlow was also upset about Michael, and turned on anyone who happened to be within earshot. "It's all right for you, you're sitting pretty aren't you? What do you know about the war? You with your little flips here and little flips there, not like my poor son, injured and watching his ship go down while he struggles to keep afloat in a stormy sea. It's time you saw a bit of action."

"That's not fair, Mr Brownlow," said Ra. "Kevin has been in very great danger – every time he goes up in his plane he meets danger; you only have to look at his kite to see what a close shave he has had."

"Oh, and when did you see his kite, eh?" jeered Joe. Alice looked in amazement at Ra. All the times Joe had tried to provoke him he never once had taken the bait, and now here he was defending her Kevin. Ra looked very embarrassed and uncomfortable.

"In the repair hangar when I went with some equipment from the factory."

Kevin smiled, and Ra looked relieved that his statement had been accepted. Alice took Kevin's hand and drew him outside.

"Oh Kevin, what are we to do? You can't ask Mam and Dad now, not in their present mood."

"No. The best thing for us is to find two seats in the back row of the stalls; it won't matter if we've seen the film already."

They arrived at the cinema just as the first house was leaving and easily found two seats on the back row. Alice didn't remember what the film was about, but looking around she imagined they must have seen as much of it as the rest of those on the back row. On the way home Kevin told her he would only be at the aerodrome for another three weeks and then he was being posted to a fighter station in Yorkshire, not many miles from where his parents ran a public house. He wouldn't have much opportunity to visit her in Lincoln.

"Please Alice, let's get married, then I can find some accommodation near my new station," pleaded Kevin.

"Oh Kevin, I would love to, but when I told my mother we wanted to marry she just went barmy; said I was too young and I haven't to mention the subject again," she said sadly.

"But Alice, you can't do this to me – I love you and I need you."

"Please Kevin, try to be patient; after Christmas they might feel more kindly towards you. Michael could be home and that should make all the difference."

Michael was shipped home in time to spend Christmas with his family. He had broken his leg when he had been thrown against the wall by the blast from the explosion which had sunk the *Ark Royal*. Although he was still on crutches, he got around very well. It was wonderful having him home again; he and Alice had always been close and they chatted for hours. Alice told him all about Kevin and their problem of wanting to marry and not being allowed even to discuss their future plans with Mum and Dad.

"Ally" – this was his pet name for Alice – "if you are sure you love him and he loves you, then go ahead and marry him; I can understand him being impatient." Michael moved his leg, grimacing to ease the pain, then sighed a long, sad sigh.

"Mum and Dad won't understand, but I do. Don't think Kevin is being unreasonable trying to rush you to the altar. Being a flying man he loses friends every week; this war doesn't guarantee a future for any of us. When you see young men your own age and friends you had a drink with only the night before being killed in this terrible war, it makes you realise that you've to grab what you hold dear and live for today, because tomorrow we may die. I met a girl in Malta; she was beautiful. Then the German fleet came too near with their shells – it was instantaneous, thank God."

"Oh Michael, I'm so sorry, I'd no idea and here I am going on about my problems. I never thought; you never mentioned anyone in your letters. Please, please forgive me."

"Silly goose, there's nothing to forgive. Yes, I was getting very fond of Melaine – not only was she very beautiful but full of fun and so brave. If we'd had more time together, who knows what might have happened?" Michael laughed. "And just imagine Mum and Dad's reaction to a foreign daughter-in-law."

Chapter Two

The next morning a letter arrived from Aunt Annie, who was also Alice's godmother. She was her dad's sister, and having no children of her own liked to spend Christmas with her brother's family whenever possible. She wrote now to check if there would be room to accommodate her over Christmas, now they had lodgers. Ra and Martin had leave over the Christmas season and were with their families, so Michael had his own room back for a short while. Aunt Annie would sleep in Alice's bed, and Alice would have the camp bed under the window. Alice looked forward to her aunt's arrival – she had always been her favourite and Annie was inclined to spoil her.

The Tuesday before Christmas, Alice went to work as usual. She was glad to be out of the house – Mum was fussing over Michael and getting flustered over the Christmas arrangements. Kevin was coming down for a couple of days and staying at the public house only five minutes' walk away from the Brownlow house. Alice wanted him to spend Christmas Day with her family but her parents wouldn't hear of it. Michael said he would try to change their minds but Alice didn't think he would have much success.

When Alice got home that night Aunt Annie had arrived with Uncle John. All the sleeping arrangements had to be reorganised. Michael said he would sleep in the shelter and Auntie and Uncle could sleep in his room with the twin beds. Mum wouldn't hear of it, and besides, the shelter was always cold and damp. In the end he had the camp bed put up in the sitting room.

Aunt Annie and Uncle John lived on the outskirts of a small village in the Lake District. Uncle John had retired from teaching at the village school just before the war started, but when so many young people joined the forces he came out of retirement to ease the shortfall of teachers. Living in the country there seemed to be no shortage of eggs and chickens, and so the villagers used the age-old system of barter and exchange. Aunt Annie kept bees and some chickens, so honey and eggs would be exchanged for bacon and cheese. This year, in the third Christmas of the war, she had surpassed her previous efforts and to supplement their rations had brought a large turkey and a piece of ham, about two pounds of farm-made sausages, two dozen fresh eggs, a large cheese and a jar of cream.

"How many of us will there be for Christmas dinner?" she asked.

"Just the family," answered Nelly.

"What about Kevin?" asked Michael.

"Who is Kevin, a friend of yours?" asked Aunt Annie, turning to Michael.

"Well I don't know yet, I haven't met him but he and Alice are in love and want to get married. He's staying at the George so he can see her over the Christmas holiday."

At this, Nelly flushed with indignation. "Hmm, married indeed."

"Well Nelly, if this young man has come a long way to be near Alice at Christmas the least we can do is share our turkey with him; there's far too much for just us few. I thought you would have your lodgers with you; that's why I brought such a big bird," said Annie.

Alice couldn't believe her ears. Through Michael and Aunt Annie's manipulation, Alice and Kevin were going to spend Christmas Day together after all. How she wanted to give Michael and Auntie a big thank-you hug, but it would have to wait for a more opportune time.

At about eight o'clock that night, the doorbell rang and there was Kevin with a bunch of pink and mauve chrysanthemums in one hand and three parcels in the other. Alice invited him in and introduced him to Michael and her aunt and uncle. They had a very pleasant evening, with everyone in a festive mood. Kevin had brought Mr Brownlow a bottle of whisky and his wife a box of chocolates. Alice's parcel had a pair of silk stockings wrapped around a small box containing a brooch of Kevin's squadron badge. Alice could see Auntie Annie liked Kevin, and he and Michael were getting on well also. Michael was saying what a good job our fighter pilots had done in driving off the enemy planes when their ship had been under attack while bringing them home. The fact that it was flying the Red Cross made no difference to the enemy. He turned to his dad.

"You should have seen them Dad; darting like wasps, time and time again and in such small crafts. I wouldn't like to be in one all alone – gosh, if anyone's brave in this war it's them chaps. They've got guts."

"Kevin's a fighter pilot," Alice said proudly.

"I'm afraid the only heroes in our lot are dead, so count me outside your praise," said Kevin.

Christmas Day was cold and dry. Everyone had wished for snow but this year had to be content with a keen frost. Aunt Annie and Alice helped to prepare the Christmas dinner; it was to be a real banquet. Kevin came at 11.30 and took Michael and Joe for a drink. Uncle John declined the invitation as he was strict chapel and therefore didn't drink apart from a drop of Auntie Annie's homemade wines, which were probably far more intoxicating than anything the boys would be drinking at the George.

At one o'clock sharp dinner was to be served, and at five to one the men returned from the pub. They all sat around the table and Nelly served the meal, but Joe had the honour of carving the turkey. Alice often thought that although a woman got pleasure from looking after her family, she had to work very hard; almost like a slave at times. It was a wonderful meal, though – they had roast turkey stuffed with sausage meat at one end and chestnut stuffing at the other, roast and creamed potatoes, sprouts and buttered carrots.

When the first course was finished Mrs Brownlow brought in the Christmas pudding. Joe poured some of the whisky Kevin had brought him over the pudding and set it alight. A blue flame encircled the plate and rose to form a halo which still burned as Nelly served everyone. What a memorable meal it was, truly up to pre-war standards, thanks to Auntie Annie's generosity.

In the afternoon they played Monopoly. It was like old times, with Michael owning Park Lane and a couple of hotels, Joe with all four railway stations and Alice managing to acquire the waterworks. At teatime Nelly surprised them all by producing a box of crackers she had found in the attic when she had been putting some of Michael's things away.

"We may as well enjoy these while we have the chance," she said.

"It's been a wonderful Christmas," whispered Kevin as they said goodnight at the front door. "I'll see you tomorrow, and do you think I could ask your dad for permission for us to become engaged?"

"Well, they both seem to have mellowed towards you, so you could try."

"Good. I'll be here at ten in the morning, with my boots blacked," he added with a grin.

"When I was a young man courting the lady who is now my wife, it was customary to name the date of the forthcoming marriage when the engagement was announced. Alice is too young to marry, and besides, it's not sensible in wartime. Chances are you would have children and who in their right senses would bring children into a world like this? What security could you give a child or wife? No, the answer must be no; when the war is over, or when Alice is twenty-one, that's when you can marry her and not a minute before."

"But Mr Brownlow, I love Alice, and what's more, she loves me. And people do get married in wartime."

"That's enough. You asked if you could marry Alice, and I've said no; that's the final word on the subject. The matter is now closed. If you want to take my daughter out, I've no objections, but forget about getting married. It's out of the question."

Kevin came out of the sitting room looking very depressed. Alice had hoped that her dad would have been more reasonable than her mother, but she should have realised that this subject had been well discussed by both of them. They went for a walk to the park, and there were some ducks on the pond but they hadn't brought any bread for them. Kevin and Alice were so sad and disappointed. Alice had thought that after yesterday, when everyone was getting along so well together, her parents would have let them become engaged. Perhaps Dad knew that an engagement would be the thin edge of the wedge.

"What about getting a special licence from the magistrate?"

"Oh Kevin, I couldn't, I just couldn't. Think how hurt Mum and Dad would be!"

"Then you don't love me!"

"Yes I do – oh Kevin, you know I love you. Please, let's give them a few more weeks. They're sure to come round, and Michael and Auntie Annie are both on our side. They may be able to change their minds."

Boxing Day was very different from the day before. Yesterday they had all been happy, but now Kevin was quiet and deeply hurt. Joe had disappointed him, and Alice had hurt him by not readily agreeing to his suggestion to apply to the magistrate for permission to marry. They wandered aimlessly about the park; there was a cold wind, and they were hungry, having had no dinner.

"What do you want to do?" asked Kevin.

"I wouldn't mind a hot cuppa."

"Come on then, we'll try the station. There won't be anywhere else open today."

As they sat in the sulphurous, smoke-filled station, Kevin squeezed her hand. "Sorry luv, I didn't mean to upset you. I can understand you not wanting to hurt your parents. We'll wait just a little longer, and if they haven't relented by Easter, then will you agree to us going to the court?"

"Yes darling," she said, and sealed the promise with a passionate kiss.

The second Sunday in January was particularly depressing. The snow had been falling for the past four days, and was now turning to slush. Underneath the snow were patches of ice, making walking difficult and dangerous. Some people had put ashes down, which made walking easier, but as soon as Alice got used to walking on ashes she came to the icy patches.

Kevin had returned to his new fighter station on the outskirts of York. He wrote as often as he could, his letters full of the love they shared and his many plans for when they were married. He said there were quite a few villages near to his RAF station where it would be possible for them to rent a room once they were married, or if Alice didn't want to stay in nearby Linton, she could stay with his parents at their public house in Harrogate. Occasionally in his off-duty periods he went into York, after which his letters were full of the wonders of that medieval city whose history stretched back as far as the Roman occupation in AD 71.

Ra had gone on another of his mysterious courses. He never discussed them, but no one else from the factory where he was employed ever went away to train. The radio continued to churn out the depressing news of the war, interspaced with the music of Ivy Benson and the sound of the Glen Miller Orchestra. Martin taught Alice to play chess and by the end of the weekend she knew all the different moves the chess men could make – she wasn't any good at strategy but nevertheless enjoyed the challenge.

Monday brought a little excitement into the sewing room. Janet Forster, who also spent her days sewing the long seams of parachute panels alongside Alice, had become engaged to a sergeant pilot who was serving at the station Kevin had recently left. Everyone was touched by the magic the little ring conjured up as it twinkled on her third finger.

"When is the great day?" asked Daisy.

"Twenty-first of March, and you are all invited to the wedding. Oh, and Alice, Bob says Kevin and some of the boys who were posted are going to try to be there."

Alice could hardly wait for Kevin's next letter to confirm what Janet had said. She missed him dreadfully. At Christmas just being together was enough, or at least she thought so at the time, but now she felt ill with longing for his touch and to have her hand in his. They had talked so much then that now they didn't need words: a look or a special smile across a crowded room could convey so much that they could have entire secret conversations without speaking.

What a memorable day the 14th of February was. Kevin sent Alice a huge Valentine card, and with it a formal proposal of marriage. Alice showed her mum and dad the card and pleaded with them to reconsider their decision. She told them she loved them and didn't want to hurt them, but she loved Kevin and was definitely going to marry him.

"What you do when you are twenty-one, young lady, is your concern but until that time and while you are still under my roof, I'll say when you get married and who to."

"But Dad, this is the 20th century, not Victorian times."

"Less of your cheek, and hurry up or you will be late for work."

This was another typical reply. Why couldn't her parents talk to her instead of at her, as if she was a child? They had to let her marry Kevin – they needed each other. She couldn't go on just filling in the time, week after week. Without Kevin she felt dead inside.

When Alice got to work she poured out her troubles to Daisy. She didn't know how she would have coped without Daisy's sympathetic ear.

"Your dad did say as long as you are under his roof, didn't he?"

"Yes," Alice replied.

"Well, why don't you move out, then?"

"Oh Daisy, I couldn't, think how hurt my parents would be. I'll wait until Easter; Kevin agreed that we should."

It was all right Daisy talking about leaving home: her parents were dead and she lived with an aunt who let her go her own way and never interfered. Alice knew that deep down her parents loved her and only wanted her to be happy and secure.

Janet's wedding was arranged for the coming Saturday. It was to be at 2.30 in the afternoon at St. Denis' church, with a reception to follow in the nearby church hall. Kevin and his friends were coming, and they had managed to get enough petrol for the old Austin 7 that had belonged to one of the boys who had been killed the year before. March was normally a wet and windy month, but this day there was spring in the air, with only a gentle breeze and lots of sunshine. In the park the daffodils nodded their golden heads, the rockeries were awash with purple aubrietia and in the borders the forsythia stretched up its golden arms towards the deep pink of the nodding flowering current. Daisy and Alice went straight to the church as Kevin and his friends didn't know what time they would arrive. It was arranged that they too would go direct to church. The girls were both wearing their precious new silk stockings and were careful not to snag them when getting on and off the bus.

They arrived at the church at twenty minutes past two and chose a pew near the back in case the boys arrived after the service had started. The church was rather dark as most of the old stained glass windows had been removed for safekeeping and the window openings had been boarded up, leaving only two clear glass windows to let in some light. The church was filling up: about eighty people had been invited and many neighbours and friends from the factory had come to wish the happy couple all the best in their new life together. The groom sat in the front pew on the right-hand side with his best man. Behind them were five older people who were presumably the groom's parents and aunts, and behind them were a number of RAF boys in their blue uniforms, accompanied by their wives and girlfriends.

On the left side of the church, the bride's family had just taken their places near the front. Now with only three minutes to the half-hour, the church was almost full. Janet's twelve-year-old sisters were the bridesmaids, and were waiting in the porch for the arrival of the bride. They were identical twins and looked very pretty in their rose pink satin dresses and pink flowered headdresses interspersed with silver leaves. The organist was playing Bach's *Air on the G String*. The congregation kept looking round to see if the bride was coming. It was now well turned the half-hour. Suddenly there was a commotion and the organist brought Bach's music to a swift close and started to play the opening bars of Wagner's *Bridal Chorus* from *Lohengrin*. Everyone stood up and peered surreptitiously round to see the bride enter the church. All they could see were five boys in blue trying to look invisible as they were hustled into the pew. A moment later Janet entered the nave with her father and came down the aisle wearing a long white dress and the veil her mother had worn at her own wedding twenty-three years earlier. She looked very lovely.

When the bridal party reached the altar steps, the priest gave an address; then everyone sang the hymn *Lead Us, Heavenly Father, Lead Us*, and the exchange of vows began. A poignant hush descended on the church as the Reverend Elrod commanded Bob to take Janet's left hand.

Kevin reached for Alice's hand and at the appropriate time in the service, said very quietly, "With this ring I thee wed," and slipped a ring onto her third finger.

Alice was so moved she couldn't see; her eyes filled with tears of joy and happiness. All she could whisper was, "Oh, Kevin." He squeezed her hand and continued to hold it throughout the ceremony. When at last Alice was able to look at her left hand and the ring, there was a beautiful red stone surrounded by sparkling diamonds on a band of gold.

When people share a common trouble or disaster such as war, there is a mutual bond that brings them closer together and so it is natural for them to help each other. Janet's wedding reception was proof of this. Looking at the buffet laid out on the long trestle tables placed at the side of the church hall, it was hard to believe there was a war going on, or that food was rationed and in short supply. Friends, neighbours and relatives had all contributed: maybe an ounce of tea or margarine or a few sultanas and currants or a precious egg. The appetising spread was unbelievable. Alice had forgotten how many different buns and cakes there had been before rationing was introduced, yet they were all there: butterfly buns with fluffy cream, pink and white meringues, iced buns, vanilla slices, coffee kisses and lots of large sponge cakes with various fillings. Amongst the savouries were pork pies, sausage rolls, vol-au-vents filled with chicken, shrimp and mushrooms, and mountains of sandwiches filled with cold meats, cheese and salad. To complete the spread were the jellies and trifles. What a wonderful feast. When Alice showed Daisy her ring she made her promise not to mention it to anyone yet, because this was Janet's day and Alice didn't want to steal the limelight from her.

When everyone had finished eating the tables were cleared and the entertainment began. A dance band had been hired and one of Janet's uncles entertained everyone with his magician's tricks. He took a long piece of rope, folded it and cut it into three pieces, then tapped the end with his magic wand and hey presto, held out the complete piece of rope. He was very professional with his easy-flowing patter. A friend of Janet's mother got up and sang *Roses of Picardy* and everyone joined in the chorus; then she sang *My Hero!* from *The Chocolate Soldier*. While she was singing this in her beautiful contralto voice, one of the RAF boys, who also had a fine voice, joined in and then by popular request they both sang the duet *Indian Love Call* from *Rose Marie*. To follow the cabaret there was dancing: they did the military two-step and the St. Bernard waltz followed by a Paul Jones, as well as the modern dances. It was a wonderful wedding reception.

As Kevin was returning to Yorkshire with his friends very early the next day, he and Alice slipped away unnoticed from the reception so they could have some precious time to themselves. They strolled through the dark streets, past the church, along Dane Street and across the school playground towards the shelters. When they reached the doorway, Kevin pulled Alice to him and kissed her passionately.

"I wonder if this door is unlocked?" said Kevin as he groped his way in the pitch black. After much fumbling, they heard the creak of the hinges as the door swung open.

"Alice," he called, "come on, there's nothing for you to fall over."

She moved cautiously forward and within seconds they were once more in an embrace. After a few minutes, Kevin lit a match and they were able to find their way to the long seat that ran along the wall. They had never been quite so alone before, and now were able to relax. Kevin removed his cap and spread his coat over the bench for them to sit on. They kissed and embraced each other; then he undid his tunic as the brass buttons were digging into Alice. Oh, it was wonderful just being so alone together. At this moment nothing else in the world mattered. Alice ran her nails along Kevin's spine and felt him shudder; then his hands were undoing the buttons on her dress. She felt her breast swell under his gentle caress, then her bra went tight as he unclipped it. Never before had she experienced anything like this. Kevin cradled her naked breasts in his hands, fondling and kissing them and gently nibbling her nipples. She should have stopped him but the more he did, the more she wanted him to do. She groaned and panted as Kevin eased her knickers over her hips, then he managed to undo his trousers while still holding her tight and kissing her.

"Alice, I want you, now." Then he pushed her down onto the narrow bench and laid over her. He fondled her, then it was no longer his fingers and she felt him enter her. As he pushed hard a burning pain brought tears to her eyes and she sobbed as they held each other close.

"I'm sorry darling, I couldn't help hurting you but I promise it won't be painful next time."

"Kevin, it was wonderful," she whispered. "Hold me tight."

"Alice, you've got to marry me, promise, and soon."

It was the easiest promise to make; she loved him so much and longed to be his wife – well, now she was his wife, at least unofficially.

"Will anyone be able to tell?" she asked anxiously.

"No, of course not silly, they'll put that glow of happiness down to your being in love with the most handsome of men." He laughed, then in a more serious tone he added, "Alice, tomorrow when you wake up and remember what we've just done, please darling, don't feel ashamed. I love you, I think I loved you from the first moment I saw you at the dance, and I'll always think of you from this moment as my wife. So my darling, please hurry and name the day, and then we can make it legal and you can make an honest man of me." They kissed, then reluctantly made their way back to the church hall.

Most of the guests had left the reception by the time they got back, but Daisy and her Aunt Doris were there, and of course Kevin's friends. Someone had made some coffee and filled a flask for the boys to take with them. They would be driving through the night. After demolishing a pile of sandwiches and two large jugs of coffee the five boys piled into the tiny Austin 7, with two on the back seat and a third laid across their knees with his knees tucked under his chin. The driver and navigator sat at the front. It would be a long journey, and with such a heavy load they would be lucky to reach thirty miles an hour.

Chapter Three

March gave way to April; Easter came and went, but still Kevin hadn't been able to get some leave and so any thoughts of marriage had to be postponed. Alice continued to receive three letters a week from him, and reading between the lines she could tell Kevin was just as downhearted as she was, but true to form, Kevin was ever the inveterate clown with a smile painted on his face; always looking on the bright side. In one letter he had written *The weather will be warmer at Whitsun. I want the sun to shine on my bride.*

For a time Kevin's letters sustained her, but by the middle of April she was so low in spirit that she couldn't eat and never slept through the whole night. Sometimes she would wake from a nightmare, or just wake up feeling cold and lonely. Then one morning Alice woke up feeling dreadfully ill. She sat on the edge of the bed and the room started to spin, and she just managed to make her way to the bathroom where she was sick. On Friday morning when they were due to go to the canteen for the coffee break, Alice went dizzy again and Daisy grabbed her just in time before she fell onto one of the machines.

"You can't go on like this," said Daisy. "Just look at you: all skin and bone, and you must have lost a stone in weight since Kevin left."

"I can't eat. I do try, if only to stop my mother going on at me, but I feel so sick."

"Well, I think you need a check-up; you ought to see a doctor."

"I don't like going; besides, there is nothing wrong with me."

"You should leave that for the doctor to say. I'll make an appointment for you, and to make sure you turn up, I'll come with you."

"Oh, I don't know – perhaps it's flu? It'll pass."

"No it won't. You come with me tomorrow, I'll meet you at two."

And so it was arranged. A visit to the doctor wouldn't do any harm, and perhaps it was just nerves because she did worry about Kevin flying. And now that Michael had returned to his ship, she had no one at home who understood.

Dr Denton had been the family doctor since before Alice was born. He was nearing retirement now, but with the shortage of doctors due to the war, he was likely to continue in his profession for some time to come. He delivered his usual friendly chat to put his patient at ease, and Alice told him about her depression and feeling ill. He sent her behind the screen to undress, then gave her a thorough examination. When she was dressed again, the doctor bid her sit down and asked about her boyfriend. She blushed and told him all about Kevin and their plans to get married and about all the difficulties with her parents and the frustration of Kevin not being able to get leave. He heard her out very sympathetically.

"I think you know what is really the matter with you, Alice, don't you?"

"No – that is, I'm not sure," she stammered.

"I see. Well now, you told me that your young man came to your friend's wedding in March, and that he hasn't been able to get leave since?"

"That's right, doctor," Alice replied.

"When was your last period?"

"About a week before the wedding, I think."

"Hmm, nearly eight weeks ago. Well my dear, I congratulate you: your baby will be born in time for Christmas."

"Oh doctor – I can't be! Oh dear, what will my mother say? Could it be something else?"

"My dear child, you must be brave and face up to the facts, and the fact is that you are going to have a baby. Now I suggest you go home and break the news to your mother, and ask your young man to get special leave so you can be married."

Alice didn't remember leaving the surgery, but a while later she became aware that she was sitting in the Tudor café drinking tea with Daisy.

"What am I going to do, Daisy? Mum will go mad; she may even turn me out."

"Oh, come off it. Pull yourself together – of course your mum won't turn you out! It'll be a shock, no doubt, but when she gets used to the idea she'll look forward to spoiling her grandchild. Anyway, if she was to turn you out you could always stay with my aunt and me."

They sat for such a long time that the waitress came up to them to see if they wanted more tea, but eventually at four o'clock they left the café. Daisy went to the pictures and Alice made her way home and went straight to her room. She lay on the bed and sobbed into the pillow. What should she do? She loved Kevin deeply and was pleased about the baby, but what was her mother going to say? Where were they going to live, and how could they get married when Kevin was always on flying missions? At teatime there was a knock on her door and her mother came into the bedroom. She could see Alice had been crying.

"What's the matter with you, then?"

"Nothing," Alice replied.

"Nothing? And I suppose it's 'nothing' you've been crying about, eh?"

"I've got a headache, that's all."

"Oh, and since when has it been necessary to visit the doctor for a headache?"

"I… Who said I've been to the doctor's? I've been out with Daisy."

"You were seen going into Dr Denton's surgery with your friend, but she lives at the other side of town and is hardly likely to have a doctor up here, is she?"

Alice didn't answer. She was upset and afraid she would have to tell her mother, but how? She seemed very angry.

"I hope it's not what I think it is. I'll have no bastards in my house."

Alice gaped at her. She knew; she must have been suspecting this for the past few weeks.

"It won't be illegitimate," Alice cried. "Kevin and I are getting married."

"Huh, he'll not marry you; you're just his plaything. It'll be a bastard, do you hear me? A bastard!" she screamed. "I'll have none here – what have I brought up? All these years, slaving to bring you up decent, then you turn out like this, you slut; you harlot!"

She went out, banging the door behind her. Alice was broken-hearted.

"Oh Kevin, what am I to do?" she cried. She must have sobbed herself to sleep, for when she awoke it was dark. She closed the curtains, then put on the light to see the time: it was half past nine. Alice undressed, ready for bed. She was thirsty and hungry, and realised she hadn't had anything to eat since lunchtime.

As she went to the top of the stairs, all was very quiet. She couldn't see a light anywhere. Alice crept down the stairs and into the kitchen, found some corned beef, made herself a sandwich and a cup of cocoa and took her supper upstairs to bed. She was grateful there were no air raids that night; it would have been intolerable if they had had to share the small shelter, feeling as she did.

The next morning Alice woke with a splitting headache and felt dreadful; all the more so because soon she would have to dress and go down and face her parents. She rested for a while; then after she had heard both Ra and Martin go downstairs, got up and went to the bathroom and got washed and dressed.

When Alice entered the kitchen, everyone had reached the toast-and-marmalade stage. She sat down as usual and poured herself a cup of tea. Both boys spoke to her and went on to talk about a film they had been to see. Her mother said nothing but got up and started to clear the table. A lump came into Alice's throat: normally her mother would have cooked her breakfast along with the others and kept it warm for her, but today Alice hadn't been included. As soon as she could, Alice made her escape and went to her room.

At eleven o'clock her father called and told her to get downstairs. Alice summoned her courage and went down into the kitchen. Ra and Martin had gone out, and there were only the three of them in the house.

"Well, what have you to say for yourself?" asked her father.

She hung her head. What could she say except, "I'm sorry"?

"Sorry? Well, sorry isn't good enough; shaming your mother and me. You'll have to go; I'll not have people pointing a finger at us."

"Go?" Alice stammered. "Where to? Where can I go?"

"Out of this house, that's where you can go, you young hussy," shouted her mother.

All this time Alice had been standing just inside the kitchen door, and now she put her hands behind her to grab the door handle to steady herself.

"But I haven't anywhere to go. Please let me stay," she cried.

"Never, do you hear me? I told you yesterday, I'll have no bastards in my house. You can get yourself out, and today. I can't bear the sight of you. Go on, go; out of my sight."

Alice made her way up the stairs. She couldn't see where she was going for the tears in her eyes. She had never thought that her mother, of all mothers, would have turned on her so. She knew her mother would be upset and hurt – that was understandable – but to turn her out, and on a Sunday when most places were closed, and with no time to make arrangements? Alice found an old suitcase of Michael's in the attic and put her few belongings into it – they were mainly clothes, but she did have a sewing box that Michael had made for her during his last term at school. She carefully bound this with an old scarf to stop the lid from opening, and wrapped it in an old newspaper. When all was packed, she looked around the room she had called hers since she was five. There was nothing more she wanted to take. The little ornaments and pictures her parents had given her over the years as presents no longer belonged to her, as she no longer belonged to this house. Alice heard the front door close, and then the sound of footsteps coming up the stairs. A few minutes later there were voices on the landing; then the footsteps descended the stairs and all was quiet. It was dinnertime and she could smell the aroma of roast beef – her mother must have carried it through into the dining room. Alice felt hungry, but she couldn't face being turned away, not in front of Ra and Martin. Alice stood listening at the top of the stairs, and when all was quiet, made her way down with Michael's case in one hand and her sewing box under her other arm and went through the front door and turned to the right, along the street and away from the house that was no longer home.

As she walked a fine drizzle began to fall, her tears blending with the raindrops as they ran down her cheeks. Alice's legs moved automatically; she was in a trance and walked and walked, not knowing where to go or what to do. No one passed her by; everyone must have been at their Sunday dinner. She felt lost and so alone; Alice was cold, wet and hungry and her arms were aching from carrying her belongings. She heard a train hoot in the distance; it was like a sign and she made the first decision of the day. She would go to the railway station and have something to eat at the buffet, then find a seat in the ladies' waiting room and have a rest and get warm.

Nostalgia swept over her as she entered the station where she had waved goodbye to Kevin after his Christmas leave. A train must have just arrived, and the station was thronged with a milling crowd. The acrid smell of sulphur and smoke filled the air. People were making their way from the platforms, and there were many servicemen with their wives or sweethearts proudly at their side, some carrying young children. One man she saw in khaki had a boy of about six sitting on his shoulders and a little girl of perhaps two in his arms. He looked like a man who had been given the world. Alice wondered if Kevin would look like that when she met him with their child. She went straight to the buffet and bought some watery soup and a cheese sandwich, then went to the ladies' waiting room where she managed to get a seat near to the fire. Having put her case and parcel carefully at the side of her chair, she curled up and had a short nap.

The announcement over the loudspeaker advising would-be travellers that the train for March and Peterborough would be leaving from platform one in five minutes roused her from her sleep, and after the general stirring and bustle as people gathered their belongings and made their way to the platform, she found herself alone in the waiting room. The fire was choked with ash and had ceased to give out any warmth. Alice looked around for something to use as a poker. Hanging near to the door, and over the fire bucket filled with sand, was a triangular fire alarm with a straight piece of metal to sound the alarm. Carefully she removed this and managed to poke the dead ash through the fire bars, and in no time the fire glowed bright red and made the room warm again. Alice pulled her chair in front of the fire and took stock of her position. What was she going to do? She couldn't stay here, and she had only £5 12s 6d to her name so couldn't go to a hotel. Then she remembered Daisy's words of the previous day: "You can always stay with my aunt and me," she had said. Alice would have to take her up on her offer, she thought, but then hesitated. Daisy lived with her Aunt Doris, and maybe Doris wouldn't want the likes of Alice under her roof – after all, her own mother wouldn't have her. Alice had only met Aunt Doris once, at Janet's wedding, and she had seemed very nice, but everyone had been so happy at the time. It would be different now, and surely she wouldn't be too pleased to give shelter to a fallen woman.

Daisy had always made out that her aunt was a very easy-going woman, but she might have been exaggerating. Only yesterday, she had stated so firmly that Alice's mother would never turn her out, but she had been wrong. Perhaps Daisy would be wrong about her aunt, too. Alice's mind went off at a tangent. She imagined herself walking the streets, sleeping in the park and having to clothe her baby in cast-off clothing, until eventually she slept again. Alice was dreaming that she was one of Fagin's boys; the Artful Dodger stealing from the rich passers-by. Unfortunately she was caught and the beadle was shaking her by the shoulder.

"Sorry miss, you can't stay here. The last train went over an hour ago and I'm going to lock this room up." The voice belonged to the hand that was shaking her awake. It was the stationmaster, complete with a bunch of keys.

"I'm sorry, I must have fallen asleep," she said.

"Which train were you waiting for?" he asked.

"Oh, I wasn't waiting for a train," she stammered, "I was waiting for my friend." Alice gathered up her suitcase and sewing box and made her way out of the now-deserted railway station. It was already dark and when she looked at the station clock, the pointer had just jumped to half past eight. Alice was beginning to feel hungry – she had only had the one cheese sandwich at lunchtime and the sandwich the night before. After hesitating for a few moments, she decided Daisy was her only hope. With a sense of purpose she walked away from the station and turned towards the poorer part of town, often nicknamed Packman's Puzzle. Alice turned round one corner after another, through alleyways and along passages. When she passed the Rose and Crown with its blackout curtains drawn carefully across the windows, she crossed the road and turned left after the fish shop. If it had been any night but

Sunday she would have been able to get some fish and chips, but at least she was getting nearer to Daisy's.

Just past the fish shop was a streetlamp, and in its dim light she was able to make out the name of Felton Street, where Daisy lived at number 33. Alice had never visited her home and didn't know which side of the road it was on. There was no one about and the night was very dark. She went up to the door of the first house but couldn't find a number; then tried the next one. This was number 10, and the third house had a number clearly painted in white – 104 – so she gathered that number 10 had a digit missing, and also realised that the odd numbers were on the other side and 33 would be nearer to the far end of the street. Felton Street was one of those narrow backstreets built at the time of the growth of the factories, when houses were built as cheaply as possible and with no set standards to house the growing army of workers from the country. Most were still owned by the factories and little had been done to improve them since they were first erected. Alice crossed to the other side. The road was very uneven and the potholes were full of water from the downpour of rain earlier in the day, and she splashed her way through several puddles before she reached the other side. Alice could hear children crying as she passed one house, and from another came the sound of a wireless. She peered through the dim light at each door she passed, but there wasn't any sign of house numbers. If she didn't see a number soon she would have to knock on one of the doors and ask. Just as she passed the postbox she saw the outline of a woman coming towards her, and when she was near enough, Alice asked her which house was number 33. She had passed it, so she carefully counted the doors back to where the woman had directed her.

With trembling hands Alice knocked on the door. The sound of laughter from the wireless filled the air. She waited and then knocked again, this time louder. After what seemed ages, someone pushed a bolt back and the door opened about six inches. There was no light on behind the door, but from the glimmer of the streetlamp Alice recognised Daisy's Aunt Doris.

"Is Daisy in, please?"

"Yes, just a minute. Daisy, yer wanted," shouted the woman, and promptly closed the door. Again Alice waited, and then Daisy opened the door. She gasped when she saw Alice.

"Alice? Well, of all people, I never expected to see you in Felton Street."

"I've left home."

"Left home! Why?" Then she seemed to realise what had happened. "Have you left home, or have you been turned out?"

"They don't want me there anymore. Oh Daisy, please help me; I don't know what to do." Alice broke down and sobbed. Daisy was by her side immediately, putting her arms around her shoulders and comforting her.

"I never for a minute thought she would turn you out; I mean, she is your mother and all that sort of thing. Wait a minute, I'll have a word with Auntie."

Once more Alice stood alone in the dark. What was she going to do; supposing Daisy's aunt wouldn't let her stay? Tears filled her eyes. She felt so unwanted, and was beginning to think it would be better if she could be killed in an air raid, like the people in London who were dying every day due to the constant bombings. Someone was coming to the door again, and there was the sound of a door curtain being pulled to one side.

"Come in, and stand still while I close the door and pull the curtain. Then I'll put the light on." Alice felt, rather than saw, Daisy moving about. Then she switched the light on and Alice was standing in a very small, shabby room; obviously the living room.

"Come and sit down, you look all in. When did you have a meal last?" asked Daisy.

"Oh, I'm all right really – I had a snack at the station around lunchtime."

"Lunchtime? That's hours ago, and you're going to be a mother! Should be eating for two, and not even eating enough for one. How are you going to look after a baby when you don't look after yourself? Put your things down there, then come and sit by the fire while I find you something to eat." Alice sat down, thankful for the chance to take the weight off her feet. As she waited, she surveyed the room. What a mess. Her mother would have gone mad: there was dust over everything and judging by the things that were strewn about the room on the chairs and the sideboard, she was beginning to think the drawers and cupboards must be empty. The only cheerful thing in the room was a lovely array of pink tulips in a crystal vase, which had been placed in the centre of a table covered with a green chenille cloth. There wasn't much of the cloth visible because there were so many magazines and newspapers on the table, as well as playing cards.

"Here we are then, come and get yourself outside this little lot." With this command, Daisy's Aunt Doris set down a tray on the table, first pushing aside some of the papers. When Alice sat down for her meal, she was surprised by the feast that had been set before her. There was a lovely omelette, as light as air with grated cheese on top and some warmed-up peas and potatoes, and on a side plate was some thinly sliced brown bread and butter and a cup of tea near to it. Aunt Doris, as she was told to call her, sat and talked to her while Alice ate. She said Alice would be very welcome to stay until she had a chance to sort out her problems, and she could share Daisy's room – it was small, but she assured Alice they would manage. She mustn't worry, but when Alice had the opportunity she would need her to get her ration book; still, there was no desperate hurry, not with her job. Aunt Doris laughed.

Alice had just finished her meal when Daisy rejoined them. She had been washing her hair, which was now firmly rolled up in Dinkie curlers.

"Feeling better for that, eh?" She nodded her head at the now-empty tray.

"Yes thank you; your aunt certainly makes a nice omelette."

"Well, so she should – she's the cook in charge at the NAAFI club in the barracks." That explained why Doris wasn't in a hurry to obtain Alice's ration book. Also the omelette would have been made from fresh eggs, not the dried kind the less fortunate had to make do with. The three women sat around the fire talking for a while; then at 9.30 Daisy and Alice went upstairs to bed.

It was a very small bedroom with just enough room to walk between the single iron bedstead, which was pushed against the wall, and an old wooden chest of drawers that had at some time been painted with dark brown paint. The only other piece of furniture was a cane-bottomed chair placed against the bed.

"Which side do you want?" Daisy asked.

"Oh, I don't mind, whichever you prefer."

"You had better have the wall side, I'll be up before you. Auntie likes our guests to have a lie-in in the mornings." She giggled.

It was Daisy's light hearted gaiety that helped Alice through the next few days.

On Monday morning, after a sleepless night, Alice ached all over and had a temperature. Daisy made her stay in bed and Aunt Doris brought her a hot water bottle, a flask of hot coffee and a packet of sandwiches for her lunch.

"We've to go to work now luv; you caught a chill yesterday, and no wonder, wandering about in all that rain. We'll be back about six."

Daisy had given Alice a tablet with her morning cup of tea, and it must have been very powerful because she soon fell asleep and when she awoke it was just turned quarter past two. After Alice had eaten the sandwiches and drunk the coffee she felt much better and was able to sit up and write to Kevin, telling him what had happened at home and the cause of it all, without, she hoped, sounding too distressed. Daisy and her aunt were very kind to her, and while the house was scruffy and untidy, the warmth of their very genuine friendship blinded Alice to her surroundings.

On Thursday Alice returned to work and was given a sealed envelope addressed to her. She wondered what it could be – no one received letters at work, and this one hadn't come through the post, for there were no stamps or postmarks on the envelope. With shaking fingers she opened it and took out the contents: it was her ration book and her identity card. She looked at them, and then through the pages to see if there was a letter, but there was nothing. Tears sprang to her eyes and ran down her cheeks. Until now she had thought she would be forgiven, and had even imagined that her mother might regret turning her out and would beg her to return home; surely once she had got over the shock her mother would have forgiven her. But this was final; the last link had been severed.

Alice had now been at Felton Street for two weeks, and had persuaded Daisy and her aunt to let her do the housework while they saw to the shopping and cooking. Aunt Doris and Daisy were so very much alike: neither liked housework and they were both content to live in a perpetual muddle, yet both were such superb cooks that even a powdered egg omelette turned out to Cordon Bleu standard. Alice managed to sort out the old magazines and papers and discovered that under the debris the furniture was of good dark oak, and when polished it looked very fine indeed. Daisy's aunt complimented her on the hard work but insisted that any work not done on Saturday had to be left, as in her opinion Sunday was a day for relaxation and enjoyment.

Alice didn't feel like enjoying herself. She had received one short letter from Kevin, saying how sorry he was for causing such distress and insisting that she shouldn't worry as all would be well. At the end of the letter he wrote, *when our child is born we will look back on this time and laugh*. He must have been in a hurry; it was such a short letter and he didn't seem to understand how desperate Alice was feeling. She knew she couldn't stay here with Daisy and her aunt, for as kind as they were, there just wasn't enough room. Alice had been praying that Kevin would perform a miracle and say he had found somewhere for them to stay, but there was no mention of her moving up to Yorkshire to be near him. She felt very depressed.

On Saturday morning when Daisy had gone shopping and her aunt was at work, Alice had the house to herself and was determined to clean the fireside really well. She raked the ashes from the grate, and was in the middle of putting black lead onto the range when there was a knock at the door. She hesitated to answer it, for as usual she had managed to get a fair amount of the black lead on herself, but the knocking continued and Alice was forced to answer it. As soon as she raised the catch, the door was pushed open and she was swept off her feet into Kevin's arms.

"Darling, I thought I would never find you; I've been looking for hours and I've walked miles in this maze of streets."

"Oh Kevin, you should have warned me; I would have met you! I'm such a mess."

"You look lovely. I like the eye makeup, but should it be on your nose and cheek?"

"Oh, you. Well, come in and don't look at the shambles – I'm just trying to clean the place up."

"Daisy said you were to leave everything and come with me. I saw her queuing at the Co-op and she told me how to get here."

"But I must just finish the fireplace and get the fire going."

"No, you get washed and changed and put your overnight things into my case. I'll see to the fire," commanded Kevin.

Luckily she had a kettle of hot water handy to clean herself with, otherwise she would never have got rid of the black lead on her face. By the time she was ready with her things packed into Kevin's case, he had a nice fire burning. Alice was in a daze, and so happy – here she was with Kevin, and they were to have the next thirty-six hours together. Alice left a note for Daisy on the table and then they set off.

"Where are we going?"

"I've booked us into a hotel in Great Yarmouth for tonight, but first we must call on the vicar and see about our banns."

The Reverend Elrod made them very welcome. Kevin explained their plight, and the vicar told them that they would need permission to marry from the magistrate as Alice was not yet twenty-one, but added that as her parents had disowned her and she was pregnant, it would just be a formality. He was wonderful to them and urged them to make the application right then and there in his study. While they were busy filling out the forms, the vicar wrote a letter in support of their request. Kevin was due some leave soon and they arranged to be married at 3pm on Saturday 7th June 1942.

The young couple arrived at the station with only five minutes to spare before their train left for all stations east. Alice had been this way many times and recognised each station as they approached, and told Kevin exactly where they were. All the noticeboards and signposts had been removed for fear of an invasion, as Churchill didn't want to make it easy for the enemy should they ever land on British shores.

At last the train pulled into the station at Great Yarmouth and they walked along the seafront to the hotel. The tide was out, but they couldn't walk on the sands as they had been sealed off with large coils of barbed wire to guard against German infiltration. They had a wonderful time. The White Rose Hotel was small but very comfortable, and Kevin signed the register, telling the landlady they had just got married and Alice hadn't yet changed her ration book or her identity card to her husband's name. Alice felt so proud and respectable – she really did feel married to this wonderful man. The room was delightful; it was at the front of the house and from their window they could see the sands and the sea, and in the distance, the grey outline of a ship on the horizon. Alice looked down at the band of gold on her left hand. Kevin had brought her wedding ring with him – it was just on loan until they could make it official, but he knew that Alice would feel more comfortable wearing it now, as although they could fob people off about the name on her identity card, they could hardly say that they hadn't bothered to get a ring.

When they went downstairs into the dining room, there were only four other people there: a couple in their late forties, a retired gentleman and a sales rep. Mrs Grey, the landlady, served them herself; they had a nice homemade vegetable soup followed by steak and kidney pie, green beans and new potatoes, with Creamola pudding to follow. They went to bed early, and it was lovely to be together without feeling guilty; knowing that no one would disturb them until the morning, at least assuming there was no air raid. They lay enclosed in each other's arms, and if Alice turned in her sleep Kevin would tighten his grasp on her and wake her up, and then they made love again. In the morning Kevin put his hands onto Alice's tummy, trying to feel the baby.

"Alice, when the baby comes, if it is a girl, will you call her Estelle?"

"I've never heard of that name before."

"It means 'star'. I think she will be our star."

Alice leaned over and kissed Kevin gently on his nose.

"Will you, please?" begged Kevin.

"If that's what you want, then that's what we will call her, but what if we have a son?" she laughed.

"Why, you'll call him Kevin after his wonderful dad," he replied with a grin.

"We may change our minds before then. Anyway, you'll be here to name the baby yourself."

The weekend went all too quickly, and Kevin and Alice left Great Yarmouth on the milk train, which meant leaving the hotel at four in the morning. Mrs Grey had been so kind; she even got up to make them a hot drink and gave them a packet of sandwiches to eat on the train. It was a very tiring journey, and the train stopped at every station until they arrived in Lincoln at half past six. The young couple got a taxi to Felton Street to save time, and Kevin would need to take another train to York as his pass ran out at 19.30hrs.

Aunt Doris and Daisy were already up and had a nice cooked breakfast waiting for them. Alice took her things out of Kevin's case; then Daisy and her aunt tactfully decided that they had the washing-up to do so Kevin and Alice had a few moments alone to say their goodbyes. Alice watched as he walked up the street, and when he reached the corner he turned and waved. Then she went indoors, so sad to see him go that tears were running down her cheeks.

It was a very long and exhausting day at work, and Alice thought it would never end. After the evening meal she wrote a long letter to Kevin; writing to him brought him closer, and she relived their wonderful weekend all over again in her thoughts. When she had finished her letter to Kevin she wrote to her Aunt Annie. This was the first time she had written to her since Christmas and she wasn't sure if her aunt knew about the baby, or that she had left home. It was a difficult letter to write, but by the third attempt she had recalled how her aunt had convinced her parents to invite Kevin to share the turkey with them at Christmas. Alice knew Aunt Annie liked Kevin, and so she took the plunge and poured out all her sorrows and problems to her. She told her about this last weekend, and invited her to their wedding. It was to be a small one, with only about six guests, and Kevin thought they might go over to his parents' for the honeymoon so Alice wouldn't meet her new family until after they were married.

The next three weeks were very busy. Alice applied for and was given some extra clothing coupons and a permit to buy bedding and other household necessities. On one pair of pillowcases she embroidered lovers' knots in each corner.

Kevin had applied for married quarters, but the few there were had already been allocated to airmen with families, and now he was searching the nearby villages for accommodation so they could be together. Every day they wrote to each other, and one letter she got from him had been written while he was airborne. The writing was terrible, but the words were beautiful.

On Tuesday the 3rd of June there was no letter for Alice. She went home at lunchtime to see if it had been delivered in the midday post, but was unlucky. On Wednesday there was still no news, and by Thursday Alice was frantic. Daisy, as usual, was a tower of strength and that evening walked to the telephone kiosk on the main road and phoned Kevin's station in Yorkshire. Alice was in such a state of nerves, and was afraid something had happened. Daisy left home at seven, and by nine still hadn't returned.

"That's just typical of our Daisy, she'll be standing gossiping, just when we are waiting for her," grumbled Aunt Doris.

Alice walked to the end of the street, and as she turned she saw Daisy coming towards her from the other end. They waved; then Alice ran towards her. She could see by her friend's face that it was bad news.

"What is it? Is he… is he…?"

Daisy put out her arms and caught Alice as she fainted.

They must have been near to number 33, for when Alice came round she was sitting in the chair by the fireplace. Daisy had phoned the orderly room at Kevin's aerodrome and asked if it was possible to speak to him, there had been a lot of mumbling in the background and then a voice had asked who she was and why she wanted Kevin. She told the orderly officer and he asked her to phone back at eight o'clock. Not wanting to return home without any news, Daisy had walked around the park and filled in the hour by watching some pensioners play bowls. At eight sharp Daisy once more

44

phoned the orderly room and when she asked to speak to Kevin, Chris Newton, Kevin's friend, picked up the phone.

"Hello Daisy, they told me you had phoned. I'm glad it's you and not Alice." Chris had explained to Daisy that Kevin had been on a mission and hadn't returned, and that he was sorry but there wasn't much hope. The commanding officer would want to write to Alice, and had asked for the address. Poor Daisy – always so cheerful, but now she had the hard task of breaking the tragic news to her friend. She had rehearsed what to say; then thought it didn't sound right and rehearsed some more, but in the end it hadn't been necessary. Alice had guessed.

"Try to be brave, luv – Kevin would want you to be brave," Aunt Doris said as she stroked and patted Alice's hand. "Daisy, run up to the Rose and Crown and ask them to phone for Dr Denton. She needs to be seen by someone – a shock like this, well, I don't know, but she could lose the baby."

Alice looked up. She felt as if her head was filled with cotton wool and the noise of people talking seemed to come from a long way off. She didn't speak; *couldn't*. It was as if she was in a glass cylinder and she could see but couldn't move or speak; almost like standing outside herself, watching but not understanding.

Dr Denton came at ten o'clock. He took her temperature and checked her pulse.

"This is a very sad business, a very sad business indeed," he said, shaking his head.

Daisy helped Alice up the stairs and stayed with her until she had taken the tablets the doctor had left her. The room spun round, and she knew no more.

Chapter Four

As they crossed the Channel into France, Kevin spoke into his mouthpiece.

"Here goes; we should be landing in about fifteen minutes. Must keep radio silence from now on."

The night was clear, and the first quarter of the moon shone brightly, bathing the fields below in a soft light. Kevin scanned the ground and was soon able to discern the outline of the church with its narrow spire. Then he noticed the river shining in the moonlight. As soon as he saw the bridge he started counting the fields: one, two, three, four – ah yes, there was the wood on the left. He pushed his joystick forward and the nose went down for the descent. As he went over the wooded copse, the torches shone on either side of the field to light his way down and he was able to make a smooth landing. As the little plane came to a halt and the engine fell silent, the lights were extinguished. Half a dozen men moved from the shadows to unload the plane. Raoul handed his suitcase and the wireless transmitter to one of the waiting men; then climbed out of the rear cockpit. Kevin handed down some guns and ammunition, then climbed down to stretch his legs and handed a bundle of letters to Jean Pierre. Then, with fond farewells to his friends, he climbed back into the plane and within minutes was airborne.

Raoul and his friends watched until the plane was out of sight. The night was still, with only the owls in the nearby copse calling to each other to break the silence. He picked up his case and the wireless transmitter, while the others handled the rest of the equipment and ammunition. Stealthily they made their way to the cemetery to hide their luggage in the family vault. They heard the anti-aircraft fire, and saw a bright glow in the sky.

"Oh God, no," said Raoul. "Why tonight of all nights?" He shook his head, and with an anxious look on his face asked, "Does Lille know about the vault?"

The others looked at each other.

"There's no reason why she should, but she just might. Why do you ask?" said Louis.

"I'm not sure, but I have a strange feeling we may have been betrayed."

"You think that could have been the Lysander; that glow in the sky?" asked Jean Pierre.

"It was in that vicinity. I hope to God I am wrong," answered Raoul.

Raoul had been sent to France with the purpose of helping to reform the group that had been devastated when their leader Marcel and three others had been arrested. The two Dubois brothers were now in the hands of the Gestapo, and Marcel had taken his pill before he could be tortured into betraying his friends, but Lille the wireless operator had been released. Raoul was not at all happy about this. Why had the Germans let her go? They only released members of the resistance if it was advantageous to them. Why hadn't Lille come this evening? She was due to be flown to England with Kevin, but had sent word that she was ill. Just suppose she had known that the little plane was to be blown out of the sky as soon as it was clear of the field – and yet why, if the Germans knew so much, why weren't they here tonight to arrest the others? It didn't make sense.

They made their way in the darkness to the old cemetery, where the vault was built into the side of the disused chapel. They carefully stored the guns and ammunition in the hole that was revealed when the stone effigy of a bygone Le Nain was eased from the wall.

"I think we had better lie low for a while. Be careful, all of you, and I'll get in touch with you in a few days," said Raoul.

When the others had moved out into the darkness and were out of earshot, Louis put his hand onto Raoul's arm to detain him. They had been friends since childhood.

"It grieves me to even think this, Raoul, but I'm not happy. First Marcel and the Dubois brothers, and now maybe Kevin. He's made several visits to us, bringing you with him on more than one occasion. Something is happening and it's not to our good. I think we should change our hiding place."

"Have you anywhere in mind?"

"No, not really. I don't think it would be wise to take them to the farm."

They walked on in silence, then of one accord turned towards the river.

"Do you remember this spot?" asked Raoul.

Louis smiled and nodded his head. "You remember Old Barnard? He used to hide his bottle of cognac in the river away from his wife, and when he wanted a drink he'd pull it from the water by the string tied around the neck of the bottle," he reminisced.

"Hmm, I wonder..." said Raoul hesitatingly.

"Now what bright idea have you got?"

"I wonder if we could find something waterproof to put the guns and ammunition into? Then we could drop them into the river," said Raoul.

The two friends sat down amongst the riverside bushes, pondering on the problem.

"Maurice, voilà! His old cottage!" cried Louis excitedly.

"But that was pulled down before the war."

"Yes, but there were cellars. The site is overgrown now with weeds and shrubs, but I'm sure we could find a way into those old cellars. And" – he paused – "none of the others were here at the time. It would be just the two of us who knew where our cache was."

"It's too late tonight; dawn's only an hour away. I hope tomorrow night won't be too late," said Raoul as he stood up, giving his friend a helping hand.

Halfway through the following morning, Louis and Raoul moved the sheep down the narrow lane to fresh pasture. With a little help from the sheepdog, the flock strayed onto the waste ground where a house had once stood. As the two men moved amongst the sheep they located signs of old walls just discernible among the weeds and tall grass. The shrubs once bordering the garden were now sizeable trees, the old orchard had gone wild and the plum, apple and pear trees now stood about twenty feet high. The area once occupied by the kitchen was overgrown with grass, weeds and gorse bushes. Louis lay flat on the ground as he explored under the gorse bushes.

"There's something here!"

Raoul bent down and placed both hands on a nearby sheep. They had to be careful; someone could be watching them through binoculars. He bent down further and saw that where Louis had moved some grass sods, there was a trapdoor giving access into the cellar. He straightened up and let the sheep go, looking all around as he did so.

"Can you lift it? I don't think we are being observed."

"We had better leave it for now. The top layer of earth and grass will have to be transferred onto a board so we can re-cover the area quickly without leaving any telltale evidence of what's beneath," answered Louis.

The sheep, having now served their purpose, were quickly rounded up and returned to their grazing field. When they returned to the farm Louis went about his farming business and Raoul went into the barn and set to work on making a cover for the trapdoor.

That night there was a thunderstorm, and between flashes of lightning, the night was inky black. No one was likely to be abroad on such a night. The two men, equipped with a spade, a sharp knife, a crowbar and torches, made their way across the fields to the site of the old cottage. They had brought a tarpaulin sheet with them to work under, thus protecting themselves from the rain and shielding the light from their torches, but once they had decided on the area to be cleared they worked in darkness. The cover, made earlier by Raoul, was now filled with soil as the turf from the ground under the gorse bushes was placed on top. At last the trapdoor was clear of earth; it lay six inches below the surface of the surrounding earth so when the cover was put into place, no one would guess it was there.

"Any idea how big the cellar will be?" asked Raoul.

"No, I've never been down, but old Maurice kept his wine down there and stored his fruit and vegetables over the winter," answered Louis.

They pulled at the ring on the trapdoor, but the door wouldn't move.

"What a good job we've brought a crowbar with us. If you hand it over I'll jam it into the groove," said Louis.

"Here you are; I'll scrape around the sides and get rid of some of this soil," answered Raoul as he handed the crowbar to Louis.

They worked diligently for another ten minutes; then tried again to move the door. They slotted a piece of rope through the ring, and standing one on either side of the door, heaved and pulled. The door moved a little; then fell back into place. After a short rest they again tried, and this time the door opened an inch or two and Raoul managed to place the crowbar into the gap to keep it open.

"Give me your knife; I'll try to clear these hinges. Do you have any oil in your tool bag?"

"Yes, it's only a little can but there should be enough for tonight," answered Louis. After some scraping and much pulling and heaving, the door was lifted to its full extent, revealing a gaping chasm of three feet by four feet. The two friends smiled; then looked around them to check if anything was amiss. The rain fell relentlessly, but all was quiet and there wasn't a light anywhere. Securing a rope ladder they had prudently brought with them around the base of a nearby tree, Louis started his descent into the unknown, while Raoul adjusted the tarpaulin.

"It's safe to use a light now," called Raoul as he switched on his torch, shining it down into the cellar. Louis reached the bottom of the ladder and lowered himself a further eighteen inches onto the stone-paved floor. Raoul quickly followed. They found themselves in a room of about twelve feet square by seven feet high; the walls were whitewashed but dusty cobwebs hung everywhere. The air was damp and musty. Shelving lined the walls; there were some wine racks on them and on the lower shelves were some wooden boxes, rusty tools, one or two old pans and a bathtub. Raoul and Louis explored the shelves.

"Well, well. Look what I've found," called Louis, holding up a bottle of wine.

"I wonder if it's drinkable? Pity we haven't any glasses," replied Raoul. "This place is ideal: there's plenty of room to store all our kit and maybe hide some of our passengers."

"We could certainly fix up some bunks, but what about the cold and damp? You know they aren't in the best of health when they reach us," said Louis.

"Yes I know, and you're right to think of their comfort but given the choice I am sure they would all choose this place as it is now rather that a cell in the Gestapo HQ," answered Raoul. They continued searching.

"Help me to move this box," cried Raoul. Louis rushed to his friend's side. No wonder Raoul was excited: behind a large wooden box was what looked like a door. The two men pulled at the box, but it wouldn't move.

"If only we could get behind it, we might just be able to move it sufficiently to investigate that door," said Raoul. "What time is it?"

Louis looked at his watch. "Oh dear, much later than we thought – it's ten to three. Time we were getting back."

They quickly climbed the ladder and within ten minutes had the trapdoor closed and the cover in place. When they had collected all their equipment Louis and Raoul made their way back to the farm across the fields, but keeping close to the hedges so as not to be silhouetted in the dawn light.

Raoul settled down at the farm with his friend and his family. His papers were in order, with a background story that he was a cousin who had lost his home and family when the RAF had bombed Calais and he was therefore very much anti-British. He helped on the farm and discreetly mapped out his plan. The vault had been checked and found to be OK. There had been no unwanted visitors.

After five days Raoul was ready. He contacted London, doing his own transmitting and warning them that should they receive any messages from Lille they must be treated as suspect because Raoul had no intention of using her.

News reached the group that the Dubois brothers were being transferred to the prison in Le Mans to await public execution. Raoul had instructions to rescue them if possible. He visited each member of the group in turn, giving them their instructions. The only member he didn't contact was Lille; instead he sent Edith, Jean Pierre's wife, to see her and find out what had happened. Lille wasn't well; she had lost weight and was so afraid she dared not go out. Lille begged Edith to persuade the group to smuggle her across the border before the Gestapo came to arrest her again. When Raoul heard her request he was convinced she had made a deal with the Nazis to secure her release, but he didn't blame her – it was well known that women faced terrible humiliations and torture in the hands of these monsters. Yet although he understood, he couldn't condone it. Had she betrayed her friends, or had she been clever, just playing for time? If this was so, then she must be transported away for her own safety and that of the group. Just suppose it was a ruse to gain information about the escape routes out of France?

That night, when Louis and Raoul were having a nightcap, Raoul discussed his problem with his friend.

"Well, it's clear to me: whatever she has done, none of us are safe while she is around."

"Yes Louis, I agree, but supposing we got her into Spain and she had double-crossed us? We won't be able to stop her going to the German Embassy and telling all she knows."

"What if we were to kidnap her? She wouldn't be able to give anyone the tip-off then, and if we get her to England in Henri's boat your people would intercept her and make sure she did no harm. On the other hand, if she hasn't betrayed us, we will be carrying out her wishes and getting her out of France, so we will have nothing to upbraid ourselves for."

"You're right; we'll carry out your plan, but we must grab her tomorrow. Should we use Gerrard and Ramon, do you think?"

"Yes, they'll be ideal for the task, but they will need Edith to help them; she knows the house well. We could keep Lille in Maurice's cellar."

"No we couldn't; think, man – it will be a full moon, so what chance have we of gaining access without being observed? If only there was another way in..."

The two sat in silence for some time, both in deep thought.

"I wonder what's on the other side of that door in the cellar? It could be another room, or maybe it leads into the cellars of the old monastery – after all, the bell tower ruins are only a hundred metres away from where the cottage stood," mused Raoul.

"Now we may have some luck there – Jules Betton's daughter works in the registry office, so she may be able to look up the old records in the archives. There's bound to be something on the monastery buildings there."

At the appointed time the rope secured to the tree was fastened to the lorry, and with a little further persuasion from the men who had earlier loosened the soil around its roots, it was gradually hauled onto its side across the road that ran through the wood. Behind the bushes men were crouched ready to spring into action. The rain fell relentlessly, and Raoul looked anxiously at his watch. Where were they? They should have been here by now, and if the Germans had changed their plans at the last moment all would be in vain.

In the distance two pinpoints of yellow light showed in the darkness. Nearer and nearer they came, and at last there was a squeal of brakes as they came up to the fallen tree. The driver switched his headlights fully on, but they weren't very powerful. An officer alighted from the cab, drawing his pistol from its holster, and the driver joined him, carrying a torch.

"Funny, it falling down like that – we haven't had any high winds," said the lieutenant. "Come." The two Germans walked to the back of the lorry where two more soldiers, armed with machine guns, guarded four handcuffed prisoners.

"Come with me, we must clear the road."

"What about these?" questioned one of the guards, motioning to the four half-conscious bodies laid on the floor of the lorry.

"They won't be any good," jeered the officer.

As the Germans moved towards the fallen tree, Raoul and Renni, one of the French Resistant fighters moved quickly and jumped into the back of the lorry, while Jules Betton stealthily climbed into the cab. The German driver had left the engine running, so Jules put the lorry into reverse and accelerated. Immediately the officer took aim, but the grenades lobbed at them by Louis and Jean Pierre exploded where they stood. The operation was a success.

When he had reversed as far as the clearing, Jules turned the lorry around; then drove hard until they reached the quarry where Gerrard waited for them in his butcher's van. Raoul and Renni helped the two airmen down from the lorry and into the van. The two Dubois brothers, Arno and Claude the eldest were in a very poor condition after enduring brutal torture. They had to be lifted gently from the vehicle and laid in the van. While all this was happening, Jules was busy siphoning the petrol from the lorry; then when all was clear he released the handbrake and pushed the lorry forward so it rolled over the edge and fell into the quarry, exploding into flames as it reached the bottom.

They reached the chapel around midnight. Edith was waiting for them with Lille, who had been taken there earlier and told to stay with Edith if she valued her life. Edith had brought flasks of hot coffee and some cheese rolls for the men when they returned. Later, when Louis arrived with a file and wire-cutters, the handcuffs were removed from the four rescued men.

"I still can't believe it, we're safe!" cried the young navigator, gently rubbing his wrists where the steel bands had chafed his skin.

"They were going to shoot us as spies and they knew we were prisoners of war, the bastards," the air-gunner added.

"When were you captured; how long ago?" asked Raoul.

"I'm not sure how long it was – we've been woken up night and day; kept locked up in the dark for hours. It could have been days or weeks, I've no idea," answered the air-gunner.

"Well, can you remember the date you left your 'drome?"

"We left England on the 24th May."

"Just over three weeks. Well, you're in remarkable shape. Where is your aerodrome?"

"Near Cambridge. Does it matter?" the young navigator answered crabbedly.

"Yes, it bloody well does matter – I want proof that you are what you claim to be," snapped Raoul.

"Yes, I suppose you do; I'm sorry. It's just that that's how they started their questioning, so it's a bit of a raw nerve you touched. We are both stationed at RAF Waterbeach; I don't suppose you will have heard of it. It's a small village near Cambridge," said the air-gunner.

"As a matter of fact I know it quite well; I have stayed in the village hotel."

"Hotel? That's a laugh – I'd hardly call the Sun Inn a hotel."

"No, neither would I," laughed Raoul, now convinced they were genuine POWs. "Have your coffee and roll, then try to get some rest. We will be moving you on tonight," he said, motioning to Renni and Gerrard who followed him to the other end of the chapel where they conferred over the next move. They had not expected the two POWs. Suddenly there was a loud thud, everyone seemed to freeze, and then Edith moved over to the pew where Arno had been half-laid on the seat. The young man must have moved as he dozed, and in doing so had fallen to the floor.

"Oh dear God, Raoul come quickly," cried Edith, who had some nursing experience. As Raoul bent over the inert body, Edith whispered to him.

"He is very weak. We must get him help; he needs a doctor."

"Louis, do you have your cognac flask with you?"

Louis shook his head sadly. "Sorry Raoul, it's empty."

Claude, Arno's brother, helped by Raoul, moved into the narrow pew and sat beside his brother, supporting him in his arms.

"Come on old pal, don't let them beat you now. We have come this far; hang on. Edith and Louis will get you help."

"I've got some smelling salts," said Lille as she proffered the little brown bottle.

"We'll have to move soon," said Gerrard. "I have to be at the abattoir at six."

When Gerrard, Lille, Rennie and the two RAF boys had left, the others returned to their homes, with the exception of Raoul and Edith who stayed behind to look after the Dubois brothers. Louis had gone in search of the doctor. They made Arno as comfortable as possible on the floor; then Edith dressed the terrible sores on Claude's back where the whip had cut into his flesh. Arno had also been beaten, but knowing him to be so much younger than his brother, the Nazis had tortured him further with kicks and burned him with their lighted cigarettes while Claude, helpless, was forced to watch.

Around eleven o'clock there was a light tapping at the window nearest to the bell tower. Raoul rose from the floor where he had been resting and moved silently to the door and waited. A moment later there were three sharp knocks at the door, and when it was opened, old Dr Debrett squeezed past, carrying his bag. Raoul led him to the back of the chapel to where Claude and Arno lay.

"Are you all right for the time being?"

Claude nodded.

"Then I will see to your brother first."

"Apart from making him comfortable, doctor, I haven't treated him. He's so ill, I thought it best to wait till you had seen him yourself," said Edith.

The old doctor got down on his knees to examine the semi-conscious man, who moaned as, with practised hands, Debrett gently felt the rigid abdomen and took his rapid pulse.

"I'll have to get him to hospital – he needs an operation. There is some internal bleeding and I think they may have ruptured his spleen; there is a great deal of bruising."

"But doctor, you know that's impossible – if he turned up at the hospital you, Arno and the rest of us would all be in peril," said Raoul.

"Of course, I wasn't thinking."

The doctor got up and moved away, and Raoul followed him.

"Without the operation he will die, and soon."

"Could you do it yourself? Edith has some experience in nursing and I am willing to help," pleaded Raoul. The doctor put his hand up to his chin, gently rubbing his lips with his thumb as he pondered on what to do.

"It's possible," he said at last, "but not here. I couldn't do it under these conditions."

Again three sharp knocks were heard. Raoul went quickly to the door and pushed back the bolt, and Louis squeezed through the opening.

"Hope I'm not intruding, but Marguerite is worried about Arno. How is he now?

"Not well; he needs an operation. I am willing to do it if we can find somewhere suitable; where we can have round-the-clock nursing."

"Can we get him to the farm?" asked Louis, turning to Raoul. "I've got the cart outside with plenty of hay to cushion and hide them."

"But what about Marguerite and your children? Think of the danger you will be putting them into," answered Raoul.

"It is her idea. She remembers Arno being born."

"What do you think, doctor?"

"It's our only chance. I'll give him a shot of morphine, then you can lift him onto the cart, keeping him as still as possible. I have three appointments at the hospital this afternoon, but ring my surgery and ask for me to visit your wife, Louis – say she has terrible pains in her stomach. I'll be there about teatime. Have the kitchen table scrubbed down and plenty of boiling water handy." Having issued his instructions, the doctor hurried away and Raoul and Louis looked about for something to use as a stretcher.

"If only these pews weren't so well made. I can't see anything we could use," said Louis.

"What about that strip of carpet up by the altar?" asked Edith. Raoul went to investigate – yes, it would do, even if it was thick with dust.

"Edith, you had better go home now. Try to get some rest but be sure you're at the farm by five o'clock," said Raoul.

Very carefully, so as not to disturb the dust, the carpet was laid at Arno's side, then Louis put his hands firmly around Arno's feet, while Raoul put his arms under his shoulders. Very gently, both men lifted him onto the strip of carpet, then gingerly lifted the makeshift stretcher and carefully carried the young man to the waiting cart and laid him in the hay, covering him with more hay. Raoul then went back into the chapel to get Claude. As he was unable to walk, Raoul gently raised him in a fireman's lift so he wouldn't hurt his back and carried him to the cart, then covered him with hay so both men were hidden from view.

When all was ready, Louis climbed up onto the driving seat and set off for the farm. The road was very narrow, and as it was only used for farm carts, he was unlikely to meet any other traffic. Raoul decided to walk back to the farm by crossing the fields, so wasn't over-burdening the old horse with his weight. He reached the farm a good fifteen minutes before Louis and advised Marguerite about the forthcoming operation.

By the time they heard the clip-clop of Louis' old carthorse coming into the yard, Marguerite and Raoul had prepared a bed in the cellar, skilfully hidden behind wine barrels and boxes. The kitchen table had been cleared and scrubbed down and the large kettle had been put on to boil. Raoul bid Claude climb onto his back, then with his arms clasped around his thighs and under his buttocks, lifted him up and carried him into the kitchen. Louis and Raoul cleared the hay away from Arno and once again lifted the makeshift stretcher and carefully transferred the young man from the cart and carried him into the kitchen, laying him on his side on the old settle. Arno moaned as they put him down, but when Raoul had a closer look at him, he was unconscious.

"I've got some broth keeping hot; I'm sure you men can do with something inside you," said Marguerite as she busied herself cutting wedges of bread and ladling out the rich, tasty broth. They ate in silence; then Louis looked at the clock on the mantel. It was quarter to four.

"I'd best be getting along to the school and collect the children. I'll take them to my mother's; it's best they're kept out of the way for a few days."

"I'll go, I've put some things in a bag for them," volunteered Marguerite.

"No, you stay here and keep out of sight. Remember you are supposed to be ill."

When Louis had gone, Raoul and Marguerite got Claude down into the cellar. Raoul laid him on the bed and helped him turn onto his side to take any pressure from his injured back, which was even now oozing with blood.

"I'll get the doctor to have a look at you once he has seen to poor Arno. He will most likely give you something to help you sleep," said Raoul.

"Poor Arno, I can remember him being born. Such a beautiful baby, and when he was small everyone loved him. Do you remember when he dived into the village pond to rescue Madame Cartier's hat that had blown in the wind?" Marguerite reminisced.

Claude nodded. "He always thinks of others, never of himself; oh Marguerite, they were awful to him." Tears welled up in his eyes and spilled down his cheeks. "I had to watch, and every time they asked me a question and I refused to answer, they burned him with their cigarettes. I screamed for them to stop, but they didn't take any notice," Claude sobbed.

Marguerite tried to comfort him. "Arno wouldn't forgive you if you had told them anything. There's nothing more you can do at present, so just try to rest, there's a good chap."

Edith arrived on her bicycle at half past four, closely followed by Louis, who had explained to his mother the need for the children to be kept away from the farm for a few days. The old lady was glad of any excuse to have her grandchildren stay with her. Edith bent down to look at Arno.

"Well he's still with us, thank God. I hope the doctor won't be long. Have you got a tray we can use? A metal one would be best," she said.

Ever since she was a small child, Edith had dreamed of becoming a nurse. She loved caring for people and didn't mind the sight of blood, but she hadn't had much schooling and when it came to exams had failed miserably. After a little while, the low purr of Dr Debrett's Renault was heard.

The next five minutes were all bustle. The doctor wanted the fire built up; then the windows were blacked out, although it wouldn't be lighting-up time for a couple of hours. The doctor was taking every precaution: he didn't want anyone peering through the window and he wanted as much artificial light as possible. At last the door was locked and bolted, the instruments were sterilised in boiling water and the plasma drip was ready to insert into Arno's arm as he lay stripped of his blood-soaked clothing.

"Doctor, I'm sorry but I'm not used to…" Louis pointed to the table as he changed colour and turned his head away.

"It's OK Louis, we understand. You go and help your wife in the cellar; she'll be glad of your company," said the kind doctor. "Right, are we all ready?"

Edith and Raoul nodded.

"I'm going to put him out with chloroform. Watch carefully Raoul, you will need to do this if he shows signs of coming round while I am busy."

Edith had washed Arno's body where she judged the doctor would make his incision, but the doctor also swabbed the area with methylated ether. As he took the scalpel from Edith and moved it towards the bruised flesh, Raoul bit his lip and screwed his eyes shut. When he opened them seconds later, the doctor and Edith were busy clipping back the tissue and muscle around the gaping hole under Arno's ribs. Time and time again, Edith held out the kidney dish to receive the bloody swabs before emptying them into the nearby bucket.

"I'll have the silk suture." The doctor took the needle from Edith, and again went into the hole in Arno's side. "Ah, there we are – scalpel please." Like a professional, Edith handed the instruments to the doctor and was ready with a bowl when the messy bag which had once been Arno's spleen was removed.

"How are things at your end?" the doctor asked Raoul.

"OK. I gave him a couple of drops a few minutes ago, and his pulse is weak but steady."

"Good. I think it's time we put him back together. Pass me the sulphanilamide; then I'll want the catgut this time."

The clips holding back the muscles had been removed, and with deft hands the doctor eased them back into place, stitching the severed ones with catgut, which would dissolve as the muscles knitted together. Finally, using the silk sutures and with needlework any woman would be proud of, he closed the wound.

"Well, that's that job done. If we can get him onto his side, I'll see what I can do to his back."

When they had succeeded in getting Arno onto his right side, it was the doctor's turn to feel sick. A weary sigh escaped his lips.

"Oh God, what a terrible mess; it's even worse than Claude's. The wounds have started to fester. Better get me a bowl of warm water, and put a tablespoon of salt in it."

"I think he's coming round, doctor; shall I put some more drops onto the pad?"

"Oh dear, yes; just three drops should be enough. I need a few more minutes and I would like to get him downstairs before he comes round."

Raoul was fascinated by the way Edith and the doctor worked together. Each wound in turn was cleaned and smeared with white zinc ointment, and when all had been done a large piece of gauze covered in ointment was placed onto Arno's back, followed by lint and cotton wool to protect the area as much as possible. The dressing was then secured with bandages made from torn old sheets.

"That's all we can do. I'll just disconnect the drip, and then we must get him into the cellar."

"Will he manage, sharing a bed with Claude?" Raoul asked.

"No, I can't risk any undue pressure if Claude was to turn in his sleep. He must be on his own," replied the doctor.

"I'll slip down and ask Louis and Marguerite. They will know what they have that is suitable," added Edith.

While Louis and Edith carried the old bed-chair from the attic down to the cellar and lined it with a bolster and pillows, Raoul and the doctor dressed Arno in a shirt, a pair of long underpants and woolly socks.

"It is essential to keep him warm, to guard against shock," stressed the doctor.

"All is ready in the cellar. Shall I help Raoul carry Arno down the stairs?" asked Louis.

"In a minute Louis – what are we to use as a stretcher?" asked Dr Debrett.

"Oh, I thought we could just lift and carry him."

"No, we must take care not to open any of his wounds."

"What about the cupboard door?" asked Raoul, pointing to the store cupboard in the corner of the kitchen.

"The screwdrivers are in the barn. I'll get one," said Louis as he hurried from the room.

Ten minutes later, Arno was laid as comfortably as possible in the bed-chair with the bolster along the length of his back and a pillow to his front to make sure he didn't roll onto his back. The doctor fixed up another drip, then sat and waited with the others for him to regain consciousness.

"I've done what I can for now," he explained. "Arno is very weak and very ill, and the next forty-eight hours are crucial. We must keep him warm and quiet, and someone must be with him all the time. Hopefully he will sleep, but I don't know what mental damage he has suffered. If he becomes distressed, then you must wake him; just talk quietly and try to reassure him. Don't give him anything to drink. If he asks for water, wet his lips with a sponge, but again I must stress that he can't have anything to drink. I'll call in the morning and give him another shot of morphine."

Arno moved his head. His eyelids fluttered and a moan escaped his lips.

"He is coming round now. Claude, come here where he will see you – he will need your encouragement if he is going to make it."

Claude managed to sit up, then carefully bent forward and touched his brother's hand. "Arno, it's me, Claude. You're going to be OK. We are safe now."

Arno's eyes focused on his brother. He blinked two or three times, smiled, then slipped into sleep.

"I'll go now. See you in the morning, and goodnight to you all."

"I'll let you out, doctor, and thank you for all you've done," said Louis.

Raoul helped to clear up in the kitchen, then went to bed for the first time in two days. Edith, who had also stayed awake the previous night, waited until the plasma drip was finished and then disconnected it.

"Edith, you go to bed now, you must be very tired. I've put some blankets on the settee in the parlour for you. I'll stay up tonight, then you can take over in the morning," said Marguerite.

It was to be a long night for Marguerite. When everyone had retired to bed, she made herself comfortable with cushions and a blanket on one of the apple boxes. Shortly after midnight she was awakened by Claude, who was having a nightmare and screaming, "No, no." Marguerite rushed to his side and gently woke him up.

"Ssh, Claude, it's OK now," she comforted him with her soft, soothing voice. "There now, wake up."

"They were burning Arno," he sobbed.

"Look, Arno is over there. He's still sleeping; we mustn't disturb him. Would you like a warm drink?"

The young man nodded his head. "Yes please. Marguerite, do you think Arno will get better?"

"I don't know. The doctor said he was very weak, but the damage wasn't as extensive as he had first anticipated. We will have to wait and see. Here, drink this – I brought a couple of flasks down earlier, just in case you should wake up."

After a while Claude drifted into sleep, but Marguerite sat with her eyes wide open, staring into space. Suddenly Arno started to moan. Again she got up, this time to look at the young lad. He was only twenty. Arno lay on his right side, propped up to protect his back and his left side. He looked grey, and his forehead was cold and clammy. Marguerite knelt beside him, talking quietly to reassure him. When he was calm, she went up the stairs into the kitchen, making herself a cup of coffee and filling a hot water bottle for Arno. She wrapped the bottle in an old cardigan and placed it at his feet.

"Water," whispered Arno.

"I'm sorry, you can't have anything to drink yet but I can wet your lips for you with this cold sponge. Would it help if I held your hand?"

Arno clasped his fingers around the proffered hand, and Marguerite was surprised by how much strength he had. In time Arno relaxed into a sound sleep. Marguerite wondered if she could now extract her fingers, which were cramping, without disturbing him. Carefully she unwound Arno's hand from hers and stood, massaging the small of her back. It was 4.30, and Louis would be getting up to do the milking in another hour's time. Oh, she was so tired, but the others had all been awake the previous night – the night of the rescue. She bent over Claude, who was in a deep sleep, and then she checked on Arno. He too was sleeping.

Louis and Raoul both rose early, and after making coffee for breakfast, Raoul took two mugs down into the cellar for Claude and Marguerite. Claude had a temperature, and Arno was restless.

"I'll stay now, if you want to get some rest."

"No, I'm all right – you and Louis have plenty to do. I'll stay until Edith is ready to take over," answered Marguerite.

The evening milking was finished and supper was about to be served when there was a knock on the kitchen door. Louis went over and greeted Father Joseph, the new young priest at St. John the Baptist's church in the village.

"May I come in?" asked the priest. "Sorry to come while you are having supper, but it was awkward for me to get away earlier."

"Come and sit down, Father. Will you dine with us? There's plenty for all," invited Marguerite. The priest gladly joined them at the table – the food at the refectory was inclined to be poor and unappetising. Everyone chattered to make him feel welcome, but each wondered why he had come. He had only been at the church for six weeks and wasn't well known.

When the meal was over and they had moved away from the table, Father Joseph hesitated, then, touching Louis on his arm, said quietly, "Dr Debrett asked me to call."

Louis looked at the priest in bewilderment.

"The sick men, especially the younger one… he thought I might be of some help," he added quietly so no one else heard. Fear was visible on Louis' face as he begged to be excused and went outside in pursuit of Raoul. Within seconds Raoul came back into the kitchen and asked the priest if he might have a word in private, outside.

"I can't understand, Father, why Dr Debrett should ask you to call. What do you want exactly?"

"You are right to be careful, my friend. Dr Debrett is a friend of my parents; he has known me all my life. He spoke to me in the strictest of confidence, you understand. The young men, they are both very ill and he thought I might help supplement his treatment in a way. Could I try, please?"

Raoul nodded. "Come this way, they are in the cellar."

The young priest nodded a polite 'good evening' to Edith; then bent down over Claude. "How are you, my friend?"

Claude looked up at the priest and saw the compassion on his face. "I feel so responsible, it was I who encouraged Arno to join us. It will be my cross to bear."

"If God gives us a cross to carry, He always makes sure our backs are strong enough to bear the burden. At Arno's age there are no grey areas, only right and wrong, and he would have chosen the same path even without you. Put everything into God's hands. When we ask for His help it is never refused," said Father Joseph. Then he turned to the younger man. "Arno, let us put our hands together and pray."

Arno moved slightly, bringing his hands together. Father Joseph enveloped them with his own as he knelt at the side of the sick man and quietly prayed for courage and faith in God's love. Then he put his hands on Arno's head and blessed him. When he got up he went back to Claude and laid his hands on Claude's head and asked for God's forgiveness and faith to make him whole, then he went up the stairs and into the kitchen.

"I must be on my way. The other farms I have visited today have been asked for a contribution towards the church's Saints' Day Fete; I thought it a good cover story for coming here." He then left.

When all was locked up for the night, Louis and Raoul joined Edith and Marguerite in the cellar with the sick men. Claude had managed to walk a few steps and the clammy fever had left Arno.

"It was when Father Joseph came," said Edith. "He seemed to take the tension away with him."

"Yes, when he laid his hands on my head, I could feel a hot sensation burning through me, then I relaxed and felt at peace," said Claude, Arno agreed; the same sensation had happened to him.

The following day Arno was allowed to drink water, and in the evening had an egg beaten into a glass of milk. Edith returned home to her husband Jean Pierre, and life returned to normal at the farm.

Five days after the operation Dr Debrett called to see his patients, and while he was there Father Joseph came. Raoul was in the yard repairing the barn door and so was the first to see him.

"Good afternoon Father."

"Hello, I'm glad I've seen you. I've been wondering: how are you going to manage when the children return home?"

Raoul looked at the priest. Why was he asking him? They weren't his children. The priest must have read his thoughts.

"I ask you because I understand you're the one in charge; the leader." He paused and looked into Raoul's eyes, then continued. "Moving men under cover of darkness isn't so difficult I know, it goes on all the time, but sick men, that is an entirely different operation."

"You seem to know a lot. I had no idea Dr Debrett was so well informed," said Raoul haughtily.

"Please, you mustn't blame the doctor – it's because he doesn't know that he asked me to help."

"Oh, and can you help?"

"Yes I think so, but I'll need your assistance. Before I came here I was at the monastery near Tallouse. One of the monks is a qualified doctor; he runs a small hospital in the cellars. A friend of ours has a barge on the canal nearby. If you could get the two brothers safely to the north of the bridge at Gerrond I could arrange for Jacque to be waiting there on the river with his coal barge. I had a walk along the riverside this morning, and there's a clump of bushes which would give ideal cover if you got there first."

"Thanks. I'll see the others, but we must wait for Dr Debrett to give the go-ahead."

Two nights later, Claude and Arno, wrapped in warm, dark clothing, were lifted onto an ingenious contraption similar to a sedan chair for two, but without the refinements of a roof and side walls. On this they were carried by four men through the woods and across several fields. As they approached the road they needed to cross to get to the river, Pierre whispered to warn them of the convoy of lorries in the distance.

"Quick, lie down. Sorry lads, but can you crawl towards the hedge?" asked Raoul.

The six men lay prone in the darkness for what seemed hours.

"What's keeping them, Pierre? Can you see?"

"They've stopped," he answered.

"I think they've got a puncture. One or two are smoking; I can see the glow of their cigarettes," said Louis, who had incredible eyesight.

"We'll have to wait, I dare not take a chance at crossing the road, not with that moon shining. Why couldn't it have rained?" said Raoul.

Half an hour later the German convoy began to move. Slowly it approached the spot where the men were hiding. The second vehicle was being towed by the first lorry, its front wheels jacked up with chains, making speed impossible. At last the last taillight was out of sight.

"Come, we must hurry – I hope Father Joseph is with his friend and they are still waiting for us. We must have been hanging around here for over an hour."

Raoul and Louis helped Arno and Claude onto the carrying frame; then Jules and Pierre joined them in lifting the frame and carefully carrying the sick men across the road and into the wooded area that led down to the river. There was no barge in sight. With a sinking heart, Raoul thought they were too late, he realised a barge couldn't moor in this stretch of river without drawing attention. Suddenly there was a movement in the bushes and a young man dressed in a sailor's dark jumper, and with a beret on his head, came towards them.

"You've made good time, all things considered," said Father Joseph.

"Oh Father, I thought we'd missed you. There was a convoy."

"Yes I know, it would seem someone had scattered nails on the road just before the convoy came. No doubt they'll have been swept up by now, leaving no trace; it's just a pity they chose tonight." The priest then put his hands to his mouth and hooted three times, just like an owl.

"We must wait a little longer; the barge is out of sight of the road."

Within minutes, the barge came quietly into view, turned round and backed into the place where the men were waiting. The brothers were gently but quickly lifted on board and the barge moved away downstream. Raoul firmly shook Father Joseph's hand.

"Thank you, we couldn't have done without your help. May we call on your services again in the future?"

"Saving life is the same as saving souls; I'll be glad to help any time, but care and discretion must always be observed. I'll bid you all goodnight." With that the priest disappeared into the night and the four friends made their way home.

"I must confess, I'm glad to see them go: it will be a relief for Marguerite and the children can come home again. I've missed them," said Louis.

"Yes, we can get on with our work now. The Leconec factory are working on some bearings for the Nazis; we must slow down production. Any ideas? Raoul asked.

They reached the edge of the wood and crossed the now-deserted road. After they had crossed the second field, Jules Betton and Jean Pierre bid them goodnight and turned towards the village, and Raoul and Louis returned to the farm.

Chapter Five

Daisy pulled her old dressing gown round her and tied the belt as she went to answer the door.

"Oh! It's you, you don't know, oh… I'm sorry, you had better come in."

Aunt Annie stepped over the threshold into 33 Felton Street. What a strange greeting. She looked around the small living room. It had a forlorn look, and there was no bustle or excitement in the air.

"Is Alice at the hairdresser's then?" she asked.

"No, she's in bed," answered Daisy.

"In bed? Shouldn't she be getting ready? It's half past eleven."

"Please sit down. I don't know how to tell you, but the wedding is off."

"Off? It can't be! I don't believe it; Kevin wouldn't let her down."

"Kevin… Kevin is dead," Daisy sobbed.

Aunt Annie jumped up and put her arms round the young girl who had been such a tower of strength to her niece in her hour of need.

"Oh my God. Oh Daisy, please luv, don't cry. Just tell me what's happened."

Daisy told Annie how she had heard from Kevin's friend that Kevin had failed to return from a flying mission, and how this morning Alice had received a letter from his commanding officer.

"The doctor left some tablets for her. We made a cup of tea and gave her two, and she was asleep when I went upstairs at eleven," said Daisy. "Would you like a cuppa?"

"Yes please; after a shock like this, I think I need one."

They sat for ages, talking; then Daisy's Aunt Doris came back from the hairdresser's.

"Oh, I am glad to see you – I couldn't let you know; I didn't have your address and Alice was in such a state we couldn't ask her. I'm so pleased you've come, she does need you," said Aunt Doris.

"Would you mind if I went upstairs to sit with her?"

"Of course not, but there's only a rickety chair so you won't be very comfortable. Daisy will show you the way."

"Thank you, I'll manage. I just want to be there when she wakes up, poor bairn."

Alice awoke when the clock had just turned two. She turned over; then opened her eyes.

"Auntie?" she said in a small, quivering voice.

"Hello darling. Oh, my poor child," said Aunt Annie as she rose from the chair and went to sit on the bed where she cradled her niece in her arms.

"Oh Auntie, I want my Kevin," she sobbed, her whole body shaking. For the first time since hearing the terrible news, she was able to cry. After a while, aunt and niece regained their composure.

"How did you know, Auntie? Did Daisy send for you?"

"No luv, no one sent for me. I was coming to see you."

"Oh yes, the wedding. I asked you to come, didn't I?"

"It was a terrible shock. I just can't believe it."

"Have you read my letter from his commanding officer?"

"No luv, but Daisy told me you'd received one."

"Please, Auntie, I would like you to read it to me," said Alice, holding out the buff envelope.

Aunt Annie took the letter from Alice's outstretched hand and began to read.

My Dear Miss Brownlow,

It is with deepest regret that I have to tell you that Flight Lieutenant Renwick was reported missing, presumed dead, on the 4th of June 1942.

He was a first class pilot, and a good and loyal friend. I came to know him very well. He talked about you to me and had great plans for your future. His fellow officers had the customary collection for a present for a happier occasion, but in the circumstances we would like you to accept the enclosed cheque. If there is any way I can be of help to you in the future, please do not hesitate to get in touch.

Yours sincerely,
Raymond Ellison
Squadron Leader

Aunt Annie looked at the enclosed cheque, and her eyes widened at the amount.

"They must have thought a lot of him: £25! You'll do well to save this for when your baby comes."

"Why Auntie, why had it to happen to us? Mum said it would be a bastard! Oh Auntie, what am I going to do? If only Mum and Dad could be like you." She broke down, sobbing, and Aunt Annie clasped her firmly in her arms.

She let her cry for a time; then asked, "Do they know, your mum and dad? Do they know about Kevin?"

Alice shook her head.

"Well I'll go and tell them; they may feel differently when they know. Now you try and go to sleep. I'm booked in at the George for tonight but I'll come and see you in the morning." She bent down and kissed Alice's wet cheek, then went downstairs.

"Oh, Daisy was just about to bring a tray up to you; I've made a few sandwiches. Would you like a drink? I was hoping Alice would eat something – I am so worried about her," said Aunt Doris.

"Yes, so am I. I'm going to see her parents tonight – between you and me, they are the last people I want to talk to but I have promised Alice. Thank you, I would like a cup of tea."

The evening sun was about to set as Annie turned into Melbourne Road where her brother Joe lived with his wife Nelly. She had put off the visit as long as she could by having her evening meal at the hotel. She was angry and sad at her brother's weakness in always following his wife's lead, and wasn't quite sure how she would handle the situation, but someone had to try to bring some peace into her niece's life. She rang the bell and after a short time Joe opened the door to her.

"Well, of all people, fancy seeing you here! Come in lass, come in."

They went into the living room where Nelly was sitting listening to *Saturday Night Theatre* on the wireless.

"Well, this is a surprise! What brings you to Lincoln?"

"It depends. What brought me to visit Lincoln at this time of year was Alice's wedding, but that's not why I'm here."

"Oh, I am surprised, I never thought he'd marry her," said Nelly.

"I can't think why you should say that – they both pleaded with you to let them marry. Anyway, he hasn't. He can't."

"I don't think Nelly and I want to hear any more. We've washed our hands of her," said Joe.

"You didn't let me finish. He can't marry her because he is dead."

An ominous silence filled the air, broken by Nelly's shrill retort. "Well that's nothing to do with us. She's made her bed; she must lie in it."

"It's everything to do with you; both of you. Alice is your daughter and she needs you now more than ever. If you hadn't been so unreasonable they would have been married last Easter," retaliated Annie.

"That's enough, Annie – we don't want to hear any more," put in Joe.

"No, I don't suppose you do, but that young man gave his life for the likes of you. Why are you always such a coward? You sneer and scoff at others, but you should look at yourself. You could have gone in the last war, but no, you were 'too young' – too young be blown; there were younger lads than you went, and now you say you are too old! Maybe you are for the armed forces but there are lots of jobs you could do, but like all the other cowards you hide in your cushy, safe job. You don't even do fire watching – frightened of getting your hands dirty, eh?"

"I think you've said enough, Annie. I want you to leave."

"Oh, I'm going, but I wonder what Michael will think when he hears how you've treated his sister?"

"It's nothing to do with Michael," Nelly shouted.

"Well, we will see where he spends his leave, then. That'll be interesting." With this parting shot, she stormed out of her brother's house, leaving the front door wide open. She was fuming. How could her own brother be so immune to his daughter's plight, and that wife of his, stuck-up bitch, called herself a mother. *Huh! I'm more of a mother than she is, and from now on I'll be one to my dear Alice.*

Annie walked through the park, trying to compose her thoughts before returning to the George. How was she to break the news to Alice that she had failed in her mission to change her parents' attitude? She had seen the hope in the girl's eyes when she had told her she would go and visit them, and she had even said that they might feel different now. How wrong she had been. Her brother and his wife had no feelings for anyone. How could they be so cruel? On reaching the George she went straight up to her room. From Kevin's description last Christmas, she realised it was the same room he had occupied when he had come to Lincoln to spend his Christmas leave with Alice. She sighed – at least they had been together then, thanks mainly to Michael and herself.

At half past nine on Sunday morning Aunt Annie was once more in the house in Felton Street. Alice was dressed and sat in the chair next to the empty fireplace. She looked very pale.

"Alice, I've been thinking – with all these air raids around here, it would be better and safer for you if you came to stay with Uncle John and me. Keswick is a safe area; we hardly ever have an air-raid warning and it would be so nice for us to have a baby in the house," said Aunt Annie.

Alice looked up in alarm at her aunt. "But what about Mum? You promised to go and see her; you promised," said Alice in an accusing voice.

Aunt Annie got up from the chair by the table and went over to her niece, gently putting her arms around her shoulders.

"I did go, honest. I'm sorry luv, I tried, but they didn't want to know."

"Didn't you tell them about Kevin? They'll want me to go home when they know, I know they will," shouted Alice.

"Alice, I'm so very sorry, I've told them everything. I tried. I even told them how upset Michael would be at the way they've treated you, but nothing I said would move them. They don't want anything more to do with you."

Alice was numb. During all of the six weeks she had been away from home, at the back of her mind she was sure her mother would forgive her, especially once she was a respectable married woman, but now that could never be: Kevin was dead. She sat, staring in front of her, dry-eyed.

Aunt Annie tried to comfort her, but she never moved. Daisy spoke to her, but there was no response. Aunt Annie turned to Daisy's aunt.

"It's as if she's in a trance. What are we going to do? I'm frightened."

"I think we should send for the doctor. There's the baby to consider," said Aunt Doris.

"I'll go," said Daisy. "I'll be back within half an hour."

Fifteen minutes later, Daisy returned in style in the doctor's car. The doctor had just returned home from church as Daisy had reached his house. Dr Denton had brought Alice into the world, and knew all the family. He shook his head. He just couldn't understand any mother turning away from a child in need, and Alice was very much in need of love and understanding at this tragic time.

"Alice, look at me," said the doctor.

Alice stared straight ahead with unseeing eyes.

"Oh dear, she is in a state of deep shock. Hmm... I can't treat her myself; I don't have the knowledge or the experience, but I have a friend who specialises in such cases. He runs a private nursing home not very far away; I think we should take her to him," the doctor said. Then, turning to Aunt Annie, he asked, "Perhaps you will come with us?"

"Now?"

"Yes, the sooner Dr Grant sees her, the sooner you can take her home with you. I can think of no place better for her convalescence."

Dr Denton stood up and gently helped Alice to her feet.

"If you could steady her at the other side, I think we may persuade her to walk to the car."

Slowly they made their way into the street and to the doctor's car.

"Could you pack her case, Daisy? I'll call for it later," said Aunt Annie.

The doctor drove first to his own house, where he left aunt and niece in the car while he telephoned his friend Dr Grant. Five minutes later they were driving out of the town and into the countryside. Alice still hadn't spoken; she just sat on the back seat of the car with her aunt, staring blankly in front of her.

The doctor, turning his head slightly, said, "Dr Grant has a nursing home just ten miles up the road; he will see Alice there this afternoon. She may need to stay for a few days."

"Whatever it costs, doctor – my husband and I will find the money."

"Well, it may not be necessary. We will see," added the doctor.

They drove on in silence. *What a pity*, thought Aunt Annie, *all this lovely scenery with the trees full of early summer blossom, and Alice, who loves the country, being totally unaware of her surroundings.*

Soon they arrived at a large stone-built house with lovely gardens. No sooner had the car stopped than the front door opened and a man in his fifties came out to greet the doctor. They talked for about five minutes, both with grave expressions. Then, with a smile, Dr Grant came over to the car and spoke first to Alice and then to her aunt.

"Come along inside, we were just about to have some tea," said Dr Grant, who then led the way while Dr Denton and Aunt Annie guided the younger woman into the house.

"If you would like to sit here on the settee with your niece, I'll get Mrs Bradley, my housekeeper, to wheel in the tea trolley."

"Thank you doctor," said Aunt Annie.

As they sat drinking their tea the two doctors made general conversation, but although they spoke to Alice she didn't respond. Staring ahead, she drank her tea and put the cup and saucer back onto the tea trolley.

"Do you think she can hear us?" asked Aunt Annie.

"In a way. Let me explain: the body is very sensitive and has its own way of coping with injury. Often when there is serious physical injury, the patient becomes comatose; this is the body insisting on complete rest. In Alice's case she has received a severe mental shock and her mind has blocked her senses, so although she can hear us her mind doesn't recognise or interpret what she hears. When we ask her to sit or stand, she will obey because these are natural responses to everyday commands, but where she has to think, her mind puts up a shutter," said Dr Grant.

"Oh I see. I think I understand, doctor."

"Well, I'll talk with her." Turning to Alice, he stood up and bid her follow him into his study.

While Dr Grant was with Alice in his study, old Dr Denton invited Aunt Annie to walk with him round the grounds of the nursing home. The gardens had been laid out with much thought and care.

"What a pity Alice couldn't be sharing this with us. She loves flowers and prefers to see them growing rather than in a vase," Aunt Annie said.

"Yes, all in good time. Let's hope she will find happiness again. These are lovely roses; the shape is perfect. Just smell the bouquet." The doctor bent down, cupped the rose in his hands and breathed in deeply. The pair continued their walk through the rose garden, through the archway dripping with purple clematis and into the herb garden which was laid out in the Elizabethan style with pebbled areas dividing the different herbs. The scents mingled and rose into the warm air.

"Oh, how beautiful – just look at this water garden; oh, and the waterfall! My, those fish certainly move fast. Look at that one there!" exclaimed Aunt Annie.

"Look at that beauty: it's a fan-tailed comet. See how gracefully the tail sweeps the water as it swims," said the doctor. Then he consulted his watch. "Time we were getting back. I think Dr Grant will be waiting for us."

"Thank you for showing me these wonderful grounds; it's all so soothing. I feel stronger already and more able to cope with Alice."

"Yes, I'm glad you realise there will be difficulties. You say your husband is a schoolteacher, in which case he will have had some experience in dealing with difficult children during his long career. You may have to treat Alice like a child for a while, and you will have to be very firm with her," the doctor said as they re-entered the house.

"We have just finished our little chat; you timed your walk well. Did you like the gardens?" asked Dr Grant, turning to Aunt Annie.

"They were truly wonderful, and so peaceful."

"If you could spare me a few moments please, before my good friend takes you both home – I think Alice will be better being with you than in a hospital environment," said Dr Grant, and he led Aunt Annie into his study. After he had finished explaining Alice's state of mind and advising Annie how to cope, he walked with them to Dr Denton's car and saw them safely on their way home. Alice was very quiet; her aunt spoke to her two or three times but in the end gave up the struggle. The evening sun was slipping behind the golden-edged clouds as they arrived back in Felton Street.

"I'd be grateful if you would let me know how Alice is getting on. Perhaps you would write to me in a week or two, but be sure to have your own doctor look at her as soon as possible and give him Dr Grant's letter," said the doctor as he bid farewell to Aunt Annie and her niece.

Doris and Daisy were eagerly awaiting their return, but one look at Alice, who was staring vacantly ahead, told them that no instant miracles had been performed.

"Well now, I'm sure you're ready for a cup of tea. Kettle won't be long in boiling," Aunt Doris said.

"Could Alice stay here another night?" asked Aunt Annie. "I'll have to check the train times and connections, and arrange for my husband to meet us in Penrith. It's a long journey and could be difficult; I just hope it won't be too much for her," she added, nodding towards Alice who sat where they had put her at the side of the fireplace, staring into space and plucking the material of her dress where it covered her thighs.

"As if you needed to ask! She's welcome to stay as long as she likes," said Aunt Doris.

Monday was a busy time for Aunt Annie. She had written to her husband John on Saturday night after seeing her brother, asking him to prepare the guest room and to meet them in Penrith as their train would arrive ten minutes after the train for Keswick had left. Now she wrote the message in readiness to telegraph her husband with the time of their arrival. She packed her overnight bag, checked the wardrobe and drawers to ensure she had not left anything and wearily trudged downstairs for breakfast. It was going to be another very long day. After checking out of the George, she made her way to the bus stop, where she caught the bus that would take her as far as the Co-op. From there it was only a short walk to

Felton Street, where she arrived at 8.30. Alice was there on her own as Daisy and her aunt had gone to work, but Doris had left a note for Aunt Annie. Alice gave her aunt the note; then sat down again, gazing fixedly into the empty grate.

Dear Annie,

We couldn't wait to see you this morning – duty calls! I have made you some sandwiches and put some chocolate biscuits into a bag; they're on the draining board.

Hope you have a good journey, and keep in touch.

"How kind, Alice – Doris has left us some sandwiches! They'll be nicer than anything we'd get on the train. Alice," shouted Aunt Annie, "You can hear me and you must answer when I speak to you."

"Pardon, what did you say?" Alice asked in a whisper.

"I asked if you had packed your belongings, are they all here? I've ordered a taxi to be here at nine o'clock."

Alice nodded her head towards the case and sewing box, fastened now with an old leather belt.

"Everything 's there."

Aunt Annie recognised the sewing box her nephew had lovingly made for his sister. Thinking about Michael, she decided she would write to him as soon as she got back home and tell him what was going on. He apparently had no idea that his sister was pregnant, or that she would have been married by now if fate hadn't stepped in.

The taxi arrived on time and set down aunt and niece outside the railway station at nine minutes past the hour. Their train was due out at 9.22, and was already waiting at the platform.

"Come along Alice, we should be able to get a window seat," said Aunt Annie. They walked along the platform. The middle carriages of the train were nearly full, but the ones nearer to the goods wagon were almost empty and this carriage had a corridor, which was considered safer for women who travelled alone.

"Here we are, we'll go into this one," Aunt Annie said to Alice, gently urging her into a compartment which was occupied by an elderly couple. "You sit there dear, I'll just put our cases up onto the rack."

Alice did as her aunt told her, and sat hunched in a corner seat. Her aunt sat next to her and retrieved two magazines from a carrier bag, giving the *Picture-Goer* to her niece and keeping the *Woman's Weekly* for herself. At 9.25, just three minutes late, the guard came along the platform banging all the doors closed. Then he waved his green flag, and with a jerk, the train set off. No one else came into the compartment. The old gentleman sat opposite Alice, reading his newspaper. His wife sat with her head resting on his shoulder and closed her eyes to doze. Alice sat in a world of her own, not seeing anything or saying anything. *Well*, thought Aunt Annie, *I'm glad I've got a good read.*

After a while the gentle swaying of the train rocked Aunt Annie to sleep, and it was with a start that she woke up as the train stopped.

"This is Nottingham; this is Nottingham," a voice announced through the loudspeaker.

"Come on Alice, take your case; this is where we get off." Aunt Annie struggled with her overnight case, her shoulder bag and Alice's sewing box. Alice just did as she was told, like a sheep she followed her aunt from the train, along the platform, over the bridge and onto another platform to await the train for Derby.

"Would you like an apple, dear?"

"Yes please, Auntie." They stood eating their apples – there were no seats on this platform; not even a waiting room. Some soldiers were also waiting for the train and Aunt Annie asked a sergeant if he would be so kind as to keep an eye on their luggage while they walked up and down to stretch their legs.

"Aye that's all right, leave them there," he answered. They walked to the end of the platform and back again, just as the announcer pronounced that, "The train for Derby will be arriving at platform three in five minutes and will depart at 11.02. Passengers for Crewe must change at Derby."

Aunt Annie thanked the sergeant, picked up the sewing box and her overnight case and moved further down the platform with Alice following closely behind. The train steamed into the station, filling the air with acrid smoke. No sooner had the train stopped than everyone surged forward, making it difficult for the passengers to alight or board.

"Keep close to me, Alice; I'll try to get you a seat."

The train was packed: in one compartment ten people were squashed together, five on each side; in another a woman sat with a shopping basket on the seat beside her.

"Is that someone's seat?" asked Aunt Annie. The woman ignored the question and looked out of the window.

"Come along Alice, you can sit here," Aunt Annie said as she lifted the basket and placed it firmly onto the startled woman's knee. A sailor sitting next to Alice was clearly amused by the incident, and gallantly stood up and offered his seat to Aunt Annie. It was so warm in the train, and added to their discomfort was the fact that they were travelling with their backs to the engine. The train swayed from side to side as it rattled over the points where one line crossed another, and the journey seemed unending. Aunt Annie looked at her niece in concern. Her face was ashen and there were tiny beads of perspiration on her upper lip.

"Are you all right dear?"

"Yes thank you, but it's so hot and I feel sick."

"Here, have this mint; it may help. Only fifteen minutes more and we should be in Derby."

The train began to slow down as it approached the station. People were moving in the corridor, and soldiers with kitbags resting on their shoulders squeezed past the passengers staying on the train. Aunt Annie stood up to get her suitcase down, but the sailor who had given up his seat for her quickly moved back into the compartment and lifted it down for her.

"Thank you, I hope you have a safe journey. God bless you," said Aunt Annie. Then, turning to her niece, "Come on Alice, we change trains here."

They squeezed along the crowded corridor, and at last they were on the platform. Aunt Annie looked up at the clock.

"Twelve o'clock; I thought it was a long journey. They're running ten minutes late. Well, at least our train isn't due until 1.53 so we've plenty of time to have a nice lunch. Let's put our cases into the left luggage office and then we'll see about our dinner."

Aunt Annie led her niece from the station to the Midland Hotel. The large Victorian dining room was half-full, and there were several uniformed officers but the majority of the diners were middle-aged businessmen in dark suits, plus a scattering of elderly ladies who chose to reside in hotels rather than battle with ration books and running their own homes without staff. The waitress dressed in black with starched white collar, cuffs and apron came to take their order, and Aunt Annie chose a cheese omelette and salad with apple pie and custard to follow. After lunch they decided to have a short stroll and look at the shops. The sweet shop was particularly attractive, with lots of chocolates and sweets on the display in the window.

"What a pity they are all made of wood," exclaimed Aunt Annie.

The Co-op window had a similar display, again with mock boxes of things no longer obtainable. At half past one they returned to the railway station, and after collecting their luggage made their way towards platform 5.

"Auntie, I'm tired; it's one train after another. How much longer will we be?"

"I'm sorry luv, but we've two more trains to catch before we get home. Tomorrow you can rest in bed for the whole day."

Again the train was packed, and they had to stand in the corridor. Alice sat on her upturned case, while her aunt stood watching and praying the girl wouldn't faint. It was so hot and stuffy. The small window openings only let in a slight movement of air until the train entered the three-mile-long Harecastle tunnel, at which point smoke and soot permeated the corridor. When the lights came on those standing near to the windows closed them, but not before a young boy got a speck of soot in his eye. Once through the tunnel the train slowed down as it approached Crewe station.

"Come on luv, we'll go to the buffet for a cup of tea; then have a rest in the ladies' waiting room. We have over an hour to fill," Aunt Annie said.

The train arrived from London on time, but it was crowded with servicemen. Some were going on leave, while others were returning to their units. This was the last train the women would have to catch, and would take them through to Penrith where John would be waiting for them. The two women waited patiently for the train to empty, while nearby about twenty young sailors poured onto the platform. On seeing the two women, one called back to the others still on the train.

"Hang on there, let these ladies through."

Aunt and niece boarded the train and were politely ushered into the now-empty compartment vacated by the sailors.

"Oh thank you, we've been travelling since this morning and my niece isn't in the best of health. Thank you all so very much."

The train rapidly filled up after the sailors had gone, but Alice and her aunt had seats next to each other and facing the engine. At Preston the rear carriages, which were going on to Aberdeen, were detached and shunted onto another line, thus leaving a shorter and lighter train for the climb up over Shap. Aunt Annie decided that now was the time to take out the sandwiches Doris and Daisy had so kindly packed for them. The air was cooler and the scenery was varied and pleasant to gaze upon. As the train raced over the North Lancashire plain, dipping down towards Morecambe Bay, they caught a welcome glimpse of the sea, and beyond the miles of sand they saw range upon range of the Lakeland hills.

"We should soon be home; just look at that marvellous scenery. It does your heart good," sighed Aunt Annie. The train took on water at Dillicar trough; then there was a further stop at Tebay for the extra engine to be coupled for the five-and-a-half-mile push up to Shap summit. The sun was setting, casting a golden glow over the mountainside. As the train slowed for the approach to Penrith station, Aunt Annie gently roused her sleeping niece.

"Come on dear, wake up; Uncle John will be waiting for us."

Chapter Six

Two weeks after young Alice's arrival in Keswick, Annie and her husband John were sitting in the garden enjoying afternoon tea under the apple tree.

"Well luv, Alice seems to be settling down all right," said John.

"Yes, I suppose she is – she looks more rested and she's eating better, but she doesn't talk to anyone, does she?"

"The doctor did warn you that it would take time. Perhaps when Michael comes she will open up a bit. You did write to Michael, didn't you?"

"Yes, but when will he get my letter, and if he's on convoy escort in the North Atlantic what chance will he have to visit us? No, the best I can hope for is a letter. I can't expect miracles."

"Where is she, by the way? I haven't seen her since dinnertime," asked John.

"She took some sugar lumps; I think she'll have walked up to Lockwood's field to see the ponies. Poor bairn, she's so locked into herself. I wonder if she talks to the ponies? The doctor did say that he thought some emotion would eventually release her from this conflict. It would never have happened if that hard-faced bitch hadn't turned her out."

"Now, now Annie, don't upset yourself; after all, we stand a very good chance of becoming grandparents in the course of time – something we never thought possible a month ago," coaxed her husband.

Annie looked lovingly at him: he understood her so well, and it had been a great sadness to them both that they were childless. They had always made much of Joe's children for that reason, and maybe this was God's way of compensating them, but it was a cruel burden on young Alice.

Alice looked at the beautiful blue sky, with little puffs of white clouds here and there. The sun shone continually, and hardly an aeroplane disturbed the peace. She went into her aunt's larder and lifted down the tin holding the sugar lumps – sugar was on ration, but five cubes wouldn't be missed. With her small bounty she let herself out of the house. Aunt Annie was used to her going for walks on her own, and she approved of plenty of fresh air and gentle exercise.

Alice was happy in her cotton-wool world. She thought of nothing and no one, so no memories invaded her mind to bring her sorrow. Each moment of each day was endured, and at mealtimes she ate the food put in front of her. When her aunt and uncle spoke to her she answered them, but they didn't expect her to say much and so she rarely spoke and returned to her quiet world. The only time her emotions were disturbed was when the two young ponies trotted up to her, as she stood leaning over the gate, and demanded the sugar lumps she never failed to bring. As they nuzzled against her a longing she didn't understand would sweep over her, making her feel sad, and on these occasions she quickly left the ponies and hurried away, not knowing why.

During the week while Uncle John was at school, Alice helped her aunt. They made jams and jellies, tended the garden and went shopping. After the midday meal Aunt Annie insisted that her niece rest for at least an hour, and then she was free to go on her lonely walks. Although she worried about her niece, she also welcomed the break from the constant strain of trying to make conversation.

Then one day a letter arrived from Michael. He had enclosed a letter for his sister saying how pleased he was to know that she was staying for a holiday with their aunt, but he didn't mention the baby or even Kevin. The letter to his aunt was very different: he had liked Kevin and thought Alice would have been happy with him; it was a tragedy made worse by the cruel and unwarranted actions of his parents. When he was back in port and had some leave he would come and see if he could help restore his sister back to normality.

Alice returned home just as her uncle got back from school.

"Hello luv, enjoyed your walk, have you?" he asked.

"Yes thank you."

They walked up the path together, and Aunt Annie came to the door to welcome them.

"I'm glad you're both early – I've had a letter from Michael and there is one for you too," she said to her niece. They went into the living room and Aunt Annie got the envelope from behind the clock and handed it to her niece. Alice just stared at the letter.

"Well, aren't you going to open it?"

Slowly Alice ran her thumb under the flap of the envelope and took out the single sheet of paper.

Dear Alice,

Hope you are keeping well. I was pleased to hear from Auntie that you are staying with her for a holiday. We always did have good times in Keswick. I envy you the peace and beautiful scenery .Our scenery doesn't change much: we have grey skies, grey seas and grey battleships, and even the seagulls are grey. It's very noisy and when there's a swell on, lots of the lads are seasick; fortunately my stomach is like cast iron so I weather the storms well. Next time we come into port and I get some leave I will come and see you. We can explore all our old haunts together.

Take care of yourself,
Your loving brother
Michael

"He's coming on leave, Auntie; Michael says he's coming to see us when he gets some leave."

"Thank God, it will be lovely to see you both together again."

Alice walked along the shore of the lake, remembering the happy times she had spent there with Michael. She laughed inwardly to herself – oh, what fun they would have. Perhaps they would get a boat and row around the island as they used to do in the school holidays. Today was extremely humid and the air was very still, and not even the slightest breeze came from the lake. At the first rumble of thunder Alice turned her footsteps towards home, but by the time she reached the school by St. John's church the heavens had opened and the rain came lashing down. Running up the steps, she sheltered in the church porch, but the driving rain came almost to the door. Michael and Alice had often stayed with their aunt and uncle when they were small, and Aunt Annie had brought them to this church, knowing that they would follow the service more easily than the one at the chapel where she and her husband were regular attendees.

It seems years since she had last been inside the church, but she bravely pushed open the door and walked down the centre aisle and sat down in a pew. Alice raised her head and looked around her at the two angels Alpha and Omega guarding the choir and sanctuary; then she gazed at the stained glass windows on her right. The first one showed the woman searching for her lost coin; then the good shepherd and the sower. She felt at peace and slid to her knees and started to pray. She asked God to bless all her family and to bring Michael safely home on leave; then repeated the Lord's Prayer. When she had finished praying, she stayed on her knees for a while longer, and suddenly a strange sensation passed through her stomach, like a strong pulse. She held her breath, and as she relaxed the feeling returned. It was the first time she had felt her baby move inside her. For weeks she had put it out of her mind that she was pregnant, but now she turned again towards the windows and saw Jesus blessing the little children. Tears ran down her cheeks: her baby would be loved by Jesus and by Alice herself, and she vowed to devote her life to making it happy.

The storm had been over for a full hour and still Alice had not returned. Aunt Annie was worried – after all, thunder sounded very like falling bombs and who knew what effect it would have on her niece. Again she went to the front door and looked along the road for the young woman. At last Alice turned the corner and came into view. Aunt Annie knew at once something had happened. Her niece looked different and moved differently; could it be that her mind had cleared? As Alice reached the gate, her aunt called to her.

"Alice, wherever have you been? I've been worried."

"Oh Auntie." Alice threw herself into her aunt's arms, sobbing.

"Why, bairn, whatever is the matter? Are you hurt? Have you had an accident?"

"Oh Auntie, what will Michael think when he finds out?"

"Michael? What do you mean?"

"If he disowns me I don't know what I'll do. We've always been such good friends."

Aunt Annie let her niece cry for a bit; then, pulling her towards the settee, they both sat down.

"Now then luv, don't you worry – I know my Michael and that's why I wrote to him and told him all that's happened. He knows you are expecting a baby and that's why he will be spending his leave with us and not going to Lincoln. Now tell me what's happened – you've never mentioned the baby since I came to Lincoln for you."

"It was in the church, Auntie – I went in there to shelter from the rain and I found myself kneeling and saying my prayers. Then I felt my baby move – oh Auntie, I want my baby; Kevin wanted it and he would have made a very good father, so I must be an extra-good mother. You will help me, won't you?"

"Yes, my dear. If only you knew just how much Uncle John and I are looking forward to being grandparents, 'cause that is what we want to be."

With the return to normality, Alice changed her ways. She no longer went for walks on her own, but stayed close to her aunt. One day they took the bus into Kendal where a friend of her aunt's kept a draper's and haberdashery shop. The lady had a good stock of wool and let Alice have some without coupons. Fully equipped with patterns and knitting needles, aunt and niece spent many happy hours sitting in the garden creating the baby's layette, and on these occasions the topic of conversation was of course babies, and Alice's baby in particular.

One Thursday after finishing their shopping they dropped into the Moot Hall where a bring-and-buy sale was being held in aid of the evacuated children from Tyneside, where many of them had been bombed out. There were some fine things donated for sale, but what caught Alice's eye was an old-fashioned swinging cradle.

"Auntie, look at this!"

"What a beautiful piece of furniture. Of course it will need a good clean and perhaps French polishing. Would you like it?"

Alice smiled and nodded her head. It was reasonably priced, as the sellers didn't always recognise the valuable pieces when they saw them. Aunt Annie paid for the cradle and arranged for Tom Hawksworth to deliver it later that evening.

As they neared the open gate, Aunt Annie said, "Well now, I wonder who's been to see us? I distinctly remember closing the gate."

They walked round to the back and found that someone had left a grey canvas kitbag propped up against the door.

"Auntie, you don't think it's Michael's, do you?" No sooner had Alice spoken her brother's name than he came walking up the path. Alice ran to him and was given a big hug.

"Michael, I can't believe it's you!"

"I've no need to ask how you are; you're positively blooming," said Michael; then, turning, he asked, "and how is my favourite auntie?"

92

"All the better for seeing you; I didn't dare hope for you to get leave so soon. It's wonderful having you here. Isn't she bonny?"

"You both look bonny; a sight for sore eyes. I'm going to enjoy this leave, I can feel it in my bones."

That evening was a celebration. News was exchanged, and after supper the indoor cricket game was brought out and played just for old time's sake. Then to seal the evening, Aunt Annie brought out a bottle of her homemade bramble wine. The next evening Michael took his sister to the cinema, and on the way home suggested to Alice that she might change her name by deed poll to Renwick so that her child could bear its father's name.

"I think Kevin would have wanted that," said Michael.

"Yes, I think you are right, but won't it cost a lot of money?"

"I don't know. You would have to contact a solicitor, and perhaps you could enquire as to whether it is possible and how much it is likely to cost. I have to go away for a couple of days, but when I get back we could see if my bank balance would stretch to pay for it."

"Thank you Michael, you are so good and kind. I was afraid you would be like Mum and Dad and not want to know me anymore."

"Thanks for the compliment! I hope I'll never be as bigoted and narrow-minded as those two. It's not going to be easy for you, bringing up a baby with no man to support you, but there will be hundreds like you by the time the war is over. Oh, and once you've changed your name it would be better if you wore a wedding ring – you did say Kevin had given you one?"

"Yes, when we went to Great Yarmouth for that weekend. I felt like a proper married woman then," said Alice.

"Well, go on feeling like a proper married woman; Kevin loved you, so always remember that."

The days that followed were idyllic for Michael and Alice. In the mornings their aunt packed a picnic for them, and as soon as breakfast was over, off they went for the day on the local bus. One day they travelled to Bo'Ness and had a sail on the lake; another day they went to Kendal. Often they would have a leisurely climb up the hills surrounding Keswick, and on these occasions Michael was always very considerate of his sister's condition, having been charged by his aunt to take great care of Alice. On Tuesday evening Michael announced his intention to visit a friend the next day, and maybe stay overnight.

"But you don't know anyone here!"

"Ally, I'm only going for the day. If we have a few drinks in the evening I'll be back by Thursday lunchtime at the latest, OK?"

With this promise, she let him go.

Midday found Michael outside the Royal Baths in Harrogate. He gazed at the fine Georgian buildings around him; then walked on in search of a café. After his meal at the Copper Kettle he wandered around the streets, looking at the licensees' names displayed over the doors of the many public houses. None of them said 'Renwick'. He had come to Harrogate with the purpose of finding Kevin's family, hoping to establish some sort of relationship between them and Alice, but first he had to satisfy himself of the reception Alice could expect. It was nearly midday closing time and he was no further on in his quest, so taking the bull by the horns he went into the next pub he came to. After paying for his beer he asked the landlady if she knew the Renwicks and where he might find them. He was in luck: the landlady had met Mrs Renwick at a lady victuallers' dinner. The Renwicks were tenants of a pub on the Ripon Road on the outskirts of Harrogate. With the address written on a scrap of paper, Michael made for the railway station where he got a taxi.

The low-ceilinged room was dark after the bright sunlight outside. Michael ordered half a pint of beer at the bar; then took his drink and sat at one of the marbled-topped tables. It was quiet, with only a handful of customers. An old farmer sat on a stool at the bar, chattering away to the landlord. Gradually the pub emptied as the other drinkers returned to their work, and the landlord called time as he put the towel over the pumps and bid farewell to the old man.

"Excuse me, could I have a word?" asked Michael.

"Sorry, I've called time; I must lock up now."

"But I've got to talk to you. I knew your son Kevin; he was to marry my sister."

The landlord hesitated. He seemed to be having difficulty breathing for a few minutes, but then he nodded at Michael and bid him sit down. After locking up, he sat down opposite Michael.

"We wondered about her. She never got in touch; not even a word of condolence."

"She couldn't – she had a nervous breakdown when she heard about Kevin. She doesn't know I'm here. I had a job finding you; I didn't know your address. I don't want to cause you or your wife any pain, but I wondered if you knew about their wedding plans?"

"Oh yes, naturally – Kevin told us they were going to spend part of their honeymoon here."

"Did he tell you Alice was expecting his child?"

"So that was why they were in such a hurry. No, he never mentioned anything. You say your sister had a breakdown – how is she? Is the baby all right? She hasn't lost it, has she?"

Michael shook his head. "No, she is still expecting and the baby is due in December. It's a long story: Kevin and Alice had been eager to get married since last Christmas but my parents were against it; they said she was too young. I don't think they thought Kevin was good enough."

"They'll be satisfied now then," said Mr Renwick with some bitterness.

"Please, don't misunderstand – I don't think anyone would have been good enough; they're terrible snobs. Anyway, when they discovered she was pregnant they turned her out. I don't know what would have happened to her if her friend hadn't taken her in. Two days before the wedding was due to take place Kevin failed to return from his mission and it was all too much for Alice. She had a complete mental breakdown and her reasoning only returned ten days ago when she felt the baby move. I didn't tell her what I had in mind because if it turned out that you'd rather not know her it would be better to let sleeping dogs lie. She has suffered more than enough."

"Well, you've taken the wind out of my sail, that's for sure. I'll have to break this news to my wife; just stay here a minute or two while I tell her."

After about ten minutes sitting alone in the bar and wondering if he had done the right thing, Michael stood up to stretch his legs just as Mr Renwick returned.

"Would you like to come through? We're just about to have a cuppa – sorry I was so long, but you'll understand it's been a great shock to my wife."

Michael followed Kevin's father into the living room behind the bar. A small, slightly stooped and prematurely grey-haired lady aged about fifty appeared from the kitchen carrying a tray that she carefully placed on the table.

"So you, Lt. Brownlow, are the bearer of this wonderful news. I'm Rosemary Renwick." Smiling, she held her outstretched hand towards Michael, who grasped it warmly.

After talking for about half an hour Rosemary went to the sideboard, took out a photograph and passed it to Michael.

"A friend of Kevin's gave us this – it was the last photo he had taken."

Michael looked at the smiling faces of Alice and Kevin. It had been taken at a wedding, and the young couple looked so very happy it brought a lump to his throat.

"When we heard the terrible news about our youngest son, something inside us died. There was this huge void – we had nothing left of him but our memories, but now we are to have a grandchild. This is truly the silver lining to a very black cloud."

"Mrs Renwick, this is far more than I'd hoped for. I'll give you my aunt's address and I'll get her to write to you – perhaps between you, you will be able to arrange a meeting with my sister." And with this parting comment, Michael took his leave.

By the time Michael got back to Keswick it was late and they were all sitting round the wireless listening to the nine o'clock news.

"The RAF have made more daylight raids on the Ruhr," the announcer declared, and Aunt Annie got up and went into the kitchen to make a bedtime drink. Michael followed her and told her of his successful mission.

"Michael, I can't believe it – you're a wonderful lad. I'll write to her tomorrow while you're out on your morning walk with Alice."

"Auntie, when you meet her, will you suggest to her that Alice should change her name to theirs? I didn't get the opportunity, and it would be polite and kinder to have their permission first."

"Yes, I'll do that; now let's go and tell Alice the good news."

Two days later Michael returned to his ship, and Alice once more returned into her shell. Uncle John and Aunt Annie became worried about her, until John had an idea.

"Alice, you know we're very short of teachers at the moment – well, I wondered whether you might like to train? It would be ideal for you: you'd have some independence and security for yourself and your child. You were very bright at school and I'd be more than willing to help you with your studies."

"Uncle, it's a marvellous idea, but honestly, can you see them wanting to employ a pregnant woman?"

"You wouldn't be pregnant by the time you're trained, and I know someone who can't wait to be nursemaid number one."

Within a few weeks Alice was busy pouring through school textbooks, preparing lessons and learning how to teach young children. Then a letter came from Mrs Renwick in answer to Aunt Annie's letter. It read:

Dear Alice,

My husband and I are looking forward to meeting you. Kevin loved you dearly, and he didn't tell us of the upset you were having with your parents but he let us know just how important you were to him. In the short time you had together you made Kevin a very happy man, and I shall always be grateful to you for that. Now you are to give us a grandchild. Please come and meet us – I hope you will become the loving daughter Kevin promised to find for me.

With love from your mother-in-law,
Rosemary Renwick

"Oh Auntie, what a lovely letter! Kevin always said his mother was wonderful, and she certainly sounds nice."

"When will you go to visit them?" asked Aunt Annie.

"I... er... I can't."

"Can't? Whyever not? Come on Alice, just think what that poor woman's been through these last few months. It's obvious she wants to get to know you, and just think of your baby – it will need relations like everyone else."

"But Auntie, I don't know her; I'm frightened and she may not like me. Anyway, I can't travel in this heat now my legs have started to swell up."

"Alice, you are being a coward and just making excuses."

Alice pouted, then snatching up her letter, she stalked out of the house. Her aunt shook her head. She understood the younger woman so well. Poor Alice – she wanted to run to Kevin's mother but was too scared to do so, and the fear of being rejected again, as her own parents had rejected her, was too strong.

That evening, prompted by her aunt, Alice wrote to Mrs Renwick, saying how delighted she would be to travel to Harrogate to meet them, but as the recent heat wave was causing her some discomfort it would be better to wait for the cooler weather. This at least would buy her some time to get used to the idea.

Chapter Seven

Raoul had a spring in his step as he walked up the hill to the clinic run by the monks. He had been in France for three very successful months, and the group he commanded had worked well together. After rescuing the Dubois brothers from the Gestapo their confidence had increased, and with it their trust in Raoul. The German operations had been thwarted in many areas. Monsieur LeBott, the grocer, had donated a stone of sugar that the rats had been at, and this was converted into syrup and spooned into petrol tanks at the German vehicle compound. The damage done to the engines took weeks to repair. The foundry making castings for some of the German weapons had an unexplained explosion in one of the furnaces, and the damage caused was so great the work had to be transferred to another town. An outbreak of food poisoning broke out at the German HQ, and the local workers who had their meals there stayed away from work on the pretext that they too were suffering, but it didn't stop them playing boules in the seclusion of Jacque's yard. The night before, the telephone wires to all key installations within an area of six square miles had been cut. Raoul had called a halt to their work and ordered a six-week holiday from further exploits as a safety measure.

It was over a year since Raoul had seen his wife. Monique was a doctor who had been in practice in Marseilles and had worked with the underground movement there, but the Germans had infiltrated the group, which ended with several of their members being shot. Monique escaped and came to the clinic to fill a vacancy left by Brother Lucien, who was the only doctor at the clinic and had recently died of a heart attack.

Father Justin welcomed Raoul and showed him into the room by the front door. "Dr Monique will be along shortly; she is just doing her round of the wards," he explained; then left.

Raoul looked around him. The room was typical of many of those found in nunneries and monasteries. The walls were whitewashed, and the small lancet-shaped lattice window had wooden louver shutters bleached white with much scrubbing and the many hours of sunshine. The bare wooden floor was also brushed white. The only decoration to be seen was a wooden crucifix made from dark oak with the figure of Our Lord carved from bone, hanging on the wall opposite the fireplace. Raoul wondered if they ever enjoyed the luxury of a fire burning in the grate. The only furniture was a table and a wooden settle. After five minutes surveying the room Raoul sat down on the settle and waited patiently for his wife to appear.

The petite young lady with glossy chestnut curls and dark brown eyes slowed her step as she came nearer to the door. Why oh why did she always feel so nervous at the prospect of seeing him? She loved him; her feelings were never in doubt, but she was afraid now of meeting him again after twelve-and-a-half months, yet this was not such a long time in comparison to the wives who waited for their husbands to return from the war zones in Africa and Burma, some of whom had already waited two years.

The handle turned and the door opened. Raoul got to his feet, a slight gasp escaped his lips and then she was in his arms and nothing else mattered.

"Darling, oh it's wonderful feeling, you in my arms again and it's not just a dream," whispered Raoul.

"I couldn't believe it when I got your card. I wonder what the censors made of your message?" laughed Monique.

"Come on, let's go outside – this place isn't conducive to passionate embraces."

"You can leave your bag there by the table; it'll be quite safe. I'm longing to show you round; it is so beautiful here and the monks are very friendly and helpful," said Monique as she gently nudged her husband towards the door. With love shining in their eyes, the young couple went out into the sunshine. As they walked up the hill through the vines, Monique chatted and pointed out places of interest: the wayside shrine, and further down the hill the stone angel guarding the well. The waters there were said to have healing properties.

"You see that house over there, next to the field with the haystack? That is the house of Madame Bercuse, where I live and where you will be staying. Madame B has given us her double bed for the duration of your stay."

"How did you explain my existence to her?" asked Raoul.

"I told her the truth. She is the only one who knows I'm married, apart from Father Justin."

"Was that wise – can she be trusted?"

"Yes darling, Madame B and I met while we were both working with the resistance in Marseilles. Her husband was one of the seven men killed by the Nazis, and she came here to live with her grand-mère. When the old lady died this spring, Madame B asked me to move in with her so we could keep each other company."

They had been walking for twenty minutes along the narrow footpath that twisted through the rows of vines, now heavy with fruit.

"Do you think it will be a vintage year?" asked Raoul, pointing to the fruit.

"I hope so. The monks will be very busy, there are so few of them left. Some have been taken away and forced to work on the new buildings to house the German soldiers."

"How many are there left? Will they be able to manage their farm and the vineyard?" asked Raoul.

"There are fifteen of them now, and that includes Father Justin, but most are old and can only do light work. Father Justin managed to convince the authorities that two younger ones we use as handymen around the clinic were medical orderlies, so they let them stay."

"I'm surprised they were so obliging!"

"Well, perhaps it is because we looked after an *oberleutnant* so well when he had a heart attack."

"You mean you have German patients?"

"Yes – German, French, English, American and a Pole," answered Monique.

"How on earth do you manage to come by such a variety of nationalities?"

"Well, the local people are the French patients and we get an occasional German from the town, usually higher-ranking officers with their gout and ulcers. The American who left us last week was a pilot with the USAF – he came to us at night via the resistance – and the two English sailors and the Pole came through the same system. The two sailors will be transferred to the convalescent ward in a day or so – that's in the monastery, so they may be able to help the brothers with the farm work – and that will leave us with only the Pole in our isolation ward."

"And when will he be leaving you?" Raoul asked. He knew Monique always liked to share her work with him. A sad look crossed her beautiful face.

"I don't know; he was very ill when he came to us – he had shrapnel wounds and other injuries including a broken jaw. Now his jaw is healing but he doesn't talk; I think he may still be in shock but he would need expert help and there is no one I dare turn to, so we are concentrating on the damage to his body and can only hope and pray that his mind will heal itself with time."

Hand in hand they continued their walk in silence, and when they arrived at a sheltered spot by the side of a stream they sat down, putting their arms around one another. Their lips met, and they passionately embraced.

"Six whole weeks, *ma chérie*. Do you realise this will be the longest time we have ever spent together since we married?" said Raoul.

"Yes, in nearly six years we've only had the long weekends or a stolen short break. Oh darling, I wish you could stay here with me."

"You mean you want me to become a monk?" he laughed. She shook her head, and with a mischievous grin said, "Hardly, darling – a monk can't do things like this." She pressed her body close to her husband's, and it was dusk by the time they reluctantly drew apart and, sighing but happy, returned to the clinic to pick up Raoul's bag; then went down the hill to Madame B's house, their home for the next six weeks.

Madame B welcomed them as only a French woman can, with a warm embrace and kisses to each cheek.

"*Bon accueil*, Monsieur Raoul, I have heard such a lot about you! I'm so pleased you have been able to make this visit. Monique, I have left a chasseur in the oven, the table is laid ready and now you must excuse me – I have a date with the Father at church."

"You don't think she is on her way to reporting me to the authorities?" asked Raoul anxiously.

"Oh darling, I would trust B with my life and yours. I have put my life in her hands before today – how do you think I got away from Marseilles?"

"Sorry, I'm not used to being in such a vulnerable position."

"Come, bring your things; I'll show you upstairs."

Monique led the way to Madame B's bedroom. It had a wide double bed piled high with feather pillows covered with white broderie anglaise pillowcases. Raoul put down his bag; then picked up his wife and almost threw her onto the bed, pinning her down with his strong body.

"Well, you are certainly making up for the last twelve months," giggled Monique, as Raoul expertly divested her of her clothes, then removed his own. When they were both naked they lay on the bed, touching and exploring one another; then they made love and slept.

104

It was quite dark when they awoke. Monique pulled on a cotton negligee; then, leaning over, she woke her husband with a kiss.

"Come along sleepyhead, we have a date with a chasseur. B will never forgive us if we don't do justice to it."

"Come back to bed. I'm not hungry for food, only for you."

"I have a busy morning tomorrow and must eat to keep up my strength, so hurry up. See you downstairs in ten minutes," ordered Monique. Raoul swilled his face; then pulled on his shirt and trousers and went downstairs to join his wife.

"Mmm, this smells good. I sometimes wonder how B gets such good food, but ask no questions and be told no lies," said Monique.

"This is good wine, is it from the monastery?"

"No, I think this is one of the bottles purloined from the cellars of the Chateau Mintre after the Germans requisitioned it."

"Monique, when you escaped from Marseilles I was relieved; I thought – well, hoped – you had finished working for the resistance. Must you keep putting your life in danger? Isn't it enough to heal bodies and leave me to help the resistance?"

Monique smiled and placed her hand on her husband's arm.

"Dearest, that is all I am doing: healing the sick within my limited powers. If B is still working with the underground movement I know nothing of it. Come, finish your supper and then we can return upstairs for a night of love."

The next few weeks passed all too quickly. Monique went to the clinic each morning, but was free to spend the afternoons with Raoul. Every afternoon they would walk through the vines and enjoy just being together. Raoul wished he could take her to the cinema in town or to the local café for a meal, but this wasn't possible. His papers were in order should they be stopped at any time, but it wasn't worth the risk of drawing attention to themselves.

One night during the third week of Raoul's stay, someone came to the house, banging on the back door. It was well past midnight. Raoul was awake instantly, and Monique turned over and woke up.

"What's the matter darling? You are so tense."

"Didn't you hear it? Someone was banging at the back door," whispered Raoul. Seconds later there was a light tap on the bedroom door and Madame B put her head round.

"Sorry to disturb you, Monique; you are wanted urgently at the clinic. Henri has brought the truck for you."

Monique kissed her husband and reassured him that this was quite normal for any doctor on call, anywhere in the world. Then quickly she dressed and left.

Father Justin welcomed her.

"They arrived just over half an hour ago; I could see at once that something needed to be done quickly. The theatre is all ready."

Monique changed into a sterile gown and entered the theatre. The young man laid on the table looked clammy and was restless. After checking his pulse Monique gave him an injection to sedate him and removed the dressing from the wound just below his right shoulder.

"Phew, what a stench, and what a mess. I'll have to open this up; if only these baby doctors would learn to leave gunshot wounds open."

The next thirty minutes was spent opening the wound and swabbing away the inflamed pus; then she cut away all the dead tissue. Once satisfied that the wound was clean Monique doused sulphadine over it and left it open to heal. The next twenty-four hours would tell.

"Take him into the little room beyond the isolation ward. I don't want him to be disturbed, and keep him sedated. I'll be back at ten."

Raoul was waiting in the kitchen when she returned. Madame B had kept him company with a pot of coffee.

"Well, I'm back to bed, and you two would be wise to follow my example."

Monique looked at Raoul and smiled. "She mothers me and she is only ten years my senior – still, she's right. I may have a busy morning; I only did the one operation but they brought four patients altogether."

Raoul offered to go to the clinic with her the next morning to help, but Monique shook her head – not many people knew of his existence. Those who had met him were told he was a cousin, and only Father Justin and Madame B knew they were married. Raoul envied his wife for her importance to the community; since he had arrived he felt he was vegetating, but you couldn't infringe on other networks of resistance. It wouldn't be safe.

Another hot, sunny Saturday afternoon, Madame B had packed a picnic and a bottle of wine for the young couple. They hadn't much time left as Raoul was due to return to Epernay on Tuesday. The time had gone much too fast for them, yet at times it had dragged for Raoul and he longed for the excitement and the challenge of outwitting the Germans. They stopped in a sheltered spot by the stream.

"I'll remember this place always," said Raoul. "It's where you became my wife again." He gently pulled Monique down beside him on the grass. "Have you thought what you will do if things happen, er… change? I mean, well… it…?" He stopped speaking, not knowing how to ask her.

"What are you trying to say, Raoul? Do you mean if the Germans win?"

"No, not that; I mean us – if… well… if it wasn't just the two of us."

"You mean a baby! Oh, but Raoul, I couldn't – how could I explain it to the monks, to the authorities? They all think I'm an unmarried, dedicated doctor; they never see me as a woman."

"Monique, you are a doctor – surely you must see that it could have happened already."

Monique, startled, sat up and stared in front of her. Her hands had flown protectively to her stomach.

"Please Monique, you must promise me that if you discover we are to have a child you will get Madame B to contact her friends and get you safely across the frontier into Switzerland. And get word to me; write to my auntie at the bank in Zurich."

They sat quietly, each consumed with the same thoughts. If only they could live a normal married life like so many other people. Even before the war their first two years of marriage had been spent studying for exams and training courses. Raoul had been selected to do research work in electronics, so his free time had also been curtailed. Now after the longest stretch of time they had spent together, they could have a child. What were they to do?

After they had been sitting pensively for some time Raoul put his arms around Monique. "Cheer up. Whatever has to be will be; where is your faith? If you are pregnant I know you will do your very utmost to protect our child, and if you aren't, why the gloomy face?"

Monique turned to him and smiled. "Come, I'll show you round the monastery as I promised."

They stood up and stretched, then after a reassuring cuddle walked hand in hand up the hillside to the monastery. On reaching the high wall they came across an overgrown path. Monique led the way through the weeds and undergrowth till eventually they came to a white wooden door. Monique put her hand into the creeper covering part of the wall and found the bell-pull. A tinkling sound could be heard a little way off.

"We must be patient; Brother Paulus is nearly eighty and very slow so it will take him a few minutes to reach the door," cautioned Monique.

"Do many people use this door?" asked Raoul.

"No, just the villagers at harvest time, and occasionally the night visitors."

"Night visitors? Do you mean that the resistance use it?"

"Oh Raoul, they are very careful and only about six of them know about it. Here comes Brother Paulus; I can hear his stick tapping on the path." No sooner had Monique spoken than the door was opened by an old monk whose back was bent with rheumatism.

"Dr Monique, how nice of you to call! We haven't sent for you…?"

"No, Brother Paulus; I hope you are all keeping well and not in need of my services. This is a social call, I have brought my cousin with me – I thought you might show us the gardens and Father Justin said you may show him the chapel."

A worried look passed over the old monk's face and he sadly shook his head. "It may be difficult. I think there is a mass being said."

"Well, we'll walk around the gardens and maybe the farm; they have their own hens and pigs," Monique said as she turned to her husband.

The old monk led them past the outhouses to the rose garden and sat on a seat by the lily pond, leaving the young couple to explore by themselves. Monique moved along the path bordered on either side with masses of colourful perennial flowers; the bees droned loudly and incessantly as they collected the nectar to take to their hives. Further on, they came to the six hives.

"These are Father Justin's pride and joy – you see that upturned wine cask over by the delphiniums? That is where he sits for hours in the summer evenings, singing to his bees."

"So the monks have their own honey?"

"Yes, and mead – it's delicious," answered Monique as she turned towards the orchard. The grounds inside the walled monastery were extensive. In the orchard were some ancient trees, but many younger ones had also been planted. Leaving the fruit trees behind, they walked round the vegetable gardens where cauliflowers, cabbages, carrots, beetroot, peas and salad crops grew in abundance.

"Well, the monks must live like lords with all this food," laughed Raoul.

"Not really; apart from themselves they feed the hospital patients and the children at the orphanage, and send baskets of vegetables to the old folks in the village."

"They really do devote their lives in the most practical way to the benefit of others. I feel quite humble," said Raoul.

"Never mind darling, I suppose we all do our best in different ways. After all, it would be a funny old world if we were all monks and nuns," teased Monique. "Hello Brother Joseph, how is Petra the sow?" she enquired.

"Come and see, she had twelve piglets yesterday."

Monique introduced Raoul as her cousin; then the monk led the way through the cowshed into a cell where a large pig lay on her side with a row of tiny pink piglets sucking at her teats.

"She looks very content. Will this be her last litter?"

"Yes, I think so – she is very old. We will be able to keep all of the young ones this time for future breeding. The Germans don't know we had her served."

Monique turned to Raoul and explained how the Germans had commandeered all the pigs, with the exception of Petra who was so very old. One of the farmers had brought his boar that he kept hidden from the Germans over to the monastery under cover of darkness hoping the sow would conceive; the Lord had been kind and now the monks once again had piglets to raise. They had learned their lesson and would in future hide all their young stock should the Germans visit the monastery again. Monique looked at her watch.

"Come, time's getting on and the mass should be over by now. I will show you the chapel and then I must look in at the clinic; I need to check the RAF boy I cleaned up the other evening."

They took their leave of Brother Joseph and returned to the rose garden where Brother Paulus still sat.

"Is the chapel free now?" asked Monique.

"Yes, I am so sorry I delayed you. Father Justin sent a message to say I was to show you everything." The old monk got to his feet and slowly led the way to the little chapel dedicated to the patron saint of France, St. Denis.

Inside the Baroque chapel, built at the beginning of the 17th century, Raoul was struck by the ornate splendour. The reredos at the high altar was a blaze of gold and silver, with painted figures in scarlet and deep blue. In an alcove stood a four-foot statue of St. Denis carved from Italian marble. Along the walls were paintings depicting the Stations of the Cross, and in the side transept was a picture of St. Francis.

"That picture doesn't look right," exclaimed Raoul.

"I was afraid of that," said Brother Paulus. "I said we should have found a larger one."

Monique explained to Raoul that the original picture that hung there was by Raphael and had been much larger, and when the Germans came the monks took it down and hid it, along with many of their other treasures. When they had seen everything, Monique and Raoul knelt in prayer; then Brother Paulus beckoned them to follow him into the vestry.

"Please, you are much stronger than I – could you push against that bookcase?"

Raoul looked perplexed but followed the old monk's instruction and pushed the end of the wooden structure. He thought at first that the wall was collapsing, but then the bookcase turned on a pivot and a three-foot hole was revealed.

"Monique, perhaps you could show the young man around. I will stay here and keep watch."

Monique took the torch from Brother Paulus and crouched down into the hole, followed by Raoul. They went into a short passage and down a flight of steps into a small, square room. Old cassocks were hung from pegs on the wall and there were some tattered old books on the lid of a very old carved cope chest.

"Well darling, what do you think?"

"Why is it so well guarded? There is nothing here anyone would be interested in; there's hardly room to swing a cat," said Raoul.

"Sorry, I was teasing you. Can you take that crucifix down?"

"Are you sure? The monks won't want me to desecrate the place."

"Please darling, do as I say. All will be revealed."

Raoul carefully took down the cross; it was very heavy and underneath the nail it had been hung from was a ring.

"Now if you pull that ring, you will see our retreat."

Raoul followed his wife's instructions and when he pulled at the ring a part of the wall swung back, revealing a large room with beds on both sides, a table and chairs in the centre and store cupboards at each end. To the side, at the far end, was a door.

"That," said Monique, pointing to the door, "leads into the caves and potholes. It connects with the clinic – this room was built by the resistance and only a handful of people know of its existence. Men could live here undetected for weeks."

"Yes, but I still wish you weren't involved."

"Darling, none of the monks or members of the underground movement would involve me. To them I am just a doctor; not even a woman doctor."

"Speaking of which, I thought you had to see a patient? It's nearly six o'clock."

They made their way back up the steps and into the chapel, then after thanking Brother Paulus they returned to the door in the wall where Monique lifted the latch so that when the door closed behind them it would lock.

"I wish time would stand still; I'm so dreading next Tuesday when we will have to say *au revoir*. We will only be able to walk down here two more times."

Raoul stopped, put his arms around his wife and pulled her close to him. "Come on, *chérie*, it's not like you to be so down. I have to return on Tuesday, but that's not to say I won't be back to see you soon."

"I know Raoul, but how soon – weeks; months? Please don't let it be another year, I've got used to you being with me and it will be so lonely when you leave." Monique wept into her husband's shoulder. Raoul comforted his wife; then gently pushed her in the direction of the clinic and walked quickly down the hill to Madame B's house.

When he entered the kitchen Madame B was just putting a chicken into the oven for their evening meal. He waited until she had poured out coffee for them both before he broached the subject he knew was dangerous to discuss, but in the time he had known Madame B he had come to like and trust her.

"B, I know I shouldn't ask you and I understand that there are things it is best not to know about, but… it's Monique. I must know that if she were to discover she is pregnant, I can count on you to ensure she gets out of France and into Switzerland. You could arrange this, couldn't you? You have contacts."

"I don't think she is pregnant, but yes, it would be dangerous for her to stay here if she was. Not everyone is against the Germans, or maybe she would be accused of collaborating with them. Did Monique tell you I was in touch with the underground?"

"No, but one only has to sample your cooking to know that you aren't reduced to rations only, and Monique did mention the wine came from the German-held chateau. Please don't worry – it's probably my training that makes me so observant."

"Monique and I have been through much together, and I look upon her as my younger sister. I'll look after her and keep her safe. You have my word."

After breakfast Raoul went into the garden and dug over the patch of earth, ready for the autumn planting. He felt better doing something worthwhile, and as he finished the last row he looked up to see Monique coming towards him with two mugs of coffee. Later that afternoon they went for their walk, but this time with a purpose.

"Raoul, yesterday when I went to the clinic, the Germans had been. They questioned Father Justin and searched the clinic – Brother Alban saw them enter and went round to the side, and with the help of Brother Clement managed to get all our special visitors into the cellar and then into the caves."

"How many visitors have you got now?"

"There is the Pole, the airman and two Jews – we are just giving them refuge, they're not ill – oh, and an American with a broken leg. The Pole is going to live with the monks; he's strong enough to help them with the lighter chores and the work will be good therapy for him. The American will have to stay out of sight for at least six more weeks so we may keep him in the monastery, but the Jews will be moving on the day after tomorrow."

"That leaves the airman. What are you going to do with him?"

"Well Raoul, I wondered if you could help; you see, he is very anxious to get back to England and I thought you might talk to him."

Raoul smiled at his wife. "You scheming minx, that's why we are going to the monastery again, is it?"

"Thank yo,u I knew you wouldn't let me down." Monique smiled.

They reached the wooden door, but today when they pulled the bell the door was opened immediately by Father Justin. "Good to see you again," he said as he shook Raoul's hand. The couple were then led straight into the chapel where the airman sat in one of the front pews. Monique introduced Raoul, but didn't mention their relationship.

"Monique tells me you are in a hurry to return to England. I'm sure you all are, but why can't you take your chance with the local underground? What makes you so special?" asked Raoul.

The airman hesitated, then after a few minutes said, "The doctor trusts you, and she saved my life so I also will trust you."

"Thank you."

"I'm a fighter pilot. It was daylight when I was shot down, and I've also done reconnaissance flights in the past. Just before I was shot at, I saw something the Air Ministry needs to know about, and that's why I need to get back to Blighty as soon as possible. Going with the local resistance could take months; they've told me so."

"I understand your plight, but the resistance is the only way out. We could hardly book you a flight through Air France!"

"But Raoul, I thought you could have him flown out, like—" Monique stopped. Whatever had come over her, to implicate her husband in this way? She wasn't being fair. "I'm sorry, I didn't think."

"I can't promise anything, but I'll try. If you get caught, don't mention Monique. If you do, I will kill you with my own bare hands."

That night when they had finished supper, Raoul asked Madame B if she would get the leader of the local resistance to come and see him under cover of darkness. An hour later Ives came to the house. Raoul shook hands, recognising him as an old friend from his training school in England. It was agreed that as soon as Raoul had secured a pickup for the airman, Ives would get him to Epernay as they had contacts in the area.

They awoke early on Monday morning to heavy rain. Monique would have to go to the clinic but promised, barring emergencies, to be back by two. These were their last few hours together and both were tense and unnatural with each other, so Raoul was relieved when his wife finally left for work. The morning was bound to drag with nothing much to do, so he went upstairs to put all his things together in the battered old case, then returned to the kitchen and attempted to read a book. About half past eleven a thump came at the back door. Madame B was out, so with trepidation Raoul went to answer it. There was no one there. He looked about, and was just about to close the door when a hand beckoned him to the shed next to the greenhouse.

"Just a precaution; it's not fair on Madame B to tell her too much," said Ives.

"I didn't expect to see you again."

"No, but we had a message from a mutual friend, so when you have the flight details, tell Father Joseph. Goodbye, my friend."

The journey back to Epernay was slow and uneventful. Raoul's mind wandered back over the last six wonderful weeks, and then his mind cleared and he was alert to take note of the old, familiar surroundings. There would be no playful remarks about leaving his wife in the company of so many unattached males – only Louis and Marguerite knew he was married. It was dark when he reached the village, but he called first at the home of Edith and Jean Pierre for the latest news. Prudently he went to the back door and gave three sharp knocks. A few moments later the door was opened by Jean Pierre.

"Raoul, it's so good to see you, come in, it's so good to see you. Look who's here, Edith," called Jean Pierre to his wife. Soon the three friends were seated round the kitchen table with a glass of wine, and Raoul was eager to know what had been happening during his absence.

"The Germans went crazy; they searched the whole town but found nothing to incriminate anyone. Then they arrested all the men – yes, even me. We had brainwashed ourselves into believing we knew nothing, and so were unable to enlighten our captors. After four days they let us go."

"I'm pleased you got away with it. They didn't torture anyone?" asked Raoul.

"Not in the way they treated the Dubois brothers, but we were all kept in solitary with no light and only half a cup of tepid water a day."

"I'm sorry I left you all to suffer. I feel like a coward."

"Well I for one was glad you weren't around – imagine if someone had blabbed who you were! We would all have suffered; really suffered! After we were released they imposed a curfew; that's the sad news. Old Dr Debrett had a call-out to Madame Rouen – he knew she hadn't much longer to live so he went out after curfew to visit her and on his return a German shot at him. He wasn't hit, but the shock brought on a heart attack and he died the next morning."

Raoul put his head in his hands. Of all the good people in the world, Dr Debrett had been one of the best.

"To think he did so much for everyone; it doesn't seem fair."

"He knew he hadn't long. I was with him when it happened, and he was at peace with himself," Edith told Raoul.

"Is the curfew still in force?"

"Yes, but if you go down by the field and round the church wall you should be OK. You know how to be invisible," cautioned Jean Pierre.

Raoul reached the farm at midnight. He didn't want to wake up the household, so he climbed onto the haystack and snuggled down for a night in the warm straw.

Chapter Eight

Alice turned over onto her back. It was the most comfortable position for her to be in now. She rested her hands on her raised stomach and smiled at the little thuds she felt as her baby moved inside her. It was the 1st of October: a new day and a new month. Alice noticed the sun shining outside. *That must be a good omen for the coming month*, she thought. On the 16th it would be her twentieth birthday; then two months later her baby would be born. Never had a baby been so eagerly awaited; not by just herself but by her Aunt Annie and Uncle John and Kevin's parents, who were all looking forward to becoming grandparents.

Alice wondered what it would be. She remembered Kevin asking her, if it was a girl, to call her Estelle; it was as if he had known he wouldn't be around when the baby came into this world. Most men wanted the firstborn to be a boy, but Kevin had wanted a girl. *Oh why did he have to die?* Alice turned and cried into her pillow; Kevin would have made such a wonderful dad.

Alice often wrote to her brother Michael – he understood what war did to people, and he had liked Kevin. She wrote as she spoke, jumping from one thing to another; talking of things happening now and also of the shared memories of happier times, but Michael understood his sister and answered her letters in the same vein.

Every Wednesday Alice received a letter from Mrs Renwick, sometimes as long as three pages. She always started by asking Alice about her health and that of Aunt Annie, and then she was away with her memories. Sometimes she talked about when she was carrying Kevin; she had craved oranges and hoped that if Alice was having cravings it would be for something obtainable, as the few oranges that arrived in England were rationed and only issued to green or blue ration books for children. She told Alice of the time when Kevin started to crawl, and of the mischief he would get into. Her letters were so warm and loving that Alice longed to meet her, but she still had the fear that Kevin's mother wouldn't like her. Alice never thought for one moment that her own parents would turn against her, but they had loved her once and if they couldn't forgive her, how could she expect strangers to? When Auntie Annie asked Alice when was she going to make the effort to meet this dear lady, Alice made excuses but her aunt remonstrated with her. Alice knew she wasn't being fair, and that maybe it was insulting to class Kevin's mother with her own. Aunt Annie had met Rosemary Renwick and they had become firm friends, and Alice wanted to believe her aunt but the hurt had gone deep. She remembered the black emptiness and the despair and the dreadful weeks lived through, which now, thankfully, she had been able to put behind her.

Now Alice's mind and memory had been restored, and she had a safe and happy home with her aunt and uncle. They showed their love in so many ways and were always ready to listen; they offered so many words of encouragement, little gifts and suggestions for the future. And the most important wish they all shared was the safe arrival of Alice's child so that Aunt Annie and Uncle John could become honorary grandparents.

If Uncle John's plans for Alice were successful she would be able to earn enough to support herself and her child, and such a career would ensure that they could spend the school holidays together. By midweek Aunt Annie was again badgering her niece to visit Mrs Renwick. Oh, if only she could, but something was holding her back. Maybe after her baby was born she would feel stronger and more self-assured. Now Aunt Annie was saying that she was going to invite Kevin's mother to tea on Alice's birthday, and that if Alice

119

wasn't present she would wash her hands of her. Auntie had never been so stern with Alice before – clearly she was running out of patience with her niece. Alice thought her aunt understood why she couldn't travel to Harrogate, but what on earth was she to do next week? Alice was a bag of nerves, yet Aunt Annie told her she was being a selfish coward and said that she was hurting Kevin in the spirit world by refusing to meet his mother.

Eventually Alice discovered a way to stop her aunt nagging at her: she got her textbooks out and started working on her studies. The examinations were to be held in March, and if she passed the preliminaries she could be a student teacher by the spring term. It was vital that Alice got as far ahead with her lessons as possible, as once the baby arrived she would be fully occupied. *By this time next year*, Alice mused, *I could be earning my living as a schoolteacher.* She'd decided that she would like to teach the five- to six-year-olds.

Five days before Alice's birthday, Aunt Annie received a letter to say that Rosemary wouldn't be able to come to the birthday tea. She had collapsed at the weekend and was taken to hospital, where she underwent an operation for the removal of gallstones.

"Well, you've got your wish: poor Rosemary won't be able to come to your birthday tea," said Auntie Annie.

Alice felt awful, and guilty too. She hadn't wanted her to come to tea, but honestly didn't wish her any harm.

"Oh Auntie, please, I'm sorry she is ill but you don't know how she really feels about me, the woman who seduced her son," Alice replied. Aunt Annie put her hands on Alice's shoulders and forced her to look at her.

"Listen, Alice – your baby is Rosemary's son's child. She loved Kevin and I know she will love you – I know her. I also know some people would tell you that by having this baby you are ruining your life, but to Uncle John and I, and to Rosemary and Harry, this baby is desperately wanted to fill a large gap in our lives. Oh yes, we are being selfish, but why shouldn't we be? John and I have been denied children of our own, whereas your parents had two, but only enough love for one. And when your baby is born it will be a little bit of Kevin restored to his parents, and you will have a part of Kevin that is your very own, so stop feeling sorry for yourself and start counting your blessings."

Alice felt humbled and ashamed and said she would write to Mrs Renwick, and when her auntie visited her in hospital she could take the letter with her.

Two days later, after returning from her visit to hospital, Aunt Annie told Alice how upset Mrs Renwick was that she was unable to see her on her birthday, and how she was afraid that Alice would think she didn't want to meet her. Aunt Annie had told her that the boot was actually on the other foot and Alice was in fact afraid to meet her, as she imagined that Kevin's mother wouldn't approve of her. Evidently Kevin's mum had become most upset, saying that Kevin had promised to find a daughter she would love and be proud of and that she had every confidence in her son's judgement. That night, after the tea things had been cleared away, Uncle John asked Alice if she would like to help him mark some essays. Alice was pleased and honoured that he had asked her.

"I'd love to, but I don't know how," she replied.

"Of course you do – here's a red pencil; just read through them and put a line through any incorrect spellings, and if any punctuation marks are missing just write them in, then award marks out of ten," Uncle John said.

"I will do my best, but will you check them when I've finished?"

"Yes of course, it will be good practice for you and I can assess your progress."

Alice must have been awake for some time without realising it. She was on her back as usual with her hands on her stomach, feeling the child moving around inside her, and then she heard the rattle of cups and saucers being arranged on a tray. On Sunday mornings Uncle John always brought tea for his wife and Alice before going along to the chapel to prepare for the morning service. This morning was no exception, but instead of Uncle John bringing in the tea, the door opened to a chorus of "Happy birthday!" from both of them. Uncle John carried in the tray, and Aunt Annie brought in four parcels.

"Eat your breakfast first; then you can have your cards and presents," said Aunt Annie.

"Thank you – oh what lovely roses! Uncle John, you are an incurable romantic, but I love you, both of you, and the best present to me is knowing I have your love."

"We've already had our breakfast downstairs, but we'll have our second cup with you," said Aunt Annie.

When Alice had finished eating her aunt laid out the parcels on the counterpane. The first one to be opened was from Michael; it was a length of blue Harris tweed material.

"Auntie, isn't it beautiful? Once I get my figure back into shape I'll make this into a skirt."

The next parcel was from Uncle John; a fountain pen and propelling pencil set. Then there was a big box from Aunt Annie; inside was a soft woollen dressing gown in scarlet.

"Auntie, oh, all your precious coupons! But it's wonderful."

"Yes, and you'll be glad of it when you have to get up during the night to feed your baby."

"Thank you, you are both so good to me. I wonder who this is from?" Alice picked up the fourth parcel. It was quite large and flat and had come by post, but the postmark had been smudged and as the address had been printed Alice couldn't recognise the handwriting.

"I wonder who it is from? Whatever it is, it's very soft."

"Darling, why don't you just open it and put us all out of suspense?" said Uncle John. Alice picked up the parcel again, and after further squeezing and poking, pulled the brown paper away and revealed a pretty blue flowered paper wrapping with a label that read:

To our dear daughter.
With love,
Rosemary and Harry Renwick

Inside the wrapping were two pairs of nylon stockings and a beautiful silk headscarf.

"Oh Alice, isn't it lovely? It's pure silk – look, it doesn't crease," said Aunt Annie as she demonstrated by rolling the scarf into a ball and letting it spring back into shape. For a moment Alice couldn't say or do anything, and then she was sobbing as if her heart would break. So much undeserved love and kindness from people she had yet to meet, but nothing from her own parents. Aunt Annie understood, and she put her arms around her niece and held her tight.

"Never mind love, just cherish those who do care."

The year moved on into November; the days shortened and heavy mists hung over the mountains for days on end. The war progressed and events were changing in the Allies' favour with Rommel's army in full retreat, but apart from Michael's letters from somewhere in the North Atlantic, the war didn't infringe upon the household in Keswick. Aunt and niece tried to have a walk each day, but most of the time was taken up with preparations for the birth of the baby; with knitting socks and bonnets, sewing flannelette nightgowns and smocking day dresses. A goose had been ordered for Christmas and the mincemeat, Christmas cake and pudding had been made. This would be the first Christmas Uncle John and Aunt Annie had spent in their own home for years – in previous years they had made the long journey to Lincoln to spend time with Alice's family, but now Alice was here in Keswick they had all the family they needed, and if some miracle brought Michael home on leave then Christmas would indeed be perfect.

Four weeks after her twentieth birthday Alice was sitting with her aunt in the living room finishing off some bootees when the front doorbell rang. Aunt Annie looked up at the clock.

"Half past two, now who could be calling at this time of day? No darling, don't get up, I'll go; I can move faster than you."

As she approached the front door she could see the outline of a tall person in uniform through the frosted glass panel. On opening the door the young officer saluted and bid her good afternoon.

"Oh," said Annie, feeling suddenly faint.

"Are you all right? I hope I haven't startled you."

"Just let me get my breath back; no, don't tell me who you are – you are too like your brother to be anyone else. You are Lawrence?" Annie said, holding the door open.

The young man had nodded his head. "I had to come. Is Alice at home?"

"Yes, but would you mind waiting in the sitting room? I'll have to prepare her – you look so like Kevin and she can't have the same shock I've just had."

Once Lawrence had been ushered through into the sitting room, Aunt Annie returned to Alice.

"Auntie, what's the matter? You look as if you have seen a ghost. Who was at the door? I hope it isn't bad news."

"No love, it isn't bad news, it's good news – you have a visitor. It's Lawrence Renwick."

"Kevin's brother? Oh, I never expected to meet him. Where is he?"

"I've shown him into the sitting room."

""But it must be freezing cold in there, and there isn't any fire."

"I'll bring him in here, but first I've got to warn you: he is so like Kevin they could have been twins. It gave me such a shock; I just had to prepare you." A few minutes later Aunt Annie re-entered the living room, followed by Lawrence, an eighteen-month-older version of Kevin. Alice stood up, gasped and sat down again.

"Hello Alice."

"Hello. Oh, for a moment I thought… Auntie told me but you are so like my Kevin." Before she could say anything else her voice had broken and she was weeping in Lawrence's arms.

"Sorry Alice, I didn't want to upset you but I had to come in uniform as I'm on my way home for ten days' leave. Kevin wrote such a lot about you in his letters; he was crazy about you, so I've come to say hello and offer my help." Lawrence sat next to her on the settee, and they chattered ten to the dozen while Aunt Annie made a pot of tea and buttered some scones she had made that morning.

"And when exactly are you going to make me an uncle?"

"Well, it depends if the baby arrives early or late. Kevin was often late, but he always had a good excuse. Christmas week is the most likely, the doctor says," Alice explained.

"It will be a super present for my mum – she spends all her spare time knitting for her future grandchild and talking about you. You've really got to meet her while I'm on leave. She mentioned your brother's suggestion to change your name to ours; it's a wizard idea. I hope you don't mind but I've spoken to our family solicitor and if you agree I will pick you up in my uncle's car on Tuesday at about ten o'clock and we can have lunch on the way there. Don't worry, I'll take good care of you."

Lawrence was so like Kevin that Alice was completely under his spell. It was arranged that she would travel to Harrogate to make the all-important change to her name and status, and just as Michael had urged her to wear the wedding ring Kevin had given her, now Lawrence also advised her to do so. Alice knew her aunt was worried about her travelling such a long way so late in her pregnancy, but she kept her fears to herself and Alice welcomed the chance the journey would afford her to get to know Lawrence better.

Tuesday was one of those rare days in November when dawn breaks in a misty drizzle only to dry out later, and by ten o'clock the sun was shining, promising a pleasant day ahead.

Lawrence arrived early, and he had brought a cushion for Alice to sit on and another one for her back, plus a woollen travelling rug to put over her legs for warmth.

"I've had strict instructions to give you the full VIP treatment, so Madam Princess, your coach awaits you," laughed Lawrence, as he bowed to Alice before ushering her into the front seat of his uncle's old Rover. It was just like being with Kevin, and she was so happy for the first time since that terrible day in June when news reached her of Kevin's death. Now she felt loved, wanted and at peace. The brothers had been very close friends and had the same mannerisms in speech and movement.

They stopped for lunch at a Commercial Hotel in Skipton. There wasn't much choice on the menu but nevertheless Alice enjoyed the steak and kidney pie followed by queen's pudding. Above all, though, she enjoyed Lawrence's company.

"If you want to visit the ladies' room, I'll just go and pay the bill and then wait for you outside in the car," said Lawrence.

"Thank you, you've no idea what it's like with a little one bouncing about inside you. I won't be long."

"Take your time, OK!"

They set off again – the next stop would be Harrogate. As they crossed Blubberhouses Moor the sky clouded over, and Alice hoped it wasn't a bad omen. Up to now, the day had been wonderful.

"Will this be your first visit to my hometown?" asked Lawrence.

"Yes, Kevin was going to bring me on our honeymoon," she replied, then sat quietly as she recalled the excitement she'd shared with Kevin when they were planning their future together. Lawrence stretched his hand over Alice's and squeezed it gently. It was exactly the kind of thing Kevin would have done.

"Cheer up, this is a new chapter. Kevin used to say that to me at the beginning of every new term at school. I hated change and dreaded having a new form teacher, but Kevin used to laugh and say, 'It's a nice clean page; you can do as you like with it.' He was right: by the end of the first day I was as right as ninepence. I do miss him," said Lawrence. Now it was Alice's turn to give him comfort.

Soon Lawrence was pulling the car to a halt outside a large stone building on a busy street where all the big shops were.

"Here we are – now don't be afraid, brother Lawrence is here to take care of you. This is what Kevin would have wanted, so come on, chin up," said Lawrence as he helped Alice out of the car.

The solicitor's rooms were on the second floor and Alice had to stop twice to rest while climbing up the stairs, for there was no lift.

"You OK?" asked Lawrence.

Alice nodded her head and took several deep breaths, and the next moment they were entering a waiting room where a white-haired lady sat. As they came through the door the woman rose and came towards them with arms outstretched and a beaming smile.

"Alice, my dear, at last – I'm Kevin's mum," she said as she put her arms around the young woman and gave her a big hug. Alice realised that all her fears concerning Rosemary Renwick were totally unfounded. This lady had a kind, open face, and she was full of love, just as Kevin had always said.

The Renwick family solicitor was like a favourite uncle. Having settled them into comfortable chairs, he asked his secretary to bring them tea and explained the procedure to Alice which would allow her to be known from that day onwards as Alice Renwick. All the necessary forms were completed and signed, and he then gave her a witnessed certificate to show to anyone in authority who needed to know. Alice would have to have her ration book changed and obtain a new identity card, and then the world would know she was indeed a member of the Renwick family.

"Come, my dear, this has been an exhausting time for you. Lawrence will drive us home and you can meet Harry, my husband and your new dad. After we've had tea and you have rested, Lawrence will drive you home," said Rosemary, putting an arm round Alice and helping her down the stairs and into the car.

It was quite dark when they finally set off on the return journey to Keswick. Rosemary Renwick begged Alice to stay the night, but she was so excited and longing to get back to tell Aunt Annie about her wonderful new family.

"I'm coming with you, I'll be company for Lawrence on the journey back to Harrogate. I can't miss the opportunity of seeing my dear friend Annie again. She was so kind to me when I was in hospital," said Rosemary.

Over the next two weeks Alice could talk of nothing else but her newfound family.

"My baby will have two sets of grandparents now: Granddad and Grandma Renwick and Granddad John and Granny Annie, plus two doting uncles. Isn't Lawrence nice? Oh Auntie, I know everything will work out all right – I can't wait for my baby to come."

"It won't be long now love: three weeks at the most, according to the doctor," said Aunt Annie. "Why not do a bit of studying? It'll help you to relax, and I don't think it would be wise for you to go out in this weather – it's blowing a gale out there. Who knows, we may even have a white Christmas."

As Christmas came near Alice felt heavy and ungainly. It was very awkward for her to get up and down, and occasionally her aunt would get hold of her hand and pull her out of the chair. The baby had to come soon, surely, but there was no sign of an imminent birth.

Two days before Christmas Alice was lying on her bed in the room just above the front door, having the afternoon rest which Aunt Annie insisted on, when she heard the doorbell ring. Her window was partly open and she heard a man's voice speaking, but couldn't tell what he was saying.

"Well, that was my name, but it is many years since anyone has addressed me as such," she heard her aunt's voice saying.

Now the man spoke louder and with more confidence. "You must be her aunt – tell me, have you got a niece called Alice?"

"Yes, but her name is no longer Brownlow."

"I don't understand – it was only six months ago and she was pregnant. I was told she had come to live with you; perhaps you could give me her address? I would like to see her, having come all this way."

Alice managed to pull herself upright and out of bed, and moved slowly to the window and opened it wide.

"Ra, hello! I'll be down in a few minutes," she called.

Just before entering the living room Alice stopped to eavesdrop on Aunt Annie and Ra's conversation.

"Have you come far?"

"From Lincoln. I went to the Brownlows' house first – I was billeted with them for a time and they seemed pleased to see me, but when I mentioned Alice and enquired about her health and whereabouts, they showed me the door. I find them very hard to understand. From there I went to the factory where we'd once worked, and I persuaded one of the office staff to give me Alice's friend Daisy's address."

Alice pushed open the door and welcomed Ra. She was so pleased to see him that she flung her arms round him and kissed his cheek, then felt herself blush as she realised what a liberty she had taken.

"Hello Alice, it is good to see you. You're looking well," said Ra.

"I will once I've slimmed down," she laughed.

"When do you expect your baby?"

"Any time now. Today, tomorrow – who knows?!"

"Well, I'm sure you two have lots to talk about – I'll just go and put the kettle on," said Aunt Annie.

When she had gone, Alice motioned to Ra to sit down.

"Your aunt said you're no longer called Brownlow – I see you're married. Congratulations." Ra's good wishes didn't ring true.

"I'm not married," she said in a quiet voice. "I have changed my name by deed poll to Renwick so that my baby can have its father's name. Michael suggested it and Kevin's family were eager for me to do so. You've seen Daisy – how is she?"

"She is very well and happy; did you know she has a new boyfriend? I think it might be the real thing. She sends you her love – oh, and she says it's your turn to write. I had to come and see you Alice, this is the first chance I've had. You see, I was with Kevin just a few minutes before he was shot down."

"I don't understand. Surely he wasn't shot down in England; they would have found his body." Alice felt weak and the colour drained from her face.

"No, Kevin was on a very dangerous mission; it was something he had done on several occasions. I can't tell you any more except that he was full of your wedding plans and was counting the hours to being with you. He loved you. I was the last person to talk to him, and I don't want to upset you but I came because I thought it would help you to know just how much you meant to him. He was a very brave man and we all miss him very much."

Alice sat and cried quietly into her hankie, then wiped her tears away. "Thank you for telling me. Maybe one day you'll tell me the full story – I always felt there was some unexplained bond between you and Kevin. When our baby comes I'd like you to be one of the godfathers – will you, please?"

"I'll be delighted, as long as the christening is in January," said Ra.

Christmas day dawned in a flurry of snow. Uncle John and Aunt Annie went to the morning service at chapel but Alice stayed at home, as although she had no pain she was certain that the baby would come soon. She laid the table for dinner – just three places as Michael was presumably still on the high seas. His last letter had hinted at repairs in port, with possible Christmas leave, but he hadn't arrived. He might have gone to Lincoln to see his mum and dad – Alice knew he hadn't seen them since the previous Christmas but Ra had never mentioned him, so he couldn't have been there when he'd visited. Alice's thoughts strayed to last Christmas and all the misery leading up to it: Aunt Annie and Uncle John had arrived and had shamed Mum and Dad into letting Kevin come for Christmas Day, and Michael had been home too and he and Kevin had got on so well together. It had all been so perfect.

After a very big traditional Christmas dinner, Aunt Annie, Uncle John and Alice were relaxing in the sitting room in front of a log fire, listening to *ITMA* on the wireless. It was very funny and they were all laughing, when suddenly Alice gasped, held her breath and clutched at her stomach.

"Alice, are you all right?"

She nodded. "I think so, Auntie – oh, oh, I think I've had too much pudding."

"I don't think it's the dinner, darling. Come on love, I'll help you upstairs and Uncle John will go for the midwife."

"The midwife?" Alice said. "Oh, I don't think it's the baby – the pains gone now. It must have been indigestion; perhaps if I had a drink of tea."

Aunt Annie went into the kitchen to make the tea, but said Alice was to tell her immediately if she got any more pain. Just as they were finishing their tea Alice had another spasm.

"Come on love, I think we should get you upstairs while you're still on your feet. Once you're in bed Uncle John can join us; I'll light a fire in your room, it's all laid ready. I can't speak from personal experience, but we might be in for a long wait – the midwife will be able to tell you when she gets here. I'll ask her if she would like some cold goose for her supper; that will make up for interrupting her Christmas Day," said Aunt Annie.

The pains came at regular intervals over the next four hours and then abruptly stopped. At two in the morning they started again, but this time they were stronger and closer together, and at precisely half past six, an exhausted Alice gave one last push and screamed as her baby came into the world. The nurse wiped the baby clean and attended to the umbilical cord, then as the baby let out a protesting cry, she wrapped it gently in a towel and laid it in Alice's arms.

"There now, you have a lovely little girl. What are you going to call her?" asked the nurse. Alice looked down at the baby in her arms and smiled. She was beautiful.

"Estelle. It means 'a star'," Alice replied with a sigh, remembering Kevin's words all those months ago.

After resting in bed for a week Alice pleaded with her aunt to allow her to get up in the afternoons, and when she had fully recovered from the birth she settled down to a routine of feeding, bathing and changing her baby's nappies. Alice was so pleased to be on her feet again, and would be able to walk the short distance to the chapel in two days' time for her daughter's christening. Alice would have preferred her baby to be christened in St. John's church, the place where she first felt the baby move inside her, but Uncle John was chapel and he has been so good and kind to her, so to please him she agreed that the baptism would take place at the chapel.

Uncle John was so pleased and proud, and he rushed off to the chapel on the Monday morning to stoke the boiler to make sure the place was warm and welcoming for Estelle's christening in the afternoon. Lawrence and his fiancée Helen were to be godparents, along with Ra, who had arrived the previous evening and was staying as Uncle John and Aunt Annie's guest for a few days. Harry and Rosemary had arranged for someone to look after their public house and had travelled with Lawrence and Helen in Rosemary's brother's Rover. What a blessing Leonard had his own garage, otherwise with petrol rationing, they would never have managed.

The party of ten assembled around the font. Mr Beckett the minister, who was accompanied by his wife, welcomed them, then proceeded to explain the order of the service and cautioned the godparents of their duties. The service started with prayers, and then the minister asked what names had been chosen and took the baby from Helen.

"Estelle Rosemary, I baptise thee in the name of the Father and of the Son and of the Holy Ghost." He then dribbled holy water onto Estelle's head and marked the sign of the cross of her forehead. More prayers were said, and soon they were all walking back home where a light meal awaited everyone.

Lawrence helped Alice to open Estelle's presents. A woollen matinee set had come from Daisy and her aunt, Rosemary and Harry bought their granddaughter a silver bangle inscribed with her name and date of birth, and Lawrence and Helen presented her with a lovely teddy bear, courtesy of a friend whose parents had a toy shop and still had some pre-war stock available to special customers. Ra brought her a beautifully illustrated children's Bible, and the minister and his wife gave a hand-knitted pram rug with blue bunnies and pink lambs done in Fair Isle. Then Uncle John wheeled in a lovely Silver Cross coach-built pram.

"We didn't know how to wrap it," Uncle John and Aunt Annie said together.

Alice's eyes filled with tears. "To say thank you just isn't enough, but on behalf of my daughter and myself we thank you all, not just for the presents but for all the love which accompanies them. When Estelle is old enough I will teach her to treasure each and every gift. This must be one of the happiest days of my life." Then before the tears came, Alice begged to be excused and rushed off to feed her daughter in the privacy of the living room.

Chapter Nine

Raoul presented his papers to the sentry at the naval barracks for the start of his return journey to France. The able seaman looked at his identity card; then at him.

"This supposed to be you?" he asked Raoul.

"Yes, I know it isn't a good photo but Commander Briers knows me very well. He is here, I hope?"

The AB lifted the phone and spoke to someone in a low voice. Then, after nodding his head a few times and grunting, he put the phone down and turned to Raoul as he got up from the chair.

"Come. You see that hut over there?" He pointed to his right in the darkness. Raoul peered into the misty void and discerned the outline of the hut.

"Yes, I can just make it out."

"Well, walk around it to your left, and you will come to the entrance. There's a shrouded light over the door."

Raoul thanked him and walked over to the building and after a few minutes arrived at the door. He knocked and a voice bade him enter. He stepped inside and Lieutenant Commander Briers warmly welcomed him. They were old acquaintances.

"We're a bit short on sail; hope you don't mind a sardine tin?" said the commander.

"Sardine tin? Does that read 'submarine'?" asked Raoul incredulously, thinking of his claustrophobia.

"Afraid so, it's the only way we can get near enough to the coast. Don't worry, you won't suffocate – we do have air conditioning," said the commander as he bent down to take an envelope from his open briefcase.

"This is for you: a little spending money. The heavier stuff is already on board. We dive at 01.50hrs; all the best. Hope to see you again." He gave Raoul the envelope and dismissed him with a shake of his hand.

Raoul took a deep breath before climbing down the ladder into the bowels of the submarine, and followed the cockney sailor along the metal-floored corridor. He was shown into a small cabin with a bunk and built-in cupboards. He sat down on the bed, and even though the air was fairly comfortable beads of perspiration trickled down from his forehead due to his claustrophobia. Soon there was movement – the journey had begun. A petty officer looked in to see if he was OK.

"We dive in five minutes. If you would like anything just press that bell and a steward will come."

Soon they had been at sea for over three hours. They had to be getting near to the rendezvous, Raoul thought, when there was a sharp tap at the door and the PO put his head round.

"Captain's compliments; would you like to come to the control room? I expect we'll be surfacing soon."

Raoul picked up his bag of belongings and followed the young man to the centre of the ship.

"Ah, there you are, well I've had a look through the periscope but the sea is empty. I can only wait fifteen minutes nad then if there is no sign of them, I must return to port," said the captain.

Raoul couldn't believe his ears. However would he survive? It was only by convincing himself that there was fresh air at the other side of the door that he had managed to keep his claustrophobia at bay.

"What's the weather like? Would it be too rough for a small vessel?" asked Raoul.

"Well, it's no duck pond, that's for sure, but an experienced seaman with plenty of grit could make it," answered the captain. Raoul relaxed. Henri had nerves of steel, and if it was humanly possible he would make it.

"Sir, I think there's something on the starboard side," called a sailor. The captain moved quickly to the periscope and swung it round. Sure enough, ten degrees to starboard was a small vessel.

"Make contact," he said to the radio operator. The transmitter burst into life with the reply signal: Henri had made it. There was a lot of bustle as preparations were made to surface. As soon as the conning tower was clear of water, Raoul mounted the ladder and gasped in some longed-for fresh air. Just ahead of him, the captain pointed to Henri's boat only a few yards away.

"We'll get his passengers on board first; then you can board and help load your stuff," said the captain. Raoul was amazed to see at least six men transferring from the small boat to the sub.

"Hello, I wondered if I would be seeing you," said one of the passengers to Raoul.

"Glad you made it – sorry it took so long but we had problems," answered Raoul to the RAF fighter pilot he had met while visiting Monique.

"The lovely doctor asked me to give you her love."

"Thanks, how was she?"

"Very well, but I haven't seen much of her until just before I left. I was moved into the monastery last September."

"With the Pole?" asked Raoul, grateful to be able to use the time to chat to someone who had news of his dear wife.

"Yes, but I don't think he is Polish – he spoke French to the monks on the rare occasions he did speak, but the few times I was with him he spoke English with a North Country accent," answered the airman.

"You ready?" called the captain, and Raoul made his hasty goodbyes and was put aboard his friend's boat.

"Raoul, good to see you, what a journey we've had. I had to leave Jacques and Petre on shore with having so many passengers; they tried to help but they'll never make seamen.

136

Could you hold the wheel while I check the engine?" said Henri. The little boat bounced over the waves – there were no fish in the hold, and with only Henri and Raoul aboard there wasn't enough ballast. True, there were spare parts for repairing radios and guns offloaded from the submarine, but they amounted to only a few stones in weight. Henri came back to the wheelhouse carrying two mugs of steaming cocoa.

"Here you are. All's OK in the hold but we had better do some serious fishing before we return to port. Can't risk entering the harbour in daylight with the hull out of the water," cautioned Henri.

The two friends chattered while they ate their sandwiches and drank their cocoa; then having secured the wheel, both set about hauling the nets over the side and for the next twelve hours they patiently fished. Just as the sun was setting Henri raised the anchor – the hold was full of fish and it was safe to turn for home.

By the time they reached the harbour it was quite dark, but Henri had plenty of experience and could easily have found his berth blindfolded. The sentry peered through the darkness at the approaching vessel; then flashed his search beam onto it. At the same time the air raid warning sounded and the first bombs of the raid descended. Soon all was blacked out.

"Well, we are in luck – the Hun will be too busy taking cover to bother about us," said Raoul.

"Yes, we might as well take your luggage with us now. Can you slip under the rail onto the dockside? I'll pass the boxes to you," answered Henri.

Long before the all-clear was heard, Raoul was safely ensconced in the cellar of Gerrard the butcher, who early next morning was to carry him in his butcher's van back to Epiney.

"Drop me near to the woods, Gerrard; I'll walk over the fields to the farm. There's plenty of cover with the hedges and I don't want to be seen in the village yet; not until I have appraised the situation fully," said Raoul.

The ground was very wet but Raoul found plenty of rough grass to walk on so he didn't leave telltale footprints. The boxes of spares were in two potato sacks that he carried over his shoulders, and they were getting heavier with each step he took. Dawn was breaking and there was no time for rest – it was imperative to get to Louis before daylight.

"Raoul, you old son of a gun, welcome back! That looks heavy, what have you brought us?" asked Louis, while shaking Raoul vigorously by the hand.

"Just some spare parts, but I did manage some real coffee and tea," laughed Raoul, as with arms around each other's shoulders, they made their way into the farmhouse kitchen where Marguerite was waiting with morning coffee.

Over coffee Louis told Raoul of the group's recent escapades. Apart from moving escaped POWs, they had started a fire in the administration offices at the German HQ and nearly all the records were destroyed. So successful was this exploit that the Germans were convinced it was an electrical fault in the wiring of the old building, so there were no recriminations. The lorry bringing the monthly rations to the barracks had been hijacked again, but because this had taken place five miles away, the village wasn't under suspicion. The intelligence gathered by the group and radioed to London had enabled the RAF to do some precision bombing.

Raoul was well pleased with Louis' report. Although there were many people in the area who had helped in several ways at different times, the group was only eight strong. These people were now assembled in the hayloft at Louis' farm.

"London are well pleased with our efforts, but even more must be done," continued Raoul after welcoming his friends. "We must be even more vigilant, and on our guard at all times. There is growing concern over the number of POWs who escape only to be recaptured, and there are fears that some are being shot, supposedly while trying to escape."

"That doesn't surprise me. Those evil devils will stop at nothing," said Jules.

"We have proof of that with the Dubois brothers – they were going to shoot them and the RAF men, and they were legitimate POWs," said Renni.

"What London wants us to do is negotiate with other groups to enable us to form a human chain escape route right into Germany. If the escapees came directly under our care they would have a better chance of survival," said Raoul.

"I don't like it," said Louis grimly. "It's too dangerous; we would be putting our heads on the guillotine."

"Why would it be dangerous? It's what we're doing all the time," said Jules.

"You mean going outside our group would be the danger?" asked Raoul.

"Yes. We know and trust each other, but outside our small circle we should only divulge what needs to be known. Linking up with other groups could have advantages, if you think about the time recently when we moved the RAF man from Limoges, but I'm not so sure about this latest plan," answered Louis.

"We need more routes and more hiding places and safe houses. Perhaps we should think about it for a few days; then I'll signal London with our decision," said Raoul.

The group chattered about everyday things for a while; then dispersed to their own homes.

Raoul slept the clock round, and Marguerite smiled as she quietly closed the bedroom door and carried the cup of coffee back to the kitchen. Louis came in from the barn.

"You had better drink this while it's still hot – I took it up to Raoul but he was fast asleep. I wonder when he last went to bed?" she said to her husband.

"It will do him good to rest. There's little to do on the farm at the moment, and if we weren't caught up in this awful war we could have had a trip to Paris, but not now," said Louis, shaking his head sadly. "Not now."

A week after Raoul's return, Father Joseph visited the farm. As usual he came just as they were about to start the evening meal.

"Come and sit down, Father," said Marguerite as she pulled out a chair. The priest smiled.

"You are most kind, and I do love your cooking."

Louis' son and daughter were also at the table, and after Father Joseph had said grace the family began to enjoy the meal. Conversation was kept to general news, and the children talked about the things they were doing at school. Later, when the children had said goodnight and been taken upstairs, Father Joseph took a letter from his pocket and gave it to Louis.

"This came to my old monastery a few days ago."

Louis read the letter. It was addressed to the abbot, and was obviously from an old friend. It was full of reminiscences of times spent together, and Louis wondered why the priest had given it to him to read. It discussed the new music they were using at the sung Eucharist, and mentioned how his congregation were praying for peace. There was a mention of the wellbeing of mutual friends, then on the second page the preparations for Lent and Easter. The Swiss priest said what a joyous time Easter was, with such a lot of young people getting married. He was to officiate at a double wedding of two brothers, Claude and Arno, to two sisters who had been their childhood sweethearts.

"Marguerite, they made it!" shouted Louis as he put his arms around his wife and swept her off her feet.

"Who, Louis, who made what?"

"Claude and Arno – look at this letter! I wondered why I should be interested in the abbot's correspondence, but this is the message; the rest is just dressing. Claude and Arno are to be married to Maria and Johann's daughters – you remember how heartbroken they were when their parents returned to Switzerland when the troubles first started."

"Oh Louis, how wonderful," she said, as tears of thankfulness ran down her cheeks. "And to think how ill

Arno was." She glanced down at the kitchen table that had been scrubbed down ready to be used for the operation that had saved his life.

Raoul looked across the table to the young priest. Here was someone outside their group who had given such valuable service; also here was proof of group's successfully helping each other. He motioned to Louis to come back to the table.

"We ought to talk," said Raoul. Louis looked at his wife, who with a nod and a smile left the room.

"Father Joseph, last year you helped us in a very difficult situation, and this evening you have brought us proof of your success."

"God's work takes many different forms," answered the priest.

"Raoul, are you perhaps thinking what I am thinking?" asked Louis.

"You read my mind, as always," laughed Raoul.

"You two friends are very close. Can an outsider join?" asked Father Joseph.

"That's exactly what we would like: we want you to join our group. We desperately need your help and contacts," said Raoul. Then the three men talked for over an hour about the different ways of getting men out of France: through Spain, Switzerland and by boat back to England.

"Outlining the route is simple, but details must only be given to those who need to know. I suggest that when other groups are involved, only one person negotiates; that way the rest of the members remain unknown and are therefore safe," said Father Joseph, whom they later discovered had worked within a large network of resistance groups covering the whole of France. Raoul and Louis were very pleased with their evening's negotiations, and had agreed with the young priest that although he would work with them he would not openly be a member.

March came in heralded by drifting snow and high winds. Louis hated being indoors all day, but apart from feeding the animals and cleaning them out there was nothing else he could do. In the evenings he and Raoul would play chess, but they became so used to each other's moves that even that became boring and frustrating.

"It's a long time since you have seen Monique. Why don't you take a few days' holiday?" suggested Louis.

"I'd like to do that very much. I haven't heard a word from her since just before Christmas," answered Raoul.

"It must be very worrying for you both, not being able to write freely to each other," added Marguerite.

"Friday, I'll go on Friday. It's better to travel when the trains are full; less likelihood of being stopped," said Raoul.

The rest of the week passed quickly. On Wednesday Jules Betton brought some old plans of the monastery buildings from the town archives – his daughter who worked there had managed to smuggle them out. The plans were laid out on the kitchen table and the three men eagerly searched for the information they needed. The church with the high altar was in the east, in the southeast corner was the abbot's house and to the southwest was the refectory and kitchens with the dormitories above. On the plans leading from the kitchen the cellars seemed to be linked to a natural cave, while the other passageways led northward to the hospitium and the gatehouse.

"That's where Maurice's cottage was," said Louis, pointing to the gatehouse.

"In that case, the hospice stood in the field you now keep your cows in," added Raoul.

"Blast the snow, how can we search the ground with over a foot of snow?" grumbled Louis.

"If this is where the hospice stood and this is Maurice's cottage, the passage must run along here," said Jules, pointing at the plan. "Look, it passes near to the ruined bell tower. I wonder if that's worth taking a look at?"

The three men deliberated for some time, then agreed to walk over the area the next day on the pretext of exercising the dogs.

It was dark when Raoul left the station. If he turned right the road would lead him through the village to Madame B's house and he would be there in a few minutes, but then he noticed a convoy of German troops lined up to cross the river bridge. *Better walk up the hill and come down through the woods*, he thought, *but how to get across the station yard?* The passengers had nearly all gone and if he hung about much longer the sentry would start to take an interest in him. Slowly, out of the darkness came the post van. The driver got out, leaving the rear door open, and took a bag of mail into the station. Raoul climbed quickly into the back of the van and squatted behind some bags of mail. He had no sooner hidden himself than the driver returned, slamming the door closed. The sentry stopped him as he was about to get into the driving seat and meticulously inspected his papers; eventually he let him go, and with a lurch, the van moved forward. Raoul craned his neck to see which way the driver would go. It wasn't the road into the village he'd taken, but the one leading in the direction of the monastery. The van swayed dangerously at each twist in the road, and after about fifteen minutes stopped and the driver left the van to enter a village inn.

Raoul quickly climbed over the mailbags and made his escape. The pathway was very slippery with mud, and it was a dark night with no starlight to guide him. He walked on for what seemed like hours; then standing well into the bushes at the side of the road, Raoul shone his torch onto his watch. It was half past nine; his train had arrived at seven. Raoul wondered if he had missed his way. If only it wasn't so cold and wet he could have laid low in the scrub at the roadside until dawn, but that could be dangerous in these weather conditions. After resting for a few minutes and flexing his leg muscles, he continued his climb, walking in the middle of the narrow road.

He had walked for some time when he heard the sound of a motorbike. Quickly he moved into the bushes and waited – first a glimmer of light and then the motorbike came nearer and passed him. With a sigh of relief Raoul hurried on to find the road the rider must have taken. A pinpoint of red light could just be seen to his right: the rear light on the bike. A few minutes later the outline of a group of buildings could be seen, and thinking this must be the monastery Raoul broke into a jog only to discover the buildings were houses on the fringe of a village. He was hopelessly lost – the postman must have come further away from the village Monique lived in than he had realised. The safest thing to do was to retrace his steps.

It had turned midnight when Raoul reached the railway station. All was in darkness, even the small light on the platform had been extinguished and there was no sign of the German convoy or any sentry. He now made his way to the river bridge, where again no sentry could be seen. The whole village was shrouded in darkness and seemed to be deserted. As he made his way to Madame B's house, walking on the grass verge so as not to make any noise, a dog barked but silence soon returned. Raoul decided it was too late to disturb the household, and finding the door into the woodshed unlocked, thankfully sank down onto the pile of straw used for the chickens' nesting boxes.

It was a surprised Madame B who, a few hours later and having gathered the eggs, was followed into the kitchen by a dishevelled man.

"Monique is not here," said Madame B. "She is at the clinic; some operation she must do."

Raoul looked very disappointed – after all the time and the trouble he'd taken getting here!

"You look worn out. I'll stoke up the boiler, then when the water is hot you can have a bath and go to bed. I'll send her to you when she gets back."

Monique did her hospital round early; she always liked to check each patient daily. This morning, being Saturday, she would normally have toured the wards and then gone home for the weekend, but today she had to remove a German officer's gall bladder, then reset an airman's arm which had been broken when he bailed out of his plane. The real problem was making sure unwanted visitors didn't see the airman.

"You look tired, my dear," said Father Justin.

"I haven't been sleeping well recently," answered Monique.

"You worry about your husband?"

"Oh Father, if only I knew where he was and if he's all right. His last message was in November, telling me he was going away."

"Pray, my dear – take your troubles to God and He will help you."

Monique smiled and drank the coffee the nurse had just brought her. Such devout faith. If only everything could be as simple.

It was nearly dark by the time Monique got home. What a long day it had been. Considering that it was her half day off, she had done more today than in a normal day; but how many days were normal in wartime?

"I've lit the fire in the front parlour," said Madame B.

"Whatever for? It's not Christmas!"

"It doesn't have to be. Why not take your coat off and go and rest? Dinner will be at six."

Monique did as she was bid, too tired to argue with the older woman. As she pushed the door open, she saw in the firelight the shape of a man sitting in the high-backed chair by the fire. The figure rose and came towards her; for a moment she couldn't move and then the spring was released as her husband caught her in his arms and pulled her to him.

The next few days passed all too quickly for the young couple. Monique did her morning round of visits to her patients but kept the rest of the days free to spend with her husband. He told her of his recent visit to England and about finding Alice living with her aunt in the Lake District, and about becoming a godfather to the baby Estelle Rosemary.

"England's a wonderful country; the natural beauty is so varied, and the lakes in Cumberland are truly breathtaking. The English are renowned for their talk of the weather, but it changes so often there's certainly always something to talk about. I promise I'll take you there when the war is over, or sooner if I get the chance," said Raoul.

"I'd like that. Whenever you talk about England you always get that dreamy look in your eyes; if I didn't know you better I would think you had a sweetheart there," replied Monique.

One day as they were taking a walk in the twilight Raoul repeated the conversation he had had with the airman just before leaving the submarine.

"Monique darling, I don't want to put you to any inconvenience, but I would like to meet your Pole."

"But you don't speak Polish," answered Monique.

"You said yourself that he speaks a little French with the monks, and the airman did say he had spoken English to him. Please, *chérie*, you can arrange it. Even if I only get his number and name, I could get the news of him to England and to his family; it could maybe help him," Raoul added as a final plea.

"All right, I'll speak to Father Justin. Friday afternoon may be the best time."

"I was planning to travel back on Friday," said Raoul. This was the first indication that his visit was to be so short, and Monique gasped – she had hoped her husband would stay at least two weeks or even three.

"Couldn't you stay until Monday? The trains will be busy then; I know you prefer to travel with plenty of people about and your papers are in order!" said Monique.

"Yes, of course my papers are in order. Oh well, I suppose a couple of days won't matter, you little wench; you twist me around your little finger and I am putty in your hands."

"Thank you darling." Monique stretched up and kissed her husband.

One evening they went to the cinema; a romantic musical was being shown, followed by a German propaganda film. They came out just before the lights went up at the end of the programme.

"Oh, I wish we didn't have to sneak around. In England people move about much more freely – yes, even in wartime, and no one is stopped and asked for their papers. Half the time they leave their identity cards at home so they won't lose them," said Raoul. "If we were in England now we would come out of the pictures, then find a fish-and-chip shop and eat our supper with our fingers as we walked through the blackout."

On Friday Madame B prepared lunch early, and soon after Monique and Raoul set off to walk to the monastery. The rain had stopped, but the trees sprayed droplets of water on them as the wind gently shook the branches.

"You know Monique, whoever your Pole is, he will have been posted as missing, presumed dead. It must be awful for his family – at least when the Germans take prisoners they publish a list of names, and the POWs are allowed to write home and receive the occasional letter."

"Yes Raoul, but we can't tell anyone who we have staying with us, and if we handed patients over to the Germans what proof have we got that they will be well treated? Some of the peasants taken into Germany to work haven't been heard of since, and some went over a year ago."

"Well at least if your Pole can tell us who he is I'll send a message to London."

"Good. Well, here we are – this door is so exposed at this time of year, with all the leaves off the trees and shrubs," said Monique as she pulled at the bell. They waited a while; then just as Raoul was about to ring again they heard the sound of the monk's stick tapping on the path at the other side of the door. Then a key was turned and the door opened.

"Good afternoon, Brother Paulus. I've brought my cousin again, and we wondered if Brother Francis is about? My cousin is going to try and talk to him," said Monique. The monk shook his head. Father Justin hadn't said anything to him about the doctor bringing anyone to the monastery, and he was very nervous, especially as there were six foreign young men living in the cellars at that very moment. What would Ives say if he found they were entertaining guests from the village?

"I don't know; no one said you were coming. You had better come with me to Father Justin's quarters," he replied finally.

Raoul and Monique looked at each other. Was something amiss? Monique laid a hand on the old monk's arm.

"Please Brother Paulus, don't be alarmed. You look so upset; what is the matter?"

"I'll take you to Father Justin."

Monique looked at her husband and shrugged her shoulders, then they both followed the monk to the abbot's study where they sat on the old wooden settle and awaited the return of Father Justin.

The slow tick of the clock on the wall measured the minutes as the big hand moved first to the quarter-hour, then to the half-hour. At last footsteps were heard in the passage outside, the door opened and Father Justin entered.

"My dear children, so sorry to have kept you waiting. I have been so busy and I confess I forgot to advise Brother Paulus of your visit. I have also been delayed in the chapel: two more guests arrived just before noon; not needing your services I am happy to say," said the abbot, turning to Monique. Raoul repeated the brief conversation he had had with the airman and formally asked Father Justin for permission to speak with the Pole.

"Monique will have told you, he doesn't talk to anyone – that is to say, he doesn't have conversations, but he does make himself understood to the monks and replies to their questions in French. You will find him in the low pigsty;

Suzanne the sow gave birth a few hours ago and Brother Francis insists on staying with her. You might try to persuade him that she will survive without him now!" laughed the abbot.

Monique led the way past the vegetable patch and through the orchard, past the barn, the cowshed and the pigsty.

"Isn't this the pigsty?" asked Raoul.

"Yes, but Suzanne is in the low pigsty. Come this way and down these steps, and be careful!" she warned.

"But surely there are no pigs down here? It's a cellar."

"Exactly – the last place to keep a pig, but if the Germans decided to inspect the animals, they would confiscate all the piglets. They don't know we have Suzanne. I should have brought a torch with me – have you got a lighter?" asked Monique.

"Better than that – here." Raoul took something from his pocket and passed it to his wife.

"Oh you are wonderful," she said as she snapped the torch into life. The dim light showed broken stones and rubble, but running alongside of the wall was the old staircase. "I'll try to shine the light in front for me, then behind for you. We will have to go slow; a broken leg will do neither of us any good," Monique warned. "Wait here, I'll talk to Brother Francis first. He's very nervous of strangers; even other patients."

Raoul leaned back against the wall while he waited. The Germans would think this part of the monastery unusable. If there were pigs down here you certainly couldn't smell them. Then Monique returned to her husband.

"I've tried to make him understand that you are a friend and want to help him but it's so difficult – he doesn't really understand everyday French. It's almost as if he has taught himself from what he has heard here in the clinic," explained Monique. Raoul followed his wife around the buttress in the wall; then along a short passage. As they turned into another passage, their way was lit by the natural light coming from the room at the end. The cave had an opening leading out onto the mountains, and it was from this opening that the late afternoon sun shone its light onto the sow lying on a bed of clean straw, her twelve pink piglets suckling at her teats. The monk sat with his back towards the passage, watching the young family. Monique put her hand on Raoul's arm, warning him to wait yet again, then she moved forward and putting her arm around Brother Francis' shoulder, spoke quietly to him. He shook his head slowly, then stood up and turned to face Raoul. Raoul stood motionless for what seemed hours, yet was only seconds. He stared at the young man's face; a face with no life in it; a face of someone known, yet unknown. There was no recognition in the brown eyes that looked into Raoul's. Then Raoul gasped just one word.

"Kevin."

Chapter Ten

"Raoul, what is the matter? You are as white as a sheet."

Raoul was shaking with shock, and he was finding it difficult to breath. Brother Francis was feeling faint and sat on an upturned barrel.

"I thought I was seeing ghosts. Monique, this is Kevin – the young pilot who risked his life to bring me to France last spring. He is English, and the father of my godchild."

"The young man you thought was dead?"

"Yes." Raoul turned again to his long-lost friend. "Kevin, do you remember me? I am Raoul; you flew me into France just before you were shot down."

Kevin looked at the man speaking in English. A strange feeling came over him, then his head started to pound and he felt faint. "I don't know, please leave me alone. My head!" The young man put both hands to his head, trying to hold in the pain.

"Brother Francis, you have had a shock. Come now, I will give you something to ease your pain and I am sure Suzanne will be all right on her own now." Monique took the young man's hand and led him from the cellar and into the garden, and Raoul followed. She escorted 'Brother Francis' to his room and gave him two tablets to help him sleep.

"Tomorrow we will talk some more, but now I want you to rest. Don't try too hard to remember anything, it will all come back in time."

When she had rejoined Raoul and Father Justin, tea was about to be served.

"We have waited for you, my dear," said the abbot. "What a wonderful outcome to your afternoon visit. How is Brother Francis?"

151

"He should sleep for a few hours. I haven't much experience of amnesia, but I am sure he remembers something." She turned to Raoul. "You speaking in English to him was possibly the first conversation he has been able to follow fully since his accident."

"Raoul has been telling me what he knows of Brother Francis' early life. I must brush up my English so I can talk with him. Perhaps tomorrow while you are doing your rounds in the clinic, Raoul could talk to Brother Francis here in my study. I could arrange to be here, if you think it would help," said Father Justin.

That evening over supper, Raoul talked about Kevin and Alice and how he had been instrumental in bringing them together.

"He was late for their first date and Alice was just about to walk away from where they had arranged to meet, when Kevin came running at top speed, full of apologies. He didn't have a very warm welcome from her parents – they are such self-righteous hypocrites, and when poor Alice became pregnant they turned her out. It was a Sunday and they didn't even give her time to find a place; if her friend Daisy hadn't come to her rescue goodness knows what would have happened to her. They've certainly had a hard time, I do hope their luck is about to change."

"Is she still with her friend?" asked Madame B.

"No, evidently Alice's aunt came down for the wedding and discovered that Kevin had died on active service two days before – well, that's what they believed at the time. Anyway, Aunt Annie – she's also Alice's godmother – went to see her brother, thinking that he and his wife would change their minds and welcome their daughter back into the family home, but they didn't want to know; as far as they were concerned Alice was dead to them. So Aunt Annie took Alice back to her home in Keswick where her husband is a schoolteacher, and arranged for Alice to take a teacher-training course so she would have some means of supporting herself and her child.

That, of course, won't be necessary now. I must get a message to London immediately so Kevin's family can be given the wonderful news."

"I'll ask Ives to call after church; you can give him the details and he will radio them to London for you," said Madame B.

"I don't go to the clinic normally on a Sunday, but I ought to show the German officer how conscientious I am," laughed Monique. "You can go straight to the monastery; I will join you there later, but please Raoul, be gentle. I don't know how long it will take for his memory to return. Don't rush him – now you have told Father Justin and me of his past, we can prompt him and let him find himself in his own time."

It seemed odd to Raoul to be walking up to the monastery on his own – in the past he had only come this way with Monique. No sooner had he reached the door in the wall and rung the bell than it was opened.

"Good morning, I have been expecting you. Father Justin said you would be here about this time," said Brother Paulus.

"Good morning. The doctor will be along later," replied Raoul.

"Do you remember the way, or shall I come with you?"

"That's all right, I just go along this path then turn left."

"I'll bid you good day then, and thank you for what you have done," the old monk said as he made his way back to the chapel.

A few minutes later Raoul knocked on the door of Father Justin's study.

"Come in and welcome," said Father Justin. "We have just returned from the morning service. I was just about to make some coffee."

"Good morning, Kevin. How are you feeling today?" asked Raoul.

"I don't know; it's difficult to explain. I think I remember something, but I don't know what; it's as if my head is stuffed with cotton wool. I feel I know you; that we are friends, but I can't remember anything we have said or done," answered the young man who hadn't been addressed in English for such a long time. It was such a joy to be able to follow a conversation without having first to translate it in his mind.

"Perhaps you would like me to tell you of my visit to England just before last Christmas? I had some official business to attend to, but when I got my leave authorised I went to Lincoln to look up old friends." Raoul watched Kevin for some reaction. "I visited Daisy to ask after Alice, and she told me Alice was now living with her aunt in Keswick, so I went there. Do you remember Alice?"

The young man shook his head.

"After Christmas I was again in Keswick, and I met some people from Harrogate."

"I was born in Harrogate," Kevin butted in.

"Yes, the people I met were your parents and your brother Lawrence."

Kevin sat contemplating this information. A smile spread over his face, then a look of horror. "Do they think I'm dead?"

"You were reported missing," said Raoul.

"Presumed dead," finished Kevin in a flat voice.

"Here we are – sorry to take so long making coffee, I must be getting old," said Father Justin as he handed them each a mug of steaming hot coffee.

"Did you find your friend Alice?" asked the priest.

"Yes, and she had recently given birth to a beautiful baby girl. I am her godfather, and she is called Estelle Rosemary – Rosemary after your mother, Kevin," continued Raoul.

"You mean my daughter? I have a daughter?" asked Kevin.

"Yes, a very much loved daughter."

"It was my idea to call her Estelle, our star." Kevin laid his head on his arm and wept as slowly bits of his past flashed into his mind.

Monique, having let herself into the room, quickly took in the situation.

"I'm sorry I'm so late, there were some problems I had to sort out. Brother Francis, Kevin – oh, it's so confusing, you having two names – I see you are remembering. Is it a lot or just bits?"

"I remember saying I wanted her to be called Estelle, if the baby was a girl. But I can't remember Alice, yet I feel she was important to me," answered Kevin.

"Don't worry, just let things drift back to you; there is plenty of time. Raoul is leaving us today, but he has told Father Justin and me about your family and Alice and all the obstacles put in your way. Be patient; we will help you," said Monique.

Raoul and Monique left the monastery shortly after. They made their way to Madame B's house where Ives would be waiting for them to give him the information to be radioed to London. Raoul also wanted to ask Ives what the chances were of getting both Kevin and Monique out of France.

"Just one more night of love, then you must go back. Oh, how I hate these partings, and when will you come again?" Monique cried as she wrapped herself round Raoul, and they came together.

It was with a heavy heart that Raoul returned to the farm at Epinay. He realised that while all these years he had been married to Monique he had loved her, now his feelings had intensified and he was deeply and passionately in love with her. It was no longer enough to visit her after long intervals; he wanted to share every moment with her, but the surest way he had of protecting Monique was to be away from her so that if he should be caught his wife wouldn't be implicated.

He had been back at the farm for over six weeks, and now spring had arrived there was much work to be done. Also during his absence Louis and Jules had penetrated the passage system linking various cellars of the old monastery, which now was in ruins. These cellars numbered six rooms in all, including Maurice's cellar. Apart from an entrance to the labyrinth at the base of the bell tower, four other openings, all well disguised, had been made. In the last two weeks over twenty allied escaped prisoners of war had been sheltered there. Henri rendezvoused with the submarine on several occasions but four was the maximum number of passengers he would take, knowing that on each return journey he would need his crew to help handle the boat and haul in the fish.

One afternoon Charlotte, the radio operator for the group, came to the farm. Marguerite welcomed her and kept her company until the men came in from the fields.

"Charlotte, this is a surprise! Anything wrong?" asked Raoul as he entered the kitchen.

"I got in touch with London early this morning. After I had given them our situation report, this message was tapped back. It doesn't make any sense to me; it must be some preconceived message known only to you. I hope you understand it, anyway." Charlotte passed a small piece of paper to Raoul.

Raoul took the slip of paper from her and read *KEVIN WELL, MONIQUE PREGNANT.* So many emotions passed through him in what could only have been a second. He folded the note and put it into his pocket.

"Thank you. It's OK, there is no reply at the moment," Raoul said to Charlotte; then went outside to walk quietly around the orchard. Marguerite and Louis looked at each other, wondering what the message was, but knew better than to ask Charlotte. The need-to-know rule was strictly adhered to throughout the group.

Later that night while they were sharing a bottle of wine, Raoul took the note from his pocket and passed it to Louis.

"Raoul, congratulations!" he said, then, turning to his wife, "Raoul is going to be a father."

"Oh Raoul, I'm so pleased for you both, you must be delighted," she said.

"Yes I am, but very worried. What if the Germans become aware of her condition before I can get her away? In their eyes she is a single woman, and some have very high morals where others are concerned. Then there are the villagers – they think she is single and that the only men she comes into contact with are the monks or maybe some German officers; either way, I've got to get her away. I'll have a word with Father Joseph tomorrow. If we can get Kevin and Monique back to England she will be safe – I know Kevin's family and Alice's aunt will look after her.

Chapter Eleven

"Four fours are sixteen, five fours are twenty, six fours are twenty-four," chorused the children as the teacher pointed to the numbers on the blackboard. It was Alice's third week as a teacher and she was loving every minute of it. Alice looked at her watch: only five minutes to home time.

"Now children, I want you to put your books away in your desks; then quietly stand in the aisle." The word 'quiet' took on a new meaning – asking the children to do anything quietly produced pandemonium, but they were good and obedient and very happy. Some of the children had experienced the war first-hand when they had been bombed out of their homes in Newcastle and were now living with foster parents as evacuees, so it was good to see them so happy.

With the children gone, Alice walked around the empty classroom checking that all the books had been put away and all the seats had been tipped up ready for the caretaker to sweep the wooden boarded floor.

"You ready?" her new friend Joan asked from the doorway.

"Yes, everything seems to be OK. I'll just get my coat".

As they walked from the school, Joan who taught the eight- to nine-year-olds, said how surprised she was to hear the tables being chanted so late in the day.

"Yes, we have arithmetic first thing after morning assembly but I was distressed when I realised they hadn't learnt their tables so each day they learn a new table and in the last fifteen minutes of the day they recite it. I thought maybe on Friday I could divide the class into two teams and have a competition to see which side knows the most. It would make learning fun," Alice explained.

"Well it seems a good idea to me, but I should clear it with the headmaster first," warned Joan. "These children have had three teachers already since last September: the first left to join the WAAF, the second moved nearer to where her husband is stationed and you're the third. I hope you will last to the end of the school year."

"There is every chance of that, with a baby to support," Alice said as the two friends parted at the crossroads and Alice hurried to be united with her four-month-old daughter.

Aunt Annie was just making a pot of tea as she entered the kitchen. "Hello dear, had a good day?" she asked.

"Yes, I must have the best and dearest children in the whole school. The twins, David and Doreen Turner, brought me a bunch of daffodils this morning."

"Tea's ready, we might as well have it now in peace. I think Estelle is teething – she couldn't settle and her little cheeks were so red she didn't sleep till well gone three. I'll ask the chemist tomorrow for something to put on her gums," Aunt Annie said.

"In that case, we can both put our feet up for half an hour. I'll carry the tray into the living room for you," Alice said.

"What have you planned for your angels tomorrow, then?" asked Aunt Annie as she drank her tea.

"I thought we might paint pictures of the daffodils as they looked so nice when I put them into a vase of water. In the afternoon they're practising the hymns for the Easter service."

"I think it would be nice if you took Estelle over to Harrogate during the holiday. I'm sure Rosemary and Harry will be delighted to see you both."

"Auntie, you are too late: I've already told Kevin's mother we are going, and I've accepted her offer of a bed for a couple of nights. I was going to tell you nearer the time."

Aunt and niece chatted for some time, and at five Aunt Annie went into the kitchen to prepare the evening meal and Alice went upstairs to change and see to her daughter.

Uncle John came home at quarter past six, feeling weary having chaired a meeting at school until after six o'clock.

"Well, I'm glad to see you – dinner will be spoilt if we wait much longer. What kept you so long?" Annie said to her husband. She didn't mean to nag, but whenever he was late she became very anxious. They ate the appetising meal and exchanged all the news and gossip of the day, and after they had finished their coffee, Uncle John asked to be excused as he had to go to choir practice at the chapel. As he let himself out of the house a gust of wind caught the door, causing it to bang; this was followed by a loud cry from baby Estelle.

"Well, that was a blessing in disguise – her ladyship can now have her bottle," Alice said as she went towards the stairs. This was the most precious time of the day for her, when she could relax and cuddle Estelle as she took her bottle of the new National dried baby milk. While she was in the baby bath Alice held her so she could kick and splash, gurgling all the time; then wrapped her in a big fluffy towel and dried and dressed her for bed. Since she had slept so long earlier in the evening, after Estelle had finished her bottle Alice encouraged her baby to play with her rattle and teething ring. Alice talked to Estelle, telling her how much her daddy would have loved her and what a brave man he was, and she knew she didn't understand what was being said but Alice wanted to tell her just the same.

The front doorbell shrilled throughout the house, and Alice heard Aunt Annie exclaim, "Well, of all people," as she answered the door. "But you were only here on Sunday! Oh I'm sorry, do come in – is something wrong?"

Then, recognising the voices as belonging to Kevin's parents, Alice lifted Estelle into her arms and carried her downstairs to her doting grandparents.

"Give me your coats and come and sit down, you could have knocked me down with a feather when I saw you standing there on the doorstep. There is something wrong, isn't there?" said Aunt Annie.

"This is a lovely surprise. Estelle won't settle so you can have a cuddle," Alice said, putting Estelle into her grandmother's arms "But it must be something important to bring you here in the evening, Dad?"

"Well, I think we have some good news – as far as I know everything is all right," said Harry.

"What about a drink everyone – sherry?" asked Aunt Annie. Then, turning to Harry, "There's a drop of whisky if you prefer."

"Yes please Annie, but I thought John was teetotal, being chapel."

"Yes he is, but he also accepts freedom of choice for everyone," Aunt Annie replied as she went over to the sideboard to get the drinks. Rosemary and Harry were so captivated by their granddaughter that they almost forgot why they had come. Later, when Estelle had fallen asleep in Rosemary's arms, Aunt Annie picked her up and laid her in the pram.

"Harry, will you tell them?" asked Rosemary, looking up at her husband. He patted his wife's hand and nodded. Alice looked at Aunt Annie with concern. Suddenly, after clearing his throat, Harry spoke.

"This morning I was busy cleaning out the pumps and Rosemary was washing the floor in the bar, when in walks this RAF officer. 'We're closed,' I told him, but he said he had some important news for Mr and Mrs Renwick concerning their son. I think we both must have changed colour, because this officer put his arm out to Rosemary and urged her to sit down and I followed suit. I thought it must be Lawrence; I said a quick prayer that we weren't to lose him too, but it had nothing to do with Lawrence. It's Kevin. This officer chap said they had heard from a reliable source that Kevin is alive, in France, and the resistance fighters are looking after him."

Alice gasped. "Kevin? Alive?" There was a buzzing in her head, she felt dizzy and then she fainted.

"Oh my poor bairn," Aunt Annie said as she knelt beside her niece. "I hope she doesn't go into shock as she did when

Kevin was first reported missing. It took her months to recover."

Alice was coming round.

"Alice, have a sip of my whisky, it will help you feel better," said Harry, proffering his glass to his daughter-in-law, as they saw her. When Alice had recovered, her aunt and Harry helped her onto the settee next to Rosemary.

" I can't believe it, oh Mam, if it's really true!" Alice cried as Rosemary put her arms round her and their tears of joy mingled.

After some time and when they had all regained their composure, Rosemary voiced her plans for the wedding when her son came home. Aunt Annie suggested that as their neighbours thought Alice was already married it would be better if the wedding could take place in Harrogate. This delighted Rosemary as it would mean she could arrange everything as if she were the bride's mother, and Alice would truly be her daughter. Harry Renwick cautioned his wife not to get carried away: Kevin was still in France and the only thing that they knew was that he was still alive. The RAF officer stressed that nothing further was known, but should more information become available, he would personally ensure they were made aware of it immediately.

It was gone ten when the Renwicks left. Uncle John had come home shortly after half past nine and when he was told the news, said a short prayer of thanksgiving. After the visitors had left, Alice changed Estelle, gave her a bottle and put her to bed. When she rejoined her aunt and uncle the bedtime drink of cocoa was being served.

"He might not want to marry me now. I was so sure he was dead," Alice said.

"We shall have to wait and see. They didn't mention if he was injured or ill, but perhaps we'll hear something definite soon. He would have to have changed an awful lot if he didn't love you anymore," Aunt Annie had said.

The weeks passed, but nothing more was heard from the Air Ministry. In July Estelle pulled herself up by the settee and balanced on her own feet for a minute before bumping down onto her bottom. She now had six teeth and was eating minced food and chewing rusks. She was a beautiful child: her fair hair was just starting to curl and her big brown eyes sparkled just like her daddy's.

When school broke up for the summer holidays, Uncle John went on his annual fly-fishing holiday with his old friend from his college days. Each year they stayed at the Horse's Head in Swaledale and cast their lines in the nearby river for trout. Aunt Annie thought it was time she also had a change of scenery and made arrangements to take Alice and Estelle to Morecambe for some sea air. It was the first real holiday Alice had had since the beginning of the war. They stayed in a guesthouse and because the landlady's father was a keen gardener there was always plenty of freshly grown vegetables to eke out the rations. Aunt Annie and Alice were able to go to the theatre and sometimes the cinema in the evenings, as Mrs Kirshaw, the landlady, was always willing to babysit for her guests. The weather was sunny, with a bracing wind which put roses into their cheeks. It was a wonderful holiday and Alice was sorry when it was Saturday and they had to return home.

"Cheer up love, all good things come to an end, but remember an end is also a beginning," said Aunt Annie as they boarded the train for Keswick.

They arrived home at about teatime. Uncle John was to be away for a few more days. As they opened the door, there on the floor was a pile of letters. Three were addressed to Alice, including a card from Cleethorpes from her friend Daisy, informing Alice that she was soon to be married and would like Alice to come to her wedding if possible, but would understand if she wasn't able. Alice recognised her brother's scrawl on one of the other envelopes. Impatient to know how he was, she slit the envelope open and read the short note –

so typical of him. He was going on leave in August for two weeks and staying in Lincoln with their parents as he hadn't seen them since before they had turned Alice out and he was feeling rather guilty. He said he would be returning to the Clyde via Keswick, so he would be able to see his beloved niece and her mother. The buff envelope with the Portsmouth postmark still lay on the table, and just as Alice was about to open it, Estelle cried.

"OK Auntie, I'll see to her; I can read my mystery letter later." As Alice got up and tended to her daughter, she whispered to her, "You can sleep in your own little cot tonight, darling, and in a few more weeks Uncle Michael is coming to see you."

By the time they had put Estelle to bed and unpacked all the dirty clothes, it was gone seven o'clock.

"Let's finish the holiday with fish and chips," suggested Aunt Annie.

"Good idea – you lay the table and I'll nip out and get them," said Alice.

When supper was finished and they had washed up, Aunt Annie asked her niece what was in the mystery letter.

"Good heavens, I haven't opened it; it must still be on the table." Alice looked, but there was no sign of the letter. Then she looked on the floor – it had to be somewhere. She moved the armchair, and there, almost hidden by the cushion, was the buff envelope. The address had been typed, and it looked very official but it didn't say *OHMS*. Alice opened the envelope and drew out a soiled white envelope, again addressed to her in capital letters. Across the top of the envelope was the instruction *Please post in England*. A queer feeling came over her, then with a deep breath she opened the envelope and took out the piece of paper which was written in an uneven scrawl.

France, 19 July 43

Dear Alice,

By now you will have heard that Kevin is alive and safe. I found him in a monastery being cared for by the monks and a very good lady doctor, my wife Monique. He has fully recovered from the injuries he sustained when he was shot down, but was suffering from amnesia and didn't recognise me at first. He has now regained most of his memory, and as soon as it is possible we will get him back to England, but I must warn you that it could take months.

Please excuse the writing – I am at sea in a fishing boat and I did not dare risk writing this before, in case it fell into enemy hands. Give my goddaughter a cuddle from me.

Your sincere friend,
Raoul

"Auntie, it's from Raoul, look!" Alice passed the letter to her aunt to read.

"When are you planning to go over to Harrogate?"

"I thought I would wait until Uncle John gets back, but I ought to let Kevin's parents see this letter as soon as possible."

"Your uncle will be home on Wednesday, but if I were you I'd rest tomorrow, then go first thing on Monday. Don't worry about me, I'm quite happy here on my own. I'll wash some of Estelle's things out tonight; then you can iron them in the morning."

It was a very happy service in the chapel that Sunday. A visiting preacher gave a very uplifting sermon and the children's choir sang *All Things Bright and Beautiful*. Alice felt that the whole world was beautiful, now that thoughts of Kevin took over more and more of her mind.

Alice decided to go to Harrogate by bus instead of the train; this way she wouldn't need to leave her seat until they pulled into the bus station, it would save negotiating the stairs and the railway lines. A thick mist obliterated the scenery when they left Keswick, but as they came down into the lower ground the sun broke through – another sunny day was ahead. There were two taxis waiting in the ranks, and Alice climbed into the back of the first one with Estelle in her arms as the driver stowed the case and pushchair into the boot. Mother and daughter would stay with Kevin's parents until Friday.

"We are always surprising each other: I didn't expect you until Wednesday, but do come in, I wouldn't mind you being here forever," said Rosemary as she scooped her granddaughter into her arms. "Lawrence is here; he's been injured – some shrapnel hit his leg but he says it isn't serious. Oh ,it is nice having you both. If only we could have Kevin as well."

"That's what brought me here early: I've had a letter from Raoul," Alice said.

Once the bar was closed after the lunchtime session and they were sitting having a cup of tea following a light lunch, Alice took out the letter from Raoul and passed it to Kevin's dad, who read it out loud.

"Well, we now know more than the Air Ministry; we should let them see this," said Harry, waving the letter.

"No, I don't think that would be wise," said Lawrence. Father and son argued on the rights and wrongs of this until Lawrence said, "You don't understand, Dad: there are thousands of men missing and unaccounted for, and when this is all over, perhaps they will be found. The ministry have told you that Kevin is alive, but he is only a number and name to them, a statistic. Raoul is obviously working for and with the resistance, and he shouldn't have let that be known. We mustn't break his confidence; it could put lives in danger. He just wanted to put Alice's mind at ease, but even then I wonder if he had an ulterior motive."

"Well, I can't see what he hopes to gain. Still, if you think we should keep this news to ourselves, then we will," said Harry.

Lawrence and his fiancée Helen took Alice with them on Thursday night to the theatre, where the repertory company were performing *Drake's Drum*. Alice thoroughly enjoyed her evening out – it was the first time she had been out with people her own age since Kevin went away. They laughed and giggled all the way back to the pub; it was a wonderful evening and a night to remember.

Alice and Estelle returned to Keswick on Friday as planned. Uncle John was pleased to see them and the precious letter, and when she told him of Lawrence's advice he nodded in agreement.

"The authorities will be told when the time is right; when Kevin reaches England. You put this letter safe somewhere and say nothing to nobody."

A few days later Michael arrived in Keswick to finish off his leave as he had only stayed five days with their parents.

"How is everyone in Lincoln?" Alice asked her brother.

"You may well ask – oh, they're all right; still as bigoted as ever. I asked them if they had any news of you, but Dad said, 'We don't mention that person in this house' and Mum stuck her nose in the air. I had to bite my tongue I was that mad; then I thought, what if they lose me too? In a way they have: I'll never go back to Lincoln to live. I saw Ken Baker; he's in the army on leave from North Africa – he's with Monty's lot. Oh, and I found Daisy's aunt in the NAAFI and gave her a message for Daisy – did you know she is getting married soon?"

"Yes, I've had a card from her, telling me about her wedding. I won't be able to go, but Auntie has given me a beautiful embroidered tablecloth to send to her," Alice said. "Anyway, come and help me to bath your niece."

"OK, but only if I get to play with the ducks," replied Michael.

"Really Michael, I sometimes despair of you – aren't you ever going to grow up? I can see I'll have to check your kitbag when you leave to make sure you leave Estelle's toys behind".

"Do you remember that green rubber fish we had when we were small? If we squeezed all the air out of it under the water, it filled with water and sunk to the bottom of the bath. You could never squeeze hard enough," teased Michael.

"Would you like to nip downstairs for her bottle while I dry Estelle and put her night things on?" Alice asked once Estelle had been bathed. "Auntie will have it ready." Alice was so happy sharing her daughter with Michael; he was fascinated by her and Estelle followed every movement he made with her eyes. By the time she had finished her bottle she was almost asleep.

"Once Estelle is settled, I'll show you my letter from Raoul," Alice said to Michael.

"Raoul, who's he? I've never heard you mention him before. You got a boyfriend?"

"No, you know him," Alice answered somewhat impatiently.

"No I don't, I've never met anyone by that name," replied Michael.

"Course you have – oh sorry, no, maybe you didn't meet him. He was one of the men we had billeted on us; we always called him Ra."

"Oh, him – some conscientious objector, according to Dad."

"That's the last thing he is. Oh Michael, you don't know, we were all so pleased to see you that we never told you our marvellous news. Kevin is alive."

"What? Oh Alice, that's wonderful news, I'm delighted for you! When is he coming home, or is he in a POW camp?"

"No, he's not a prisoner, but I don't know when he's coming back. Read the letter first, then I'll explain." She passed the grubby envelope to her brother.

"It looks as if this Raoul chap is with the resistance, but it's foolhardy of him to put it in writing," said Michael, passing the letter back to his sister.

"Yes he is, he told me last December when he came to see me. He was with Kevin shortly before Kevin's plane was hit. Kevin had just flown Raoul back to France; I gather it was something he had done on several occasions."

"You mean that when he was supposed to be on a training course, which really upset Dad, he was actually in France?" asked Michael. Alice nodded.

During the next week Michael and Alice spent most of their time together. They would pack a picnic and walk for miles, Michael often carrying Estelle on his shoulders while Alice dragged the pushchair behind. On the last night of Michael's leave Aunt Annie and Uncle John looked after Estelle so that brother and sister could go to dinner at the big hotel overlooking the lake.

"I booked a window table; I wanted it to be special. I know it would have been more romantic with the right partner, but until Kevin comes home I suppose I'm the best you've got."

Alice stood on her tiptoes and kissed his cheek, and told him he was very special to her and that she hoped they would always have time for each other. She said that just as she loved Kevin, one day Michael too would find someone to love and then they could all be friends.

"We shared our childhood and no one can take that away from us; the love and the happy times we had together. This last year," Alice told him, "you have been a pillar of strength for me."

"Yes love, you have had a very hard time and I hope you understand why I felt I had to spend part of my leave with them, but God knows when the next time will be. They make me so angry," said Michael.

Alice nodded in agreement.

"They are so hypocritical! Sorry, does it hurt for me to mention them to you?" asked Michael anxiously.

"No. I wish in a way that it did; at least then I would have some feeling for them, but the hurt went too deep. When I needed them they didn't want to know, and now I have a daughter of my own and even if she did get herself into all manner of trouble, I hope I'd always be there to help and support her. When I was younger, even then I felt unwanted –

no, don't say anything Michael, I know what I felt. Whatever you did was wonderful, but I always seemed to be in the wrong. Remember that time when I won the hundred-yards race? I thought then that Mam and Dad would be proud of me at last, but Mrs Gammage had pointed out how unladylike it was to run in a public place in knickers and vest. Then recently Uncle John invited me to the combined schools sports day and I couldn't help but smile – you know Roedean, the private school where the aristocracy send their daughters? It has moved here to Keswick for the duration of the war, so they took part in the races. There was Lady This and The Honourable That, running like hares in their unmentionables, their faces as red as beetroot and sweating like horses. I had to smile as I remembered Mum's comment about the behaviour of young ladies. They never had a bad word to say about you, though. It was a wonder I didn't hate you, Michael, but I loved you and you always comforted me when I was upset. You always were on my side."

Brother and sister continued their meal in silence, listening to the four-piece band. As coffee was being served Michael pointed out couples who were getting up to dance.

"How about showing them how it should be done?"

Michael had shown Alice how to dance when she was fourteen. When their dad and mum went out, they had pushed all the furniture to the side of the room, wound up the gramophone and put on a 78 of Glen Miller. Then off they would go, practising all the intricate steps.

Michael held Alice by the hand as he led her onto the dance floor and put his arm around her waist. Then they danced to the tune *Unforgettable* and were so engrossed in their dancing that they didn't realise the other couples had stopped and were watching them as they twisted and turned, lost in their own little world.

Chapter Twelve

Monique removed her clothes from the wardrobe and chest of drawers. Since fleeing from the Germans in Marseilles her only possessions were her clothes and a few trinkets of jewellery. Folding her silk lingerie with the Parisian labels, she carefully packed them into the suitcase along with her jewellery box. Then the few dresses that still fitted around her ever-expanding waistline were added, plus three cardigans and a spare pair of sandals. The silk nightgown she had worn on her honeymoon was three sizes too small but she couldn't bear to leave it behind, so into the case it went, along with the two roomy nighties B had kindly given her.

"That's the lot, B – you can do what you want with the rest of my clothes. It's no good making the case heavier than it is already. I shall have to carry it myself until we get out of France," said Monique.

"I'm going to miss you, we've been through a lot together. I do hope you have a safe journey; I'll be praying for you. Is Raoul coming for you?"

"No, it won't be Raoul, that would be too dangerous. He would be too protective and that could draw unwanted attention to us. Father Justin said I was to pack my case and take it to the monastery today, and when the time is right we will leave. It could be tonight or perhaps not until next week. Oh B, I'm so frightened. I've felt really safe here."

Madame B put her arms around the younger woman to comfort her.

"Monique, if only you could stay here but we have to be brave and sensible. Once your condition is made public, who knows how the villagers will react? They've never seen you with a man so they are bound to think you've been consorting with the German patients at the clinic, and you know what happens to collaborators. I promised Raoul I'd look after you and help you to get away should you become pregnant and that's what I am doing now. Be brave; I'll see you when the war is finished. I feel sure we will beat the Germans now. Off you go – Ives is waiting for you with the truck." Madame B pushed her friend outside and closed the door. She hadn't wanted Monique to see the tears running down her cheeks. Would she ever see her dear friend again?

Ives drove the truck round to the back entrance of the clinic where he normally collected the laundry. He handed down Monique's case and as he left, said that he would be in touch soon.

"Monique, you must come and meet your successor, Dr Le Roche," said Father Justin. Monique was introduced to a slim, handsome, dark-haired young man who only looked about twenty, but she was later assured by Father Justin that he was in fact a qualified doctor with three years' hospital experience, so that made him at least twenty-eight.

"When you've shown Dr Le Roche where everything is, perhaps you'll be so good as to join me in my quarters at the monastery," said Father Justin before leaving them.

Monique stayed at the monastery in Father Justin's quarters so she would be ready when someone came to guide Kevin and herself out of France. Each day she spent time with Kevin, schooling him in everyday French punctuation and some slang expressions, just in case they got into difficulty and were separated. One day there was a knock on Monique's door and Father Justin put his head round.

"They're here. I've put them into the reception room to have a meal; they've been travelling since last night."

"Should I go to them or are you bringing them in here?" asked Monique.

"I'll bring them here in about half an hour's time. Ives should be here by then; I've sent word to him of their arrival. Could you get Kevin please?"

Monique went to the guest room she had been using for the past four anxious days and collected her things together. She was terrified, yet eager to start their journey and with luck and God's blessings they should soon be free and safe. When all was done she threw a cardigan around her shoulders and went out into the early evening air to search for Kevin. Once she had located him, Kevin and Monique sat in the abbot's sitting room, awaiting their visitors with some trepidation. They would be putting their lives into the hands of total strangers.

"I wonder where they are taking us," said Kevin.

"Out of France, but where to then? Your guess is as good as mine. Raoul mentioned Switzerland once, and he said that sometimes fishing boats transfer human cargo to British fishing trawlers, but I think that's too dangerous now," Monique answered.

"Here we are," said Father Justin as he led a priest, a monk and Ives into the room. "This is Monique and Kevin." Then, turning to the strangers, he said, "And this is Father Joseph and Manuel. Manuel is to be your guide through Spain."

"I'm delighted to meet you both. Raoul has briefed me fully on the situation, and he sends you his love, Monique. Kevin, Raoul wants you to be fully responsible for Monique, especially when you reach England. Remember, Monique knows no one there. He said I was to tell you that if your parents can't find her a room, he knows Alice's aunt will," said Father Joseph. Manuel was then introduced, with the assurance that with his knowledge and experience of the route they were to follow, they would soon be led to safety.

Once the introductions were over Father Justin left the room, not wishing to hear their plans. The less he knew, the less he could divulge should things go wrong and he should be subjected to torture. Father Joseph outlined their journey. The first part would be organised by Ives, whose group would see them safely to the Spanish frontier. From then on Manuel would be in charge. He was a Spanish Benedictine monk from Barcelona and he knew the route and the people well, having done the journey on four previous occasions. They were to leave at dawn.

It was after lunchtime when they arrived at the little monastery outside Cahors. The three passengers hidden amongst the vegetables were hot, weary and stiff with cramp. Manuel helped Kevin out from under the potatoes; then they both gently lifted Monique, who couldn't move at all.

"Here, sit on this wall for a while. Your legs will get moving again by the time we've unloaded the cart," said Ives. He was so sorry that the good doctor had to travel in such awful, cramped conditions, especially in view of her own condition.

They were given a meal of cheese salad followed by acorn coffee. This was a very poor order indeed – all the monks looked very old, and perhaps they were unable to tend to their garden as it needed, thought Monique. They were each shown into a cell where Monique lay down to rest on the hard bed, thankful for the solitude and the peace.

Just as the sun set the travellers were summoned to the reception room and given a simple meal of bread, cold meats and fruit; again finishing the meal with acorn coffee. When it was almost dark a young boy of about fourteen led them through the nearby woods and across two fields, then down to the riverside. Here they sat waiting for over an hour in the cold night air, when suddenly out of the darkness they saw a barge moving slowly downstream. They quickly clambered onto the barge as it glided along. Should anyone have been watching, they wouldn't have realised that it had paused for a few seconds to get the people on board. What a civilised way to travel: they were able to walk about the limited space, but should unwelcome guests wish to board the barge Kevin and Monique had been shown the concealed cupboards where they could hide. Manuel had discarded his habit and was now posing as a member of the crew.

As they entered the city of Toulouse early the next morning they found the wharf bustling with activity, but poor Kevin and Monique saw nothing of this as they were incarcerated in their respective cupboards. Manuel opened each cupboard in turn and handed Kevin and Monique bread rolls filled with the soft cheese made from ewes' milk, and a cup of coffee. They were to remain hidden for as long as the barge was docked at the wharf. An hour later Manuel warned the passengers that their stay was likely to be a long one. Movement of German troops by barge along the Canal du Midi on their way to the Mediterranean coast was causing a delay in the basin where the barges turned round. Monique and Kevin took advantage of the delay and settled resignedly to sleep. Manuel, who often worked on the barge, helped with the unloading of the vegetables and fruit, then when the hole was empty, assisted with the stacking of the wood to be transported back up north.

The movement of the boat jolted Kevin and Monique from their slumbers and soon Manuel was inviting them into the cabin for a hot meal.

"When we've turned the boat round Anger the skipper will put us onto the towpath near a group of trees. We will have a fair way to walk but I'm sure you'll both manage all right," said Manuel.

The boat bumped into the riverbank. Manuel leapt over the side and onto the towpath; Kevin followed, clutching Monique's suitcase, and with outstretched hands both men helped Monique onto the firm ground.

"We'll have to do something about that case; it's too unwieldy," said Manuel. "Perhaps we could find a knapsack." It hadn't occurred to Monique, but she realised now that a knapsack would indeed be much lighter and not so unwieldy, and would allow her to have both hands free for climbing. Manuel led the way over barren fields and across deserted roads. Finally they came to a wooded area and found that trying to walk was very difficult due to the straggly undergrowth and the enveloping darkness.

"Manuel, please, I'm sorry but I'll have to stop a minute or two and have a rest," said Monique. Manuel hesitated; then with a wave urged them on, saying that they could rest when they were near the ridge. Kevin noticed that they had been slowly climbing a thickly-wooded hillside. He put his hand gently under Monique's elbow, guiding her through the bushes.

"This is a good place for you to rest. Don't use your torch, and if you must talk, whisper," said Manuel; then he walked away from them and disappeared.

"Do you have a watch, Monique? He's been gone ages," said Kevin.

"It's too dark to see my watch and I dare not use my torch. Kevin, I desperately need to spend a penny – the baby has been very active during our climb," whispered Monique.

"Can you manage here? I'll take a look ahead; don't worry, I won't disappear too." Kevin knelt down and crawled along the path Manuel had taken. After a few yards he came to what appeared to be a deep gully. It was lighter here, where the trees had been thinned. He looked to the left and then to the right, but couldn't see any signs of humanity – just more trees and shrubs. He turned and made his way back to Monique.

"What shall we do? It looks as if we've been abandoned."

"What can we do? We don't know where we are or whom we can trust and it's too dark to find our way. I suppose we might as well make ourselves comfortable and rest. We must have faith, after all, Manuel has looked after us up to now," said Monique.

Kevin sat with his back to the tree and Monique lay down with her head resting on his lap. Time passed, and soon it was hours since Manuel had left them. The sky was beginning to lighten, and nearby a cock crowed.

"Are you ready to move on?" Manuel had suddenly appeared from nowhere with a sack thrown over his shoulder. "Here," he said, passing a monk's habit that he had just taken from the sack to Kevin. "I've got this shawl for you,

Monique. Put it over your head and around your shoulders." Manuel then took another habit from the sack and pulled it over his own clothes. Now suitably disguised, they made their way forward, and guided by Manuel, were soon walking along a narrow country road. A cart pulled by two bullocks and driven by a young boy of about nine was coming towards them. As it drew near, it stopped.

"Monique, you are to ride on the cart – it will be easier for you. Batiste will take you to the nuns of St. Clare and they will look after you until the time comes for our next journey. Kevin and I will be staying at the monastery," said Manuel as he and Kevin set off to walk to their destination.

Sister Monica welcomed Monique and showed her to a small, simply-furnished bedroom. It was very clean, with the smell of lavender, and immeasurably more comfortable than the forest floor.

"We have hot water. Would you like a bath?"

"Yes please," said Monique.

"Good. Later I will bring you breakfast; then you must rest. In your condition you shouldn't have to make such an arduous journey," added Sister Monica with a shake of her head.

Monique appreciated the nuns' concern and their kindness. She stayed with them for three days, enjoying the much-needed rest. During the afternoon on the third day word came for her to be ready at teatime – a knapsack accompanied the message. It was getting dusky as Manuel and Kevin arrived at the back door of the nunnery. They shared afternoon tea with Monique and Sister Monica, and when it was quite dark Manuel led the way to the river where they boarded a small boat which was to take them to Foix.

It was strange to be sitting exposed in an open boat in pitch darkness, moving slowly against the current. Kevin and Manuel each took an oar and the boatman acted as cox, steering the boat around unseen hazards. After several hours on the river they emerged at a small inlet where the boatman took both oars and pulled the boat into the side. Although their legs felt stiff after sitting for such a long time there was no time to waste and the three travellers were soon on their way, climbing steadily into the hills. Manuel led them through narrow gullies and wooded copses, and when they came across a small cave he allowed them to rest and handed them food to eat. He had never brought a woman over the mountains before and this one was pregnant, so extra care had to be taken. After five days they reached the small town of Viella. They had left France and crossed into Spain, but there were many who would betray refugees, so Manuel insisted they did everything exactly as he instructed them, saying that he had promised to deliver them safely to a certain monastery in Barcelona.

Monique was weary and exhausted when they arrived. Her ankles were swollen, her heart pounded and she knew her blood pressure was high.

"I will see if Senora Amerie can put us up for a few days. She is a midwife and will know what to do," said Manuel.

"Manuel, I am not having the baby yet!" Monique tried to point out.

"Stay here; I will return soon."

Monique and Kevin concealed themselves in a pigsty Manuel had pointed out to them.

"Kevin, you seem to have an affinity with pigs and must feel quite at home here. Pigs do seem to loom largely in your life," laughed Monique.

"Now that's an idea: after the war I'll become a pig farmer," Kevin said with a grin.

Manuel must have been away for nearly an hour before he crept into the pigsty to join them.

"I'm sorry Monique, but if you rest a little longer do you think you could walk a couple of miles more when darkness falls?"

"What's wrong, Manuel, has something happened?" asked Monique.

"Senora Amerie was taken away by the frontier guards two days ago and no one knows what has happened to her. We must get out of this town. There is a hamlet just further down the hillside; we will find shelter there," he answered.

Later, when it was dark, Manuel led them through the outskirts of Viella and onto the wooded mountain slopes. They moved in crocodile fashion, Manuel at the front holding Monique's hand and Kevin grabbing Monique's sleeve as he followed behind. Thus they moved, conscious of any slip either one made. Around midnight it started to rain; Manuel was delighted as this meant that the guards and their dogs would be unable to track them down. Then Manuel stopped to let them rest as he pointed out a dark shape about a hundred yards away.

"That is where we will find shelter for a few days. There's a rock just along here where you can rest while I go and check everything is safe." He moved so fast that Monique realised just how much her condition had slowed them down.

"How are you feeling?" Kevin asked.

"If I were a patient I would advise complete bed rest, but the circumstances won't allow so, my dear friend, there is nothing else to do but summon up my strength and put my best foot forward!" replied Monique.

The rain continued to fall. The night was ominously dark, and only an odd cowbell could be heard jangling as the huge beasts moved in their sleep. Then Manuel was back.

"Come, all is well. We can stay at the farmhouse for a few days, then when you are fit to travel, Monique, I will arrange some transport for you." Manuel again took Monique's hand and guided her down a stony path. The way seemed easier now that a safe haven was in sight.

Senora Osorno had eight children of her own and was grandmother to another twenty-nine. She was aghast when she saw how swollen Monique's legs were and insisted she have her bed and rest for at least three days. During this time Kevin stayed out of sight in the barn – the farmer and his wife took a great risk in befriending them, but they were nevertheless cheerful and always willing to help. Manuel had disappeared, but on Thursday he strolled into the farmhouse kitchen.

"I've got some Spanish identity papers for you both so once we get you safely down the mountain we can travel in comfort. Monique, you will ride beside Senor Osorno on his cart when he goes to market on Friday. Kevin and I will walk over the fields – we won't be noticed; monks often travel this way. Once we reach Lerida we can get the bus to take us to Barcelona."

Everyone was up early on Friday morning. Signora Osorno gave Monique a shawl to put over her head and shoulders. Should they be stopped by the border patrols, her husband would say she was a cousin visiting them before the birth of her child. When all the vegetables had been put onto the cart, Kevin helped Monique up onto the seat; then with a wave he ran over the field to where Manuel waited for him.

The air was so pure, and the morning stillness only disturbed by the sweet call of the birds. Monique enjoyed the journey down the mountainside. The border guards glanced at the couple in the cart; then waved then on, obviously assuming Monique was indeed the signor's wife. There was much hustle and bustle in the marketplace; Monique was helped down from the cart and then Signor Osorno quickly transferred the produce from his cart onto the market stall. Then, whispering something softly to the neighbouring stallholder, he took his horse and cart away. Monique felt it would be wiser to move, and she wandered around the market looking at the different stalls. Eventually, feeling tired, she made her way towards the church and just as she climbed the worn steps leading towards the door, two monks came up to her, smiling broadly.

"Hello, are you going inside?" asked Manuel.

"Yes, I've walked round the market at least three times and now I'm feeling quite exhausted." answered Monique.

"Good – you sit towards the back. Kevin and I will go near to the Pietra; then I think coffee will be in order before we catch the midday bus to take us to Barcelona," said Manuel.

Manuel signalled to Monique to follow them as he left the church with Kevin. They returned to the marketplace and sat down at a table under the cool shelter of a mimosa tree where coffee was being served. Monique made a show of asking if she might sit at their table as all the others were full. She ordered her coffee and sat sipping it, not joining in the conversation but listening carefully to what Manuel was saying about the forthcoming journey. Monique was to sit near to the front of the bus, and Manuel would rest his hand on her shoulder as a sign when it was time to leave the bus. Once they had alighted she was to turn to the right and they would catch up with her.

The bus was due at midday, but in true Spanish tradition it didn't leave until almost one o'clock! Monique struggled onto the bus with her large basket, loaned by Senora Osorno – it contained her knapsack, which was hidden under the fruit and a napkin. She tendered the exact fare and stated the name of the square where she needed to alight, and the driver gave her the ticket without a second glance. Then Kevin and Manuel took their seats further down the bus.

The bus rattled and bumped over the rough roads. The hot July sun beat down relentlessly, making the bus resemble an oven. Monique closed her eyes, fervently praying that the journey would soon come to an end. After what seemed like hours, the bus drew to a halt in a square surrounded by sun-kissed stone buildings with intricate wrought iron grills guarding the lower windows. Monique glanced round to where Kevin and Manuel sat. They were both looking out of the window, so this obviously wasn't her stop. On the bus trundled, stopping several times on the way. At last it drew into another square, and this time the two monks stood up and walked down the bus. One rested his hand gently on

Monique's shoulder as he walked past. She let the family following them pass; then, standing up, gathered her things together and alighted from the bus. The heat was unbearable and just as Manuel turn to check if Monique was following them, she fainted and crumpled onto the dusty road.

Kevin and Manuel quickly ran to her side. Manuel told the assembled crowd that he would take her to a nearby convent, but first a cold drink was brought to her by a waitress from the pavement café.

"I'm sorry Manuel, I just don't know what happened," said Monique.

"Don't worry, you fainted – it was well timed and gave us a reason to look after you. Well done," said Manuel. "Come now, just a little walk round the next corner and we will be there; then I must say goodbye to you both. My mission will be complete."

The two men supported the young woman between them, not wishing to risk her having another fall. They had turned the corner and were walking beside a high garden wall. The green fronds of the trees could be seen towering above, and the birds sang sweetly. Soon they came to a wooden door. Manuel pulled at the bell and a diminutive nun with a brown, wizened face came to welcome them inside. A bell rang in the distance calling the nuns to prayer, however the little nun didn't take them to the chapel, but to a refectory where they were given food.

"This is splendid, I've never tasted Spanish food," said Monique.

"This is a very popular dish, with saffron rice, fish and pieces of chicken. You will have it many times, I'm sure, before you leave Spain," said Manuel. When they had all finished their meal, Manuel shook hands with Kevin and gently kissed Monique's cheek and bade them a safe journey to England. He had completed his mission.

The convent had a number of guest rooms, so Kevin was able to stay in a room not far from Monique and have his meals with her and Sister Francesca, who was a trained doctor at the convent clinic. French was the only language common to all three and when Kevin sometimes missed a salient point Monique would interpret in her not-too-fluent English. When this happened there was much amusement; nevertheless Kevin and Monique managed to increase their knowledge of the Spanish language. Sister Francesca examined Monique, checking her blood pressure, weight, heartbeat and pulse.

"Well, considering all you have gone through over the past weeks you are in remarkably good shape, but now you are in my care and I insist you have complete bed rest for a few days, and following that, a little exercise. I hope the rest of your journey will be in comfortable, easy stages."

During their stay Kevin and Monique enjoyed delicious meals with lots of fresh salads and fruit. After Monique was allowed out of bed she and Kevin walked around the grounds of the convent in the mornings when it was cool. In the hot afternoons they both had a siesta and in the evenings after their meal, with Sister Francesca as guide, they would explore the wonders of Barcelona. They visited the cathedral, staring in wonder at the magnificent carved wooden pinnacles over the choir stalls and looking at the beautiful stained glass windows. The evening sun was setting as they strolled down the Rambla de las Flores, the flower market where even at this time of day there were a myriad of huge, colourful blooms still on sale. In the harbour, staring out to sea, was the statue of Christopher Columbus and a replica of the Santa Maria, the little ship that took Columbus thousands of miles on his amazing voyages of discovery in the 15th century.

On the first Monday in September 1943, Kevin, disguised as a monk, and Monique in the garb of a nun got on the train at Barcelona with four nuns en route to Portugal. The four nuns were to attend a religious festival at a sister convent in Abrantes, which lay just over the Spanish/Portuguese border. The train rattled along the coast, and the blazing sun sparkling on the water reflected the intense blue of the sky. The first stop was Tarragona, where the porters busily loaded the local agricultural produce into the luggage van. The train chugged off and continued on its way, turning away from the coast and heading northward towards Zaragoza; then southwest to Madrid. As they approached the city Kevin and Monique looked out in wonder at the magnificent buildings graced by huge statues on the roofs; however they chose to remain silent lest someone notice their strange, stilted accents. The ticket collector checked their papers with a cursory glance and bid them a safe journey.

After a wearisome six hours the train arrived at Valencia on the Portuguese border. Again their papers were checked, this time by Spanish and Portuguese guards, and finally after forty minutes the train heaved and puffed its way into Abrantes where the nuns would leave them.

"You want the stop after the next one. Remember, after you have handed in your tickets, go straight to the taxi rank and say you wish to go to the British Embassy, No. 37 Rua de São Domingos à Lapa. God bless you both." Sister Maria kissed Monique and Kevin on both cheeks; then quickly left them, hurrying to catch up with the other nuns.

Kevin and Monique were now alone in their compartment. Darkness was falling, and Kevin reached across and clasped Monique's hand.

"We're almost there," he whispered.

"It is so silly of me I know, but I am more afraid now than I've been at any other time during our journey," said Monique.

"Yes, I understand – we have no one to rely on, just our two selves."

As the train pulled into the station at Lisbon, Kevin took Monique's carpet bag, in which the knapsack was hidden, and soon they were both standing on the platform.

"I wonder which way we go to get out of the station?" said Monique.

"People are walking in all directions; let's follow the family with the small children," suggested Kevin. They followed the family over a bridge, along a passage and down to another platform. It seemed as if the family were about to embark onto another train and were not staying in Lisbon. "Could you ask? If you spoke German, perhaps it would be safe."

Monique noticed a uniformed man, probably a porter, and asked, "*Wo ist der Ausgang, bitte?*"

The man pointed to the bridge they had just crossed.

"Come on, if we retrace our steps you can ask again. He wasn't surprised to hear German spoken," said Kevin.

At last, some fifteen minutes later, they were outside, waiting at the taxi rank. Kevin handed the card to the taxi driver on which was printed *No. 37 Rua de São Domingos à Lapa*, then got into the cab beside Monique.

"*Si, Señor,*" said the driver, nodding at the card; then as he put the car into gear and moved forward he started to whistle *Rule Britannia*.

The British Embassy looked very austere. After pulling the bell handle, the pair waited on the pavement for the door to be opened by a tall, thin man in a dark uniform.

"Please, we would like to see the ambassador," said Kevin.

"The ambassador is not at home. What is your business?"

"We need his help. We have travelled from occupied France, over the Pyrenees and through Spain, and now we wish to get to England."

"You had better come inside. This way, please."

Kevin and Monique followed the young man along a passage and were shown into a comfortably furnished sitting room.

"Please be seated; I will see who is available to attend to you."

Two hours later, after answering numerous questions, they were given a light supper and then shown to their respective sleeping quarters in the attic rooms of the embassy. The ambassador, they were told, would see them in the morning and if he was satisfied with their story, help would be given. The room Monique was shown into was tiny, with just a narrow bed, chair and dressing table, but oh, the bed was so comfortable. It was a relief to take off the long, heavy robes of a nun, but the one advantage of wearing the nun's habit had been that her bump had been hidden. Tomorrow when she dressed in her own clothes it would be very evident that she was an expectant mother.

The following day they were interviewed separately, first to tell their escape story and then to be thoroughly cross-questioned. Kevin gave his number, rank and name; then told how he had been recognised by Raoul, Monique's husband, and subsequently regained his memory. How well did he know this Raoul? Did he meet him in England, and why did he fly him into France? Round and round they went in circles, asking the same questions in different forms. Monique suffered similar treatment. Why had she come to the British Embassy, given that she was French? Her English was not very good, and she didn't always understand what they were saying to her.

"My husband is English," she explained. "He said I must go to England where I would be safe."

The questioners suggested that she would be safe in France, as she was French. She tried to tell them how the villagers would have reacted had they discovered she was pregnant, given that they didn't know she had a husband. But why didn't she stay with her husband – presumably he was free to travel in France as well as England?

"My husband didn't want to endanger my life by linking me with his present occupation," explained Monique.

"What is your husband's occupation?" they asked.

"He works on a farm, but that isn't why he is there. I don't know what he does; it is better I don't know anything, he says." The interviews went on ceaselessly for three days, during which time Monique and Kevin were kept apart, unaware of what was happening to each other. Monique was now sobbing, such was the stress caused by the questions. The man who had sat in silence throughout the questioning now bid Monique dry her eyes – there would be no more questions.

That evening Kevin and Monique were shown into a comfortable sitting room with a round table laid for two in the bay window, overlooking a rose garden. They flung their arms around each other in welcome. The secretary explained that they could use this room until their departure.

"Oh Kevin, what are they going to do with us? Where will they send us?" Monique was worried, remembering the monks who had been sent from the monastery.

"England, where else? We are both British subjects."

"But they kept saying I should have stayed in France; they don't understand. I have no home and I can't stay with B any longer." Monique broke down in tears.

"Come on little lady, it's not like you to give way. Cheer up, Raoul will have warned them we are on our way," said Kevin.

A light tap on the door heralded a maid carrying a tray. "I have brought you your supper; you will have all your meals in here. There is a bathroom three doors down the corridor to your right, should you require it."

Monique expressed a wish to go straight away.

Later that evening, the gentleman who had sat in silence throughout all the interviews came to see them.
"I have good news for you. We have checked with London and are satisfied that you are both who you claim to be. I'm sorry for the distress," he said, turning to Monique. "We gave you a hard ride, but we have to be careful – you would be surprised at some of the stunts would-be infiltrators try to pull. Arrangements are in hand to fly you out on Tuesday evening's flight to Shannon, and then on to England where you will land at Whitechurch, Bristol. As you haven't any means of identification you will each be given a letter of introduction, but you'll be met by officials and taken care of." As he left them, he paused by the door. "Oh, by the way, the gardens are quite beautiful. Please feel free to enjoy them."

Kevin and Monique were excited and apprehensive. They spent the waiting days together, walking in the garden or sitting in the rose arbour. Kevin tried to answer Monique's thousands of questions about England and the English, and all about flying. She had never been near a plane and was nervous.

On Tuesday the two were quickly hustled through the airport reception building and out onto the tarmac. Kevin hesitated as they neared the runway. On the peri-track many planes from different countries could be seen, including England and Germany.

"You are not used to seeing German and English planes side by side?" said the aide to Kevin. "Remember we are in a neutral country – this is a cesspit for spies from all nations. Sometimes it works in our favour, but some agents are without cause or principle and only seek monetary gain, regardless of the human suffering and devastation they cause."

They came to the silver Albatross plane, which resembled a large dolphin with wings and twin fins on its tail. The steward greeted them warmly and assisted Monique up the gangway into the plane. The aide, having handed Kevin two sealed envelopes marked with their names, bid them farewell, and Kevin followed Monique to their seats halfway down the fuselage.

There were eighteen passengers, but only one other lady, who turned out to be a trained nurse returning to England after working in Lisbon for the last two years. Monique wondered, in view of her advanced pregnancy, if this was pure coincidence or if it had been a wise precaution on behalf of the airline. Either way it was comforting to know that help was at hand should she give birth prematurely. Monique had never flown before, and seeing the beads of perspiration on her brow as the engines roared into life Kevin held her hand and reassured her that all would be well and that the pilot was as keen to get home safely as they were.

Until now he hadn't allowed himself to think about tomorrow – perhaps he hadn't believed that it would come. Now something he *did* understand was happening: the plane was moving along the runway, and at the end of the journey he would be back in England and would see his parents and his brother Lawrence once again. Was his brother still alive? The terrible thought ran through his mind: what if he too had been shot down? Then Monique's terrified grip on his arm abruptly returned his wandering thoughts to his present surroundings.

"Don't worry, look out of the window – we are airborne. See, the clouds are beneath us; we are quite safe. Try to relax." Kevin pointed to where the sun was setting. "Look, it's like a giant red balloon slipping into the sea."

Monique slackened her grip; then the steward came round offering everyone hot drinks and sandwiches. They ate in silence; then afterwards the steward came round again to collect the empty cups. Feeling more relaxed, Monique asked Kevin about Alice and whether he was looking forward to their coming meeting.

"To be quite honest I don't know. I've tried to remember what she looks like; I know she was nice and I loved her, but now... well, I can't put a face to her name. Oh Monique, I'm dreading it – suppose I don't remember her? I could pass her and not speak; that would surely hurt her and I wouldn't want to do that."

"Now it is my turn to tell you not to worry. Raoul said she was a lovely person, not just in looks but a really nice girl. She's suffered too, and Father Justin would say, 'Talk it over with our Heavenly Father; He will put it right.' And he will, I have proof of that happening many times."

"Thank you Monique, I feel better already. We should try to get some sleep now; we still have about four hours' flying time before we land," advised Kevin.

The roar of the engines broke through Kevin's dream. There were lights, bright lights; it was so hot and the flames leapt towards him. He screamed and struggled to free himself. Monique woke in an instant, and the nurse came to her assistance.

"Kevin, ssh, it's all right, ssh," urged Monique.

"Come, wake up, young man, you were dreaming," said the nurse, shaking Kevin vigorously.

"It's all right nurse, I'll talk to him, I am his doctor." Then, turning her attention to the patient, "Kevin it's all right; you are safe, the plane isn't on fire." Turning to the nurse, Monique asked, "Could you get him a drink of water, please?"

She had hardly spoken the words when the steward appeared with a glass in his hand. Kevin sat rigid, white-faced and perspiring.

"Perhaps a nip of brandy?" suggested the steward. Monique nodded.

"Kevin, can you hear me? It's all over; this plane is safe. Kevin, please."

Monique motioned to the others not to crowd him, saying that she could cope, and eventually got Kevin to sip at the brandy.

"I… oh, I'm sorry." Now he was shaking violently and began to stutter. "The noise of the engines; then I c-could see f-f-flames. It m-must have b-been a n-n-nightmare. I'm sorry Monique."

"Well, I'm not – it has been in your subconscious all this time. It's better to talk these things through; think about it, try to remember and tell me."

"I can't, not now; not here," pleaded Kevin.

"You'll have to do sometime, if you want to clear your mind of it," stressed Monique.

"Yes, I know, but not now. Look, there are lights down below – we are coming in to land."

Three small bumps and the little plane drew to a halt. The passengers prepared to disembark.

"If you would come to the reception building it will give you a chance to stretch your legs and get some fresh air. We shall be here for about an hour," the steward informed them.

Walking the hundred yards or so helped to loosen their stiffened muscles. Entering the building, they were directed to a lounge with a snack bar running along one side.

"What can I get you to drink? I think they sell cold drinks as well as tea and coffee," Kevin asked.

"I'll stick with coffee, thank you, although I expect I shall have to drink tea once we reach England," Monique said with a smile.

"Shall we sit over there?" Kevin pointed to some very comfortable-looking benches.

"Oh, that's better – it's wonderful to sit on a seat that isn't moving, and it is so peaceful without the noise of the engines," said Monique. They sat drinking their coffee and glancing through the glossy magazines they had found on the table and passed a pleasant half-hour, occasionally commenting on the advertisements.

"If you're both ready, we take off in about fifteen minutes," the steward advised.

This time when they took off, Monique was much more relaxed but Kevin still took her hand in his.

"One more hour, then England and home!"

"Will your family be there to meet you?" asked Monique.

"No, they won't be told I've arrived until after we've landed and been debriefed."

"Debriefed? Oh dear, what does that mean?"

"Just a few questions, but it won't be like Lisbon. Now they know we are bona fide, they'll just ask about the things they need to know. Not that I can tell them anything, but you might."

"Me? I don't know anything," cried Monique.

"You will be surprised at the amount of useful intelligence you have unconsciously gathered."

Of the original passengers who had boarded the plane in Lisbon, only Kevin, Monique and the nurse remained, although others had joined them at Shannon.

"Ladies and gentlemen, will you please fasten your seatbelts; we are now entering the Bristol Channel and will be landing in about ten minutes," the pilot announced. Kevin leaned across to help Monique fasten her belt, then fastened his own. As soon as the plane had landed the flare path was switched off, the door in the fuselage was opened and the warm, moist night air drifted into the plane. The other passengers were eager to be on their way, but Kevin and Monique hung back and were the last to disembark.

"What about my carpet bag?" queried Monique.

"I think it will be on the trolley with the other luggage. We'll collect it in that building over there where everyone is making for."

On entering the airport building a man in a navy blue uniform and peaked cap directed them to passport control.

"Sorry, we haven't got any passports," said Kevin.

The man looked up, startled; then smiled. "Your reception committee are waiting for you in the VIP lounge, Joe," he called after a passing young man. "Take these people to the VIP lounge; they are expected."

The floor was covered with a deep-piled fitted carpet and had comfortable armchairs set around four low coffee tables. A single reading lamp on a bookcase gave the only illumination.

"Good morning," said an elderly gentleman, who stood up as soon as they entered the room. He shook hands first with Monique; then with Kevin. "You must be very tired after your long journey. Captain Betty Taylor and Squadron Leader Jerry Thomas are taking you to a place not far from here where you can have a good night's sleep, then when you are rested, tomorrow – sorry, I mean this afternoon; I am forgetting it is gone half past two already – we will debrief you and get you fixed up with identity cards etc. Goodnight and good luck." He left without saying who he was.

The two officers, who were just a little older than Kevin, introduced themselves more informally; then ushered them out to their car. Jerry drove at a hair-raising speed up the hilly road to somewhere near Malmesbury. The sky was lightening with the dawn as they drove through tall iron gates and up a drive; then stopped at the door of a Queen Anne-style country mansion.

"You are to have the room next to mine. Give me your bag and I'll show you to your room," Betty said to Monique, and the two girls went off together.

"We are not so lucky, sorry – you will be sharing with me. I hope you don't snore," laughed Jerry. "Oh, where is your luggage?"

Kevin shrugged his shoulders in a very continental fashion. "I haven't any."

"Not to worry, we can sort all that out later," said Jerry.

Kevin was the first to be interviewed. The panel of four introduced themselves: they were Wing Commander Bennet, a doctor with the RAF; Major Sandstor from Army Intelligence; Miss Irene Temple from the Foreign Office and Lieutenant Colonel Mayfield, an army psychologist. The panel attempted every way they could think of to jog Kevin's memory but as he had suspected, he had nothing to tell them. All he could remember was the time he had been at the clinic, and then in the monastery. It was almost word for word what he had said in Lisbon. He was shown out to where Jerry was awaiting him.

"I'm to take you over to RAF Abingdon for a quick medical; then they will kit you out."

Monique was very nervous when she was shown into the interview room and saw not two people, as there had been in Lisbon, but four.

"Please sit down and make yourself comfortable," urged the wing commander. "You are a doctor, like myself – could you tell us where you have practised and under what circumstances?"

Monique spent the next thirty minutes describing her life as a doctor pre-war and then her experiences with the resistance fighters in Marseilles; her escape from there when the group had been betrayed and finally her work at the clinic.

"You treated German soldiers at the clinic?!" exclaimed Major Sandstor.

"Only the officers. I think they used their own doctors to treat the soldiers."

"Why was that, do you think?"

"I don't know. We would have preferred not to have the Germans there at all; it worried us, but maybe they were suspicious. We were fortunate that they didn't let the troops come for treatment; they would have prowled around while waiting to be attended and ignored our 'no admittance' signs, so they could easily have discovered our secret ward."

"Secret ward?" Major Sandstor was clearly startled.

"Well, we always referred to it as our isolation ward. It was where we treated the patients brought during the night by the resistance. The clinic was searched on several occasions but each time we had cleared the isolation ward."

"You were warned?" asked Major Sandstor.

"Yes."

"These German officers, were they friendly?" asked Colonel Mayfield.

"Most patients appreciated our care."

"But how did they show their appreciation? With gifts? The German officers, I mean."

"I think they gave Father Justin a bottle of schnapps occasionally. He didn't really like schnapps so would pass it on to our friends in the resistance. It was his private joke at the Germans' expense." Monique smiled at the recollection.

"They didn't invite you out?" asked the wing commander.

"Only Obersten Otto Klausmann insisted on ingratiating himself."

"How did he do this?"

"He ordered me to report to his office, then he said I would dine with him the following Saturday evening. I tried to tell him I may be needed at the clinic if there was an emergency but he was adamant I would be there."

"You didn't wish to spend the evening with him?"

"No, I was frightened."

"Why?"

"He was a terrifying animal, without pity or remorse."

"What happened? Did you go?"

"No, the dinner was cancelled. Later I learned that Klausmann had collapsed with a heart attack, and he never returned to his post."

"What was the size of the German unit?" Major Sandstor asked.

"I'm not sure. It was an infantry unit with about twenty officers."

Miss Temple then leaned forward. "Tell me: you were Kevin's doctor – did he say anything while unconscious or sedated? He doesn't appear to remember anything."

"No, when he came to us he had nothing to identify him. He had a broken jaw so he couldn't speak, and when he recovered he didn't appear to understand French. We thought he was Polish."

"Why did you think he was Polish? You say he had nothing to identify him as a Pole."

"We were told that when he arrived the two farmhands who had found him hanging by his parachute in a tree said he was a Pole. They had destroyed his papers along with his bloodstained clothing in case the Germans found them," answered Monique. She was beginning to feel tired.

"It was your husband, I believe, who uncovered his true identity?" asked Miss Temple.

"Yes, my husband helped escapees return to England. One, an airman, had told him the Pole had spoken to him in English. Raoul, my husband, begged me to let him talk to him, if only to get word to his family that he was still alive."

"But on the way home there was some disturbance?" coaxed Miss Temple.

"Yes, Kevin fell asleep and the sound of the engines rekindled the memory of his being shot down, I asked him to tell me about it, but he shut it out of his mind. I only hope that with proper treatment he will have total recall. In my opinion it is essential for his complete recovery," answered Monique.

The questioning was over. Monique had been in the interview room for nearly two hours. The panel thanked her sincerely for everything; then a young WAAF came to take her to the dining room where Jerry, Betty and Kevin sat waiting for her.

Later that afternoon, when for the first time in over eighteen months Kevin was dressed in the uniform of a flight lieutenant, he was sent for. Wing Commander Bennet, the doctor who had been one of that morning's interviewers, bid him be seated.

"Dr Le Grare is a very clever woman; the x-rays taken of your shoulder and jaw show them to be as good as new. You now appear to be in excellent health, apart from your amnesia. We are sending you over to a special unit who deal with this type of affliction. Would you like Dr Le Grare to be present?"

"Dr Le Grare? Is that Monique?" asked Kevin, not having heard Monique's surname before. The wing commander nodded, and when Kevin said he would feel better if Monique could be present, Wing Commander Bennet confirmed that arrangements would be made immediately for her to be accommodated nearby.

Chapter Thirteen

Kevin and Monique stayed just one more night at the Queen Anne mansion. On Thursday afternoon they said their goodbyes to Betty and Jerry and thanked them warmly for all their care and cheerfulness. They were then driven by staff car to a village midway between Gloucester and Cheltenham, where they were to stay at a local inn and await the arrival of Kevin's parents, who were expected the following day. On Monday Kevin would be starting treatment at a nearby private hospital for neurological disorders. The landlady, Mrs Petworth, welcomed them and showed them upstairs to their rooms. The inn had been a thriving coaching inn in the 17th century, and despite the low-beamed ceilings the rooms were spacious and airy. Monique's room contained three single beds and Kevin's room had a double bed and a cot.

Over supper that night, Kevin was morose and melancholy.

"I thought you would be bubbling over with excitement and happiness tonight, not down in the dumps. What's the matter?" Monique asked.

"Oh, I don't know – I can't believe I'm here. It's like listening to a conversation with cotton wool in your ears: you hear, but don't know what's being said. I feel some part of me is missing, as if I'm outside of myself, just an onlooker. I'm all mixed up inside; I wonder who I really am. All those months being Brother Francis, not speaking in English and just existing from one day to another. I'd love to see my parents again, but I'm so afraid. Have I changed? Will they feel the same as they used to? When I saw the cot in my room I felt terrified; I hope my mum isn't going to spring one of her

surprises and bring Alice with her. Monique, I'm not ready –
oh God, this is terrible!"

Monique put her hand on his arm. He was clearly very
distraught. "Kevin, tomorrow after breakfast, would you like
to stay in your room? I'll meet your mother and if she has
brought Alice and Estelle I can explain to them that you're
not well enough yet. You will need time, and a lot of patience
and understanding from them if you're to get truly well and
get rid of any traumas."

"Would you do that? That would be such a relief. Am I
being a coward? I don't mean to turn my back on my own
daughter or her mother."

"It's understandable. When you were shot down your
mind blanked your past out of your memory, and now you are
remembering parts of your past it will come back to you, but
slowly. No one is going to rush you; I won't let them. I'm still
your doctor until someone else takes over," said Monique.

Friday morning was sunny and warm. As Kevin and Monique
enjoyed an English wartime breakfast of cornflakes followed
by scrambled powdered egg on toast, they listened to the
birds singing in the trees, through the open window.

"Do you know what I find so different here, Kevin?"

"No, what?"

"The calm that is all around. There is no fear or tension in
the air. So many times I have seen lorries loaded with troops
pull up in village squares and round up innocent people, many
of them old – some were abused and all were very frightened.
Then an officer would appear and the troops moved on to
terrorise some other village. Last night when we walked
through the village people were talking and laughing and the
policeman was so friendly and wished us a good night. Raoul
tried to tell me it was like this, but I couldn't comprehend that
anywhere could be as peaceful as this, especially in wartime."

"It's gone half past nine; I wonder what time they will get
here. You will meet them for me, won't you?" pleaded Kevin.

"Of course. You go up to your room now and I'll tell Mrs Petworth to bring your parents into the lounge to me."

"Thanks." Kevin sighed in relief as he stood up and moved towards the stairs.

Monique sat in the lounge drinking the coffee that Mrs Petworth had kindly brought to her. A pile of magazines lay next to her on the settee. Deep in thought, she wondered what the future would hold. England was a foreign country to her, and although she could read and speak English it was a strain, and it certainly didn't come naturally to her. Apart from Kevin, she knew no one. It would have been a comfort to be able to write to Raoul, but this pleasure had been denied them since July 1940 when the Germans had occupied the Channel Islands and Raoul had escaped to England. She was desperate to know if her husband was still alive, and prayed vehemently that the SS would never capture and torture him. Would Raoul ever see their child, who at that very moment moved inside her, sending her coffee cup clean off its saucer? Monique had just rescued the cup and blotted the spilled liquid up with an old newspaper when Mrs Petworth came into the lounge, followed by a kindly-looking middle-aged couple. After introducing Kevin's parents and bidding them sit down, Mrs Petworth returned to her kitchen. Monique described the injuries that Kevin had sustained when he was shot down, and how the misunderstanding over his nationality had occurred, and the loss of his memory.

"I am sure he will be delighted to see Alice and his daughter eventually, but not just yet. We will know when the time is right. I am so relieved you didn't bring them with you."

"It wasn't possible. Alice has trained to be a teacher and she looks after the little ones at the local school. She couldn't possibly get away. I think she was relieved that she had a valid excuse. It is a very difficult time for her; in fact for both of them, I shouldn't wonder," said Rosemary Renwick.

"I'll show you to his room, and allow you to have some time with your son on your own – you must be desperate to see him again. I'll come for you when lunch is ready."

Monique left them at Kevin's door. Inside, Kevin sat on his bed staring into space, his mind shutting out the past and the present. He heard a gentle tap on the door and as it opened he heard his mother's voice say, "May we come in?"

Rosemary saw the dejected and bent figure of the young airman. He raised his head, and as their eyes met, he stood up. Rosemary reached out her arms to enfold her son.

"Oh, my bairn. Dear God, thank you; I never thought I would hold you again."

"Oh Mam." His voice broke, and their tears intermingled as he sobbed. All the fear, the pain and the loneliness spilled over as his mother clutched him in her arms.

"I'm sorry," he said as he wiped his eyes; then reached out to his father. "Dad."

"My son, I can't believe we're all here together at long last."

They stood with their arms around each other. Words wouldn't come, but they weren't necessary – they were joined together in their love and thankfulness for being reunited.

"I think we all need to freshen up," said Harry, clearing his throat. "Can't go downstairs looking like a funeral party, can we, eh?!"

Monique knocked on the door and came into the room. "And how are you all? It's rather traumatic meeting loved ones after being apart for so long."

"We're just fine, Monique. Thank you so much for arranging for us to meet in private – you knew we would break down, didn't you? I'm only glad we weren't downstairs amongst strangers."

"So, Kevin, the strong young man has learned how to cry! That's the best treatment you could have; you will find a lot of your tension has gone already. But enough now; if we don't get a move on we will have Mrs Petworth chasing us. I think she's making Yorkshire pudding in your honour," said Monique, laughing as she turned to Harry and Rosemary.

Rosemary had taken to Monique the moment they were introduced: such an attractive young lady and a very clever doctor. She and Harry had much to thank Monique and her husband for. Over the dinner of Yorkshire pudding, roast beef and vegetables, there was such a lot to talk about. When Kevin mentioned Raoul's hopes that Monique would be able to stay with his parents or Alice's aunt, Rosemary insisted that when Kevin was well enough to return home Monique would also be very welcome to stay with them.

"Still, I'm sure Annie will want you to stay with her. She can't get enough of babies and she absolutely dotes on her granddaughter. Keswick is a lovely part of England and it is quite a safe area, with very few air raids. I'll stay here at the inn until you are well, then we can all travel back to Yorkshire together," said Rosemary.

"Sorry son, I can't stay longer than tonight – Ted is looking after the bar for us, but I've got to be there on Saturday night. It gets a bit hectic," said Harry.

After their evening meal, they decided to have a stroll round the village and through the country lanes. As Harry walked with his son, Kevin asked him how his brother Lawrence was.

"Lawrence had a shrapnel wound in his leg; he was on crutches for a while, but he's on the mend now. He's been grounded 'cause the muscle was badly torn, and that made it impossible for him to use the pedals when he was flying. Anyway, they've promoted him to squadron leader and posted him to HQ 4 Bomber Command," said Harry.

"That's at York, isn't it?" asked Kevin.

"Yes, they are billeted in a house that used to be a nurses home. His office is in Heslington Hall; I believe it belongs to a lord but has been taken over by the RAF for the duration of the war."

"Lucky devil, I wonder where I'll be posted once I am fit? I hope it's in Yorkshire; there's plenty of aerodromes to choose from."

Rosemary and Monique strolled arm in arm behind the two men.

"I took a gentle walk every night when I was carrying my boys. I hope you will take care of yourself – exercise really does make a big difference," said Rosemary.

"Just what I've always told my patients," replied Monique.

"Oh sorry, I keep forgetting you're a doctor – well, it's common knowledge that doctors make the worst patients! When is your baby due? I'm going to appoint myself as a locum parentis."

"Please don't worry, I really have had lots of gentle exercise. Don't forget, we scrambled through the Pyrenees," she laughed.

"Well, when we go home, if you decide to stay with Annie she will make sure you do all the right things. She is the nicest, kindest woman I know. Speaking of Annie and Alice, that reminds me – I've brought some photographs of Estelle and her mother. Do you think now would be the right time to show them to Kevin? He hasn't mentioned her. Does he realise he is a father and has a daughter?"

"Yes, he knows, but he can't recall what Alice looks like, so showing him the photographs will help him enormously," assured Monique. "But wait until we are upstairs; we could have some tea in my room."

When they returned to the inn, Harry insisted they all have a drink together in the bar, stressing that he would have to leave very early the next morning. Soon last orders were called, and it was far too late to look at photos. Kevin was exhausted, and Monique thought it best to wait until the next day.

After Harry had left to catch his train, Rosemary suggested they all go into Cheltenham. Mrs Petworth had told her where they could catch a bus, and suggested a nice café where they would get a good dinner. Monique loved window-shopping, and Rosemary insisted on buying some white baby wool with her precious clothing coupons, along with some knitting needles and a pattern book. Then it was time to find the café. As it was nearly one o'clock the roast was finished, however the waitress told them there was plenty of fish left and so Monique was introduced to the great British national dish of fish and chips.

"Well, that was a nice meal. What do you think of our staple diet?" Rosemary asked Monique.

"Very nice indeed, but we would have served a sauce with the fish. Still, salt and vinegar did add a piquant taste and I really enjoyed it."

"I noticed when we were on the bus that there was a lovely park further down the road. Shall we make for that and have a rest?" Kevin suggested. "We don't want Monique's legs swelling up; she looks tired."

Rosemary was surprised at her son's thoughtfulness, but then the two young people had shared a very arduous journey.

The park was well maintained. Two elderly gentlemen were busy hoeing the borders and rose beds. The dahlias were a riot of colour. A young mother held on to her little boy by his reins as he threw bread to the ducks on the pond, and when they came to the lily pond, huge goldfish could be seen gliding gracefully between the lilies.

"This is heaven, but I would like to sit down and have a rest," said Monique.

"There's a summer house over there. We'll have a sit down and I'll explain all about the knitting pattern to you – I know you're eager to make a start."

"You haven't mentioned your granddaughter," complained Kevin.

"I can do better than that." Reaching into her handbag, Rosemary said, "I can show you what my little darling looks like." Thrusting a photograph into her son's hand, she watched him as he frowned.

Then a slow smile spread across his face as he exclaimed excitedly, "She's wonderful, and she's all mine, all mine!"

"Well, not *all* yours – I think Alice has a claim as well," answered Rosemary.

"Oh yes, and how is Alice? I hope you brought a photo of her too."

Rosemary passed the other photographs to her son. There was one of the christening party, and Monique, looking over Kevin's shoulder, saw Raoul holding his goddaughter.

"Raoul looks so contented, I've never seen him with a small child before. I can't wait for our baby to come."

Kevin passed the group photograph to Monique for her to feast her eyes on her husband, while he gazed at the lovely young mother, with a sad smile.

"Alice," he whispered. Kevin stared at Alice's photo for what seemed an eternity, until eventually his mother interrupted his thoughts and said it was about time they made their way to the bus stop.

"What do you think about Alice? Do you like her?" Kevin asked his mother.

"Like her? I love her; no one could have a nicer daughter. She is so thoughtful and kind, and she always makes me feel that I am so special. I would hate to lose her."

Sunday was a restful day. Monique relaxed in the garden, knitting for her baby, and found it very therapeutic. Kevin and his mother went to church in the morning, and in the afternoon talked on and on until Kevin's head ached and Rosemary was dizzy from answering the thousands of questions her son threw at her.

On Monday morning a car arrived to take Monique and Kevin to the hospital. They arrived at a large country house with lovely gardens full of various flowers. Twenty minutes after their arrival, they were shown into Professor Glenndenburgh's consulting room. While Kevin and Monique were at the hospital, Rosemary took advantage of the quietness to write to Harry and Lawrence. Then after lunch she wrote to her dear friend Annie and enclosed a short note for Alice, telling her that Kevin would be writing to her later when he felt a little better and had grown used to the idea of being free and back in England.

The next two weeks followed the same pattern. Each day Kevin was persuaded to lie on the couch, relax and talk through his thoughts. On the second Wednesday Professor Glenndenburgh suggested hypnotic therapy, but Kevin's mind rebelled. Then Monique suggested that she might try.

"It's no good Monique, I can't go to sleep, I don't want to."

"Kevin, on the plane you had a frightening nightmare and it will keep returning every time you are under stress. Think what it will be like for Alice living with you; living with your nightmare. You aren't being fair," Monique snapped. It was very rare that she was so impatient. Kevin sat with his head in his hands.

"We could try another way. I could give you an injection, but I will need your permission," said the professor.

"Perhaps tomorrow. I need time to think about it," sighed Kevin.

That night after dinner he begged to be excused so that he could write to Alice.

...So you see, Alice, it is very difficult to know how I feel. I was delighted to have your letter, and I do want to see you and our daughter. If only I could remember more clearly; yet today when the professor, and then Monique, were urging me to relax so they could hypnotise me, I wanted them to go away and I had this longing to be with you. Please have patience with me and try to understand.

Love,
Kevin

"Good morning Kevin. You didn't come down again last night – did you write your letter to Alice?" asked Monique.

"Yes, it's here – will you post it for me, Mam?" Kevin said, passing the letter to her. "Relax, Monique: I'll agree to anything the old prof wants to do. I just want to go home."

"Oh dear, it's raining – is the weather always so changeable?" said Monique.

"It will brighten up soon. 'Rain before seven, fine before eleven' – it's one of our sayings," replied Rosemary. "You will never be bored with our weather," she added as Kevin came into the lounge.

"No transport yet? I wish he'd hurry up."

"Why the rush, Kevin? You usually don't bother about five minutes or even half an hour."

"Because I want to get this 'go to sleep' business over with and then I can go home. We've been in England two weeks now and I'm as much a captive here as I was in France, Monique."

Rosemary tut-tutted over her son, and when the car arrived, nearly an hour late, Kevin and Monique were driven away. Rosemary decided to spend her day exploring Gloucester, and took the local bus in the opposite direction to Cheltenham. As she had predicted, the rain stopped and the warm sun soon dried the puddles on the footpaths.

"Just relax, it's only a pinprick and then maybe you will respond to my instructions."

"Kevin?" called Monique. "I think he is asleep now, professor."

"Kevin, go back to the beginning of last June. Where are you?" asked the professor.

Kevin moved his head; then shuffled his body in a lazy, restless way.

"Kevin, can you hear me? I asked you what you were doing in June last year. Can you remember?"

"I'm getting married."

"Who to?"

"Alice of course, who else?!"

"Did you get married?"

"No."

"Why?"

"Can't remember."

"I think you can. Kevin, do you remember landing a plane in a field?"

"Yes. Gave letters to Jean Pierre."

"Then what happened?"

"Left them. I was flying…"

"And then?"

"No – oh, oh God, I've been hit!" Kevin screamed. "I'm on fire; my shoulder – must get out." Another agonising scream escaped Kevin's lips, and beads of perspiration ran from his brow into his eyes.

"I'll bring him back now; he may start remembering on his own." Professor Glenndenburg wiped Kevin's brow, then softly urged him to wake up. Monique summoned a nurse to bring them some coffee; then at the professor's suggestion, Monique urged Kevin to tell them what he had remembered.

"Take your time but try to remember the smallest detail. Let your memory flood back, don't repress anything and you'll soon feel whole again and start living your life fully," she urged.

Kevin rested on the couch with his eyes closed, then after a few minutes he talked through the whole experience of his last flight, even mentioning being caught in the beam of a searchlight and the noise of the bullets hitting his machine, and the burning pain as a bullet entered his shoulder. He trembled and stuttered throughout his narrative until Monique bid him rest and gave him a drink of water. Kevin had told them not only about the shooting down of his plane, but about jumping out of the burning plane into oblivion and then coming to and finding himself dangling from his parachute, which was tangled in the branches of a tree.

"A dog barked and snarled at me, then two French farmers came and lifted me down. I kept passing out so I don't know exactly what happened, but my clothes, sodden with blood, had been cut away from me and burnt. I recognised a few words from my school French, but our teacher had never been out of Yorkshire," Kevin continued. "It seemed to go on forever. They gave me drinks through a straw because I couldn't open my mouth – I had fractured my jaw. It was always dark when they moved me, first on a cart, then in different lorries. One night I was laid in a coffin and I think I was carried – it's all a bit vague because I kept fainting; I hadn't had any food, only drinks. One morning I woke up and my whole body throbbed with pain. I put my hand up to my left shoulder, but it was dragged away. Someone muttered something in French but I didn't understand what had been said. I opened my eyes and discovered I was in a hospital ward, and then you were there, Monique," said Kevin, hunching his shoulders and heaving a huge sigh of relief.

"That's wonderful; you shouldn't have any more nightmares. All the talking you have done will have lifted them from your subconscious. It was a very nasty experience and you can now put it all behind you," said the professor. "You don't need me anymore, so goodbye and good luck."

Kevin and Monique thanked him and returned to the inn, and the professor telephoned his report to RAF Abington, saying that confirmation in writing would follow.

As they entered the inn, Monique asked Kevin what would happen now.

"Oh, someone will get in touch and tell us where to go – I hope it's home, and soon. Anyway, we'd best be packed ready to go in the morning. I'll explain to Mrs Petworth that our stay may soon be over."

"I'll be sorry to see you go, but I am very pleased that your treatment has been so successful. There's a message that someone should be here about ten – I'll bring you all coffee when he arrives," said Mrs Petworth when he told her.

Squadron Leader Walter Prentice walked into the inn just as the grandfather clock chimed a quarter past the hour, and was shown into the lounge. Kevin stood up to acknowledge the senior officer, who shook hands; then stared fixedly at Monique.

"La doctor!" he said in amazement. "You don't remember me?"

Monique looked at him, perplexed. The officer bent down and pulled up his left trouser leg to reveal a healed scar, six inches long.

"Your handiwork, I believe."

Monique relaxed and smiled. Who would have dreamt that she would meet a former patient? She hadn't recognised him: his face hadn't been injured, so she hadn't noticed it, but she did remember removing the bullet and stitching his leg. It was the last operation she had performed in Marseilles. Two nights later they had been betrayed, but had managed to escape. Monique chattered with the officer, then Rosemary was introduced just as Mrs Petworth brought in the coffee. Once they had drunk it, Walter Prentice looked at his watch.

"Time we were on our way. It will take us the best part of two hours to get to Abingdon; then after lunch, you, young man, will have an interview with the careers board."

"I only hope I get a posting up north – Yorkshire, preferably," said Kevin.

"They are normally very good; I was grounded for eighteen months, but I was posted onto a local selection committee and was able to live at home," replied Walter Prentice.

The journey to Abingdon took them through magnificent countryside. Monique was captivated by the lovely russet colours of the trees, and Kevin and his mother said in unison, "Just wait till you see Yorkshire!" The journey had been pretty smooth up to now. There were two horse-drawn farm carts in front of them, one loaded with potatoes and the other with sugar beet, and the road was too bendy to attempt overtaking them. Rosemary commented on how during the First World War most of the horses had been sent to France, however now, with petrol being rationed and in short supply, horses had come into their own again.

"Pity they chose here and now," said Walter. "I just hope they keep our meal hot for us – lunch usually finishes at 1.30."

As it happened, the two farm carts turned down the next farm track and the squadron leader was able to accelerate, and eventually they entered the dining room of the officers' mess at 1.20pm. It being Friday, fish was on the menu, served with a nice cheese sauce.

After lunch Monique and Rosemary were shown into a small comfortable anteroom to have coffee, and Kevin was taken to his interview. At half past three he returned, all smiles.

"I've been grounded for the time being, but I am being posted to the training wing at Linton-on-Ouse. I take up my new post on the 25th October; that's a whole three weeks' leave I've got." He gleefully threw his cap up into the air, catching it on his head where it fell at a rakish angle. Then a discreet cough announced the arrival of a distinguished-looking gentleman in a dark suit and horn-rimmed spectacles.

"Good afternoon, Madame Le Grare!"

Monique nodded, and shook the proffered hand.

"My name is Finchley, I work in the Foreign Office. I have met your husband in the course of his duties – he is a good servant of England and we are delighted to do all we can to make you feel welcome. I believe your husband has made his wishes known to you: you are to stay with a Mrs Trainor and her niece in Keswick. As the wife of a serving officer you're entitled to a weekly allowance; I have your payment book here, along with your ration book and identity card. I'm sure Mrs Renwick will show you how they all work. So, if you will just sign this receipt, please, I will detain you no longer. I wish you all a safe journey and a happy future." He bowed and shook hands with them all, and was gone.

"Right, if we're all ready we could make the 6.30 from King's Cross, but it could be rather crowded. It might be better if we got the 9.30 train. I know it doesn't get into York until past one in the morning but there should be a bit more space!" Walter Prentice called to them from the door.

As they drove towards London, Rosemary remarked on the lack of trains from York to Harrogate late at night.

"Not to worry, I'll phone for you to be met by a staff car. But before then, it will be my privilege to take you all to supper at my favourite restaurant," Walter replied.

As they approached London the dense traffic forced them down to a snail's pace. Looking out of the window, Monique saw many spaces where houses had previously stood. There were homes opened up like dollhouses, exposing wallpapered walls with curtains wafting in the empty window frames, the remainder of the buildings having been blasted away by the exploding bombs. These streets were nothing like the ones seen on the newsreels at the time of the coronation. The car meandered between piles of rubble and huge potholes, and at last their driver pulled into a space near the side entrance of King's Cross station. It was 7pm.

"I expect your ticket is via Birmingham to York?" Walter asked Rosemary.

"Yes, but I'll try and get a refund when I get home."

"No need, if you give it to me I will have it changed at the same time as I get these warrants turned into tickets. Perhaps you should take your luggage to that depository, then we'll have a clear hour for our meal."

Twenty minutes later they entered a restaurant in a cellar and were served with a tempting dish of lamb and herbs and a bottle of red wine. A gypsy trio played Hungarian dance music on their violins – it was a merry meal, and quite dark when they emerged into the street. A streetlamp at the distant junction showed only a ghostly glimmer of light.

"Follow me; careful where you tread. This passage should bring us into the station."

"I'm glad you know your way around London – I've only travelled through; never had cause to stay," commented

Kevin. Rosemary tucked her arm under Monique's: she wasn't risking her stumbling now.

The empty train was just being backed into the station as they arrived at the platform with their reclaimed luggage.

"You had better have these," Walter said as he handed the tickets to Kevin.

"First class!" exclaimed Kevin.

"Well, I did underline the fact to the CO that without the lady doctor, neither you or I would be here. She deserves to go first class, and your mother too, when you think what torture she's been through." Then, turning to Monique, he added, "I will never, ever forget you, and I'll always applaud your courage and skill." He kissed her hand, and shook hands with Rosemary and Kevin in farewell.

"Come on, this is the first class carriage; I don't think there will be standing room only here," said Kevin, leading the way into an empty carriage with seating for four on each side. The blinds at the window had been fastened down, and Rosemary pulled down the ones on the corridor side.

"With luck, we could have this compartment to ourselves," she said hopefully, as Monique snuggled down and Kevin sat opposite with his back to the engine. Rosemary, taking out her knitting, sat next to Monique, and just then the door opened. A bishop and his wife entered and wished them all a good evening, and the train was just pulling out of the station when an army colonel appeared with a brassy blonde on his arm. He glanced at his fellow passengers, then stared at Kevin: junior officers generally didn't travel first class.

"This is a first class carriage, my man – I do hope you have the correct ticket?"

Rosemary immediately recognised the type, and before Kevin had time to reply, sharply said, "Oh, our mistake, I thought you were a military colonel. Had I realised you were the ticket collector we would have had our tickets ready!"

The officer coloured up, and sat down beside his girlfriend.

At Peterborough more people crowded onto the train, and as the door opened Monique was surprised to see that people were squatting on the floor in the corridor.

"You're getting Pyrenees legs." Kevin smiled at Monique. "Best put them up here," and he made a place for her feet near to his thigh.

"Pyrenees legs? I've never heard of that before!" laughed Rosemary.

"It was as we were climbing through the Pyrenees that my legs started to swell." Monique smiled at the memory. The journey continued; knitting and magazines were discarded and eyes closed as people attempted to sleep. Rosemary, opening one eye, smiled to herself as the colonel and his blonde piece started to cuddle up and kiss.

When the train slowed down, Kevin gently shook Monique's foot.

"Wake up, the train's pulling into the station."

"Our papers! Oh, if the SS—" Monique panicked.

"Ssh, we're in England now, you're safe."

"*Pardon* – er, sorry, where are we?"

The bishop, who'd observed Monique's distress, smiled and looked at his pocket watch. "It's a quarter to two; we must be at York, my dear."

"This is our stop," said Rosemary. "Come on luv, we'll soon be home."

When they reached the barrier, Rosemary was just in time to notice the colonel hand in his third class ticket. *Ah well, it takes all sorts*, she thought with a sigh.

Walter Prentice was as good as his word. No sooner had they stepped into the station yard, where the cars and taxis were awaiting their passengers, than an RAF staff car pulled up. A young corporal jumped from the driver's seat, giving them a smart salute, ND Lawrence opened the passenger door and got out to welcome his brother. The last stage of the journey that had started four months ago began. Rosemary watched her two sons, with their arms across each other's shoulders, walk up to the front door, just as they had always done when they were at grammar school together. *Some things never change*, she thought as she turned towards Monique and the young corporal.

"Right, it's time we got ourselves inside, and you, young man, will have something hot inside you before you return to York."

Later, as Lawrence was about to see the driver to the staff car, Harry Renwick passed him a small bottle.

"Here, give the lad this to put in his cocoa when he's off duty." Lawrence laughed, then gave the quarter bottle of rum to the young man and wished him a safe journey.

Rosemary was delighted that the main meal was served at lunchtime. Her sons and Monique would be able to catch up on some much-needed rest, and she could call at the butcher's and chat him up – his brother bred his own sheep. Rosemary was well prepared, and in her basket was half a bottle of whisky to trade. She must have a decent-sized joint for tomorrow's luncheon – there would be eight of them around her dining table. Her dear friends Annie and John were coming with their niece Alice, and her own darling granddaughter who would meet her daddy at last.

On Saturday afternoon the brothers dressed in their civvies, ready to go out.

"Where are you two going?" asked their mother. "And why aren't you in uniform?"

"Mum, we're just going to have a look round the town. We might even catch the last half of the match, and we'd look too conspicuous in uniform," answered Lawrence.

"Hmm! Careful you don't get a white feather. Now just behave yourselves and keep out of mischief."

"Oh Mum, if I didn't know before, I certainly know I'm home now," laughed Kevin as he gave his mother a peck on the cheek before following his brother out.

"They never grow up," said Rosemary to Monique. "Men are only little boys in long trousers; even Harry gets into mischief if I don't keep an eye on him."

That was the day Kevin really appreciated he was free. The two brothers toured all their old haunts, meeting some of their old friends who were either on weekend leave or in reserved occupations. That evening, the pub was packed and all the old-timers were there, wanting to buy Kevin a drink. He tried to refuse, explaining that he wasn't able to drink too much, but Lawrence came to his aid, saying he'd help him drink a few rounds. After closing time Harry drank his last free pint, while Kevin and Lawrence crawled up the stairs on their hands and knees.

Sunday morning dawned with a watery sun. Rosemary looked up at the sky, with hope in her heart that all would go well that day.

"Did the noise disturb you?" she asked Monique, who was sitting by the table shelling peas.

"It did, but it reminded me so much of the local *taverna* when the villagers were celebrating that I felt quite homesick."

"You'll soon feel at home once you get settled in Keswick. It's such a peaceful place, and in a beautiful setting."

"What time are you expecting Alice and her family?"

"Oh, about half past eleven." She looked at the clock. "It's ten past ten already; I think it's about time my boys were up. They'd a heavy night last night but I just didn't have the heart to say anything. I thank God; it's so wonderful us all being here together again." Rosemary noisily blew her nose, hoping Monique wouldn't notice the tears that had welled up in her eyes.

"Come and sit down," urged Monique. "Kevin isn't the only one to have suffered. You've been through a terrible time, with both your sons wounded. Now it is all over you may suffer some delayed shock, so when those tears want to come, let them; it'll do you good to cry."

"Oh Monique, you must be a wonderful doctor, you understand everything so well."

Monique put her arms around the older woman who sat and sobbed, her arms resting on the table. After a few minutes, Rosemary pulled herself together and bathed her eyes at the kitchen sink. Monique, meanwhile, went up the stairs, knocked on the bedroom door and told the two brothers it was time to get up.

Chapter Fourteen

"Come on Alice, get a move on, I thought you would be eager to be with Kevin again. He will be waiting for you."

"Auntie, you don't understand – I can't remember what he looks like. If he is disfigured through his injuries, will I be able to look at him? I feel ashamed of myself for thinking this way, but I can't help it."

"Alice, no one has mentioned any scars on his face, and I am sure Rosemary would have warned you if there were any. As for not knowing what he looks like, you saw Lawrence the last time you were in Harrogate, and he is the image of his brother. Now pull yourself together, we're all ready to go."

Alice thought back to the last time she had been with Kevin, when they had spent that wonderful forty-eight hours together in Great Yarmouth. The love they had shared, and the plans they had made for their future together. They had both suffered, and Alice couldn't believe that the suffering was all over and everything would be perfect from now on. Yet things were very different now: she had her lovely daughter and a job she enjoyed, and was able to support herself and her daughter, but would that be enough? There were times when she had felt very lonely – yes, she had loved Kevin and if they still had the same love for each other when they met later today, life would be perfect.

"Alice, are you coming? Uncle John is waiting," Aunt Annie called up the stairs.

"I can't find Estelle's shoes," Alice shouted back.

"That's because you put them onto her feet half an hour ago. Come on, hurry up and stop playing for time. Rosemary is expecting us at 11.30."

It was a fine autumnal day, cold but bright; a good omen according to Aunt Annie. Alice played clap-a-penny with Estelle and sang *Horsey, Horsey* to her until she was tired; then Alice sat quietly, looking out of the window while her daughter slept peacefully in her arms.

When they reached the brow of the hill, they could see someone standing at the roadside near to the Renwicks' public house. As they got nearer, Alice saw that it was Rosemary and started to panic again. *Oh dear, what can I do? What can I say? I'm not ready to face Kevin.*

"Give Estelle to me, dear," said Kevin's mother, "and come and meet Monique. Lawrence has taken Kevin for a walk." They all followed Rosemary behind the bar and into the lounge.

"It is lovely for me to meet you, I've heard such a lot about you from my husband and Kevin," said Monique.

"I thought Kevin would be here!" Alice said.

Monique, with a gentle laugh, said, "We sent the boys out. Kevin was so nervous, he was pacing up and down, nearly wearing a hole in the carpet. I told him the last time I saw a man in such a state was when a local bully in France was about to become a father for the first time. Try not to worry, Lawrence has strict instructions to leave him in the garden; that way you can meet in private."

At that moment Alice knew that whatever happened, this attractive young woman would always be her special friend. They sat together on the settee chatting about babies, and after about ten minutes Lawrence strolled in.

"Hi beautiful," he said, giving Alice a big kiss and a hug. "Kevin's in the garden waiting for you."

"Lawrence, will you come with me? Please."

"What a pair, you're both as bad as each other. You both want me to hold your hands; we might as well play ring-a-ring-o'-roses," he said, pulling Alice to her feet, and together they walked outside, across the lawn and down the path to the orchard.

"Kevin, I've brought Alice to meet you," Lawrence called. Alice looked around, but couldn't see anyone. Then a bough creaked in the apple tree as Kevin leapt down.

"Hello Alice."

Alice smiled, but couldn't speak – this wasn't the happy clown she had known. He looked drawn, haggard and tense, and had lost such a lot of weight.

"There's a seat down that path; why don't you take Alice there? We'll give you a shout when dinner is ready," said Lawrence. As Lawrence returned to the house, Kevin came towards Alice and gently took her hand.

"Oh my darling, you're shaking. I'm sorry all I've ever done is cause you pain: first breaking up your family and then leaving you alone. Mam said you're a schoolteacher now."

"Yes," Alice whispered.

"Come on, let's sit down here like Lawrence suggested. You like Lawrence, don't you?"

"Yes, I do. He's been wonderful to me. He's so kind and he's such fun."

Kevin looked at her in surprise. "He's my best friend as well as my brother. I wouldn't stand in his way if you… I mean, if he was special to you."

Oh, poor Kevin – he looked as if he were fighting a demon. Alice put out her hand and clasped his.

"Lawrence is special, but not in the way you mean. He's got a lovely girl of his own, and I've no romantic feelings at all for him, but we are very good friends."

Kevin clutched her hands. "Alice, does that mean there's no one special in your life at the moment?"

"No, there is someone very, very special. You'll meet her soon, and then you will understand."

Kevin smiled. "You mean our daughter, don't you?"

Alice nodded.

"Thank you for calling her Estelle," he said as he pulled her into his arms. They didn't kiss – it was too soon, so he just held her close. "I watched you walk down the path with Lawrence. That's when I realised you were just as scared as I was. We need time to get to know each other again, but I'm so glad we're together again, aren't you?"

Alice looked into his dear, solemn face and smiled. "Yes, I've missed you so much – it was awful and I was frightened. Only Estelle made me want to go on living." Alice broke down and wept, and Kevin comforted her. Given time, all would be well. Then they heard someone banging on an ashbin lid.

"Come on," Kevin laughed as he helped Alice to her feet. "I think that's the dinner gong!"

"Come on you two, you're just in time for a sherry – this is a celebration," said Rosemary, putting a glass into Alice's hand.

"Where's my little girl? Don't hide her from me," said Kevin.

"She won't be long. Aunt Annie is giving her dinner in the kitchen; there's too many distractions for her in here," Kevin's mother explained. A few minutes later the kitchen door opened and Aunt Annie walked in with her great-niece in her arms.

"There now, what do you think of her?" she said as she put Estelle into her daddy's arms.

Kevin couldn't speak. He swallowed and blinked as tears welled up in his eyes, then clutched his daughter close to him.

Estelle gazed at this new man in her life, then, poking his nose and eyes with her little fingers, said softly, "Da-da-da."

"Oh Kevin, she knows you; she's never done that before! She's trying to say 'daddy'," Alice cried. Kevin smiled; he still couldn't talk. Someone persuaded him to sit down, and for the next half hour he was happy just to hold his little girl and play with her, while Alice filled in all the missing days and months of their daughter's life.

Just as dinner was about to be served, Alice prised a very tired little girl from her daddy's arms. "I'll put her down for her afternoon nap, then we can all eat in peace."

"Rosemary, how on earth have you managed to get such a huge joint? Have all your customers been paying you with their ration books?" Aunt Annie asked, as an enormous side of lamb was ceremoniously carried in.

"Well, maybe their ration of whisky! But this is a very special occasion: we're a united family once again, and I wanted to welcome Monique and show her that we English can put on as good a spread as the French."

"All the French are not good cooks. I can make an omelette, but that is about all. I will have to get Alice and her aunt to teach me – I've an awful lot to learn. I have never kept house before," said Monique.

The afternoon continued in this happy, bantering mood, until at about four, and after a cup of tea and a piece of Rosemary's fruitcake, Aunt Annie, Uncle John, Alice and her daughter Estelle and Monique departed for Keswick.

"See you on Wednesday," called Kevin as Uncle John drove them away.

As they approached Keswick, Monique was enraptured with the beautiful scenery. The sun was setting on the mountains, bathing everything in a pink, rosy glow. The trees were clothed in glorious autumn colours of red, golden and russet leaves. Derwent water was so still and calm that not even a ripple disturbed the peace and tranquillity. When they arrived Aunt Annie took Monique upstairs to the room they had prepared for her and her baby, due in the near future. She pulled open the drawers filled with newborn-sized baby clothes which had belonged to Estelle, assuring Monique they'd be delighted if she would accept them. Monique was thrilled.

"My baby will want for nothing if this kindness is anything to go by," Alice heard her say as she joined them upstairs.

For the first time since she had become a teacher, Alice started to regret her choice to teach the very young. The children in the senior school were given a week's holiday to help with the potato harvest, and Kevin was coming on Wednesday to stay for a few days. On Tuesday morning, while they were all sitting at the breakfast table, the postman called and Uncle John went to the door to collect the mail.

"Just the usual bills, a letter and a card for you, Alice – doesn't Daisy ever write a proper letter? And one for you, Monique."

"But I don't know anyone here." Then, as she opened the envelope she gasped, and her colour changed.

"Are you all right, love? You've gone quite pale, I hope it isn't bad news," queried Aunt Annie.

"It's from Raoul, my husband." She burst into tears, and Aunt Annie put her arms round her. "Oh, I'm being silly – he's well, and pleased I have arrived safely. It is the first letter he has been able to write to me in over three years; I don't know why I'm crying, but I can't help it."

"Come now Monique, you're the doctor. You must have heard of tears of relief, as well as tears of sorrow," said Aunt Annie.

In his letter Raoul had said how relieved he was to know that Monique and their child would be safe in England, and how he wished he could be with them. There was no address and she couldn't write back – there were no resistance forces with hidden radios here. All was at peace; hardly a plane flew overhead, and when they did they were all English, thank God. The card from Daisy was to let Alice know that all was well with her and her husband Tom, a flight sergeant, and Alice's letter was from Kevin.

My dear Alice,

I hope you weren't hurt or too disappointed with our meeting on Sunday. We were both scared and embarrassed, being under scrutiny from our families. After you left I went into the garden to be on my own, and I sat on the seat and pretended you were still with me. I do love you, Alice, and I hope we can be married soon. Seeing you again has brought all my happy memories of you rushing back. I can hardly wait for Wednesday to come, and I hope you share my feelings.

All my love,
Kevin

While Uncle John and Alice were at school, Monique helped Aunt Annie in the house and entertained Estelle. Aunt Annie showed her how to make bread and teacakes, and gradually she was turning into a very good cook.

On Wednesday when Alice got home from school, Kevin was waiting for her at the gate. She ran to him and he swept her off her feet and into his arms.

"My darling, this is how I wanted it to be on Sunday," whispered Kevin.

"Silly, wasn't it, us both being so scared? What's Estelle doing? Have you been spoiling her?" Alice asked, smiling.

"How could I spoil her? She's perfect, just like her mother."

Holding hands, they went into the living room. The piece of perfection was sitting on the rug with strawberry jam on her face and in her hair. After tea Kevin helped to bath Estelle and there was much splashing and laughter; then when Alice had dried her and put her nightclothes on, Kevin sat on the bed and gave her a bottle.

"I never thought I'd be doing this. It would have been something to look forward to, but for all those months in France I had no past to remember; not even memories of Dad and Mam and Lawrence, so I didn't look to a future. I just existed from day to day," Kevin said.

"I experienced something like that when I heard you were missing; then when my parents still didn't want me, I had a breakdown. I got through each day: I got up in the morning, washed and dressed and went downstairs and I ate what was put in front of me. I think I answered when Auntie or Uncle spoke to me, but I didn't *talk*. I felt as if I was down a black hole I couldn't climb out of. I used to go for walks through the fields, and because there was only the ponies to talk to I felt I was safe there; like being in a glass bowl where no one could reach me."

Sharing these experiences helped both of them to understand each other's needs, and eventually Alice took Estelle gently from her daddy's arms and laid her down to sleep in her cot. As she stood up and turned, Kevin pulled her into his arms and they kissed and embraced; his hands caressing her and gently pulling her close Alice yearned for him as much as he wanted her, but then she pulled away suddenly.

"Kevin please, we mustn't – it wouldn't be fair to Uncle and Auntie."

"But darling, I want you now. Don't you want me?"

"If only you knew just how much, but we can't, not here." Alice was shaking and trembling; she wanted him so much.

"How soon can we be married? I could get a special licence."

"Kevin, we can't do that, don't you understand? Ever since we knew you were safe, Auntie and your mam have been making plans – they want us to have a proper wedding and I do too."

"It's going to be hell for me until then. When can we be married?"

"Soon, darling, I promise, soon."

The days flew by. Alice left the classroom each day with her pupils, and on Friday Kevin was at the school gates to meet her. Saturday and Sunday were marvellous, with almost every second spent together; then on Monday Kevin caught the train back to Harrogate. The following weekend Alice took Estelle and stayed with Kevin's parents, but any plans Kevin had for them to share his bed were speedily thwarted.

"If you are so eager to be married, and I can understand your urgency, then get yourselves to St. Peter's. The vicar will see you after the service, and once you've fixed the date, your auntie and I will see to the rest," said Rosemary. "I'd suggest a date near to Christmas, then your brother Michael may be around to give you away."

"Kevin, that would be wonderful! Will Lawrence be your best man?" Alice asked.

"Next to me, he is the best man." Kevin smiled.

The vicar was delighted to see Kevin again. In the vestry, he consulted his diary. Lots of couples were hoping for leave to get married at Christmas, and he already had five weddings booked for the 24th and two for the Saturday before. They explained about wishing for Michael to be there to give Alice away, and eventually it was arranged and they booked the church for 2pm on Saturday 18th December 1943.

"It's a pity we're not allowed to ring the bells, but the organist and the choir will be available," added the vicar.

Sunday was a happy affair, but much quieter than the previous one when everyone had been present, and the joint was much smaller too. Harry sliced it into four portions; they would be having corned beef hash on Monday.

"I'll book the church hall tomorrow; then I'll be over on Tuesday to see my good friend Annie. We've already sorted out our preliminary arrangements, but now we can go firm," Kevin's mam said with deep satisfaction.

"Where will you go for your honeymoon? Scarborough might be your best option. Estelle can stay with Nana Annie," said Harry.

"Wherever we go, it'll only be for a couple of nights; then we can be with Estelle and be a proper family at last," said Kevin.

"We'll all share Estelle's first Christmas and birthday. Will you be able to close the pub?" Alice asked Kevin's dad.

"That's a tricky one, but it's usually quiet Christmas Day. Maybe Ted will stand in for us, and his wife Edna may lend a hand."

Estelle and her mother returned to Keswick by train later that afternoon. Kevin would come over on Tuesday with his mother, so that Rosemary and Aunt Annie could make their final plans for the wedding. After the news had leaked out that Kevin was alive and well and had returned to England,

Alice's friends and neighbours must have wondered why he wasn't living with them, as they all imagined they were already married. However, Aunt Annie came to the rescue by announcing that Kevin was receiving medical treatment in Harrogate, and was staying with his parents as it was more convenient. This did mean, of course, that only family and close friends including Daisy and her aunt would be attending the wedding on the bride's side. The two older women put their heads together to devise a guest list, inviting only people on Kevin's side whom Alice had met. The final figure was twenty-six, and being such a small number, the wedding reception was to be held at The Victorian Hotel overlooking the Stray.

Kevin's last week of his leave passed quickly. He spent the last weekend with Alice in Keswick, then on Monday morning travelled to Linton-on-Ouse for his second posting to that station. They soon got into the routine of letter-writing, and at home Alice became relaxed and happy – she loved looking after Estelle and giving her breakfast before going to school. The children were learning their first carols and preparing for the nativity play which was to be performed two days before the wedding. Monique was getting bigger every day, and longing for her baby to be born. She hadn't heard from Raoul and wondered if he was safe.

On Tuesday 29th of November, Alice had just put Estelle to bed when the doorbell rang. Aunt Annie, Uncle John and Monique were sitting around the fire listening to the wireless, and so Alice answered the door and screamed with delight and surprise.

"Now who can that be? Surely not Kevin. Oh dear, if it's Michael then his leave won't stretch until the wedding," Alice heard Aunt Annie exclaim.

She pushed open the door and cried, "Look who I've found on the doorstep!" and pulled Raoul into the room. Monique tried to get up from the settee, but her size made it very awkward.

"No, sit still, Monique. Raoul, it's wonderful to see you. Come and sit here beside Monique," said Aunt Annie, getting up to make a welcoming drink.

"*Chéri*, I can't believe you are here!" cried Monique. "In my wildest dreams I've never dared to hope; I have been so afraid for you."

"Well, you've six weeks to get used to my being around, darling."

Uncle John suddenly remembered some papers he needed from upstairs. Alice went into the kitchen to help Aunt Annie to prepare a meal for Raoul, and the loving couple had time alone together.

Later, Aunt Annie asked Raoul where his luggage was.

"I left it at the station. I had to see Monique first, before I found lodgings."

"Well, it's a wonderful evening – why don't you take Monique for a moonlight walk and pick up your luggage at the same time? Your home is here with your wife; there will be ample room for you both."

Three days later Monique went into labour, and in the early hours of Saturday the 3rd of December gave birth to a healthy seven-pound baby boy. On Sunday morning, Raoul, Uncle John and Alice went to the chapel, while Aunt Annie stayed at home to look after Estelle, who had the sniffles, and to keep an eye on Monique while they waited for the district nurse to call. Monique was very frustrated having to stay in bed, and desperately wanted to show her husband how much she had seen and learnt.

"Monique, think," Aunt Annie remonstrated with her. "Stop being a wife and mother and think like a doctor – what would you tell the patient to do?"

Monique nodded and smiled. "Auntie, you are so wise; I will follow the doctor's advice."

After ten days of detention in bed, Monique decided enough was enough. She got up, dressed and took charge of her son, who was to be christened Raymond Noel, being a

Christmastide baby. Kevin and Alice were to be the godparents at the christening on Monday the 2nd of January 1944, while everyone was still around.

On 14th December Michael arrived for two weeks' leave, in good time to give his sister away at her wedding and stay on for Christmas and Estelle's first birthday, but he would have to travel back on the 30th to Scapa Flow in time to release a Scottish officer who was taking his leave over the New Year. As Kevin was on the training staff at Linton and not yet operational, he often managed to get a thirty-six-hour pass so they would be able to make a foursome with Raoul and Monique to enjoy the night life of Keswick while Aunt Annie looked after their babies.

Thursday afternoon saw the school hall filled with mothers, aunts and grandparents, with an odd father in uniform enjoying his Christmas leave. There was much shuffling of feet on the stage; then the curtains were drawn back to reveal the children. Alice's pupils, being only five and six, were dressed as shepherds and angels. The seven- and eight-year-olds had the speaking parts of the three wise men and the shepherds. The main characters, Mary, Joseph and the innkeeper, were from the ten- and eleven-year-old class. The performance started with the carol *Away in a Manger* followed by *While Shepherds Watched Their Flocks*; then came the speaking parts of Joseph and the innkeeper. The shepherds came in carrying toy lambs, and as the carol *We Three Kings* was sung, the three kings, wearing ornate crowns made from cardboard decorated with coloured paper jewels, entered with their gifts. The whole performance was a great success and the teachers were complimented on their achievement.

Alice hoped the Christmas party would go as well tomorrow, and the mothers had been very generous in promising sandwiches, sausage rolls, tarts and buns. Old Mrs Scantlebury had promised to make two trifles, which she apparently did every year. Mr Bostock would be bringing his Punch and Judy puppets along, and the school had received a large bag of sweets from a factory in York, so the children ought to have a wonderful time. And after that, Alice would be able to relax and get ready for her big day.

"I hope you won't overindulge tomorrow night," Aunt Annie said to Michael and Raoul, who had become firm friends. They were both going to Harrogate to join Lawrence and Kevin for a stag night; then staying over for the wedding. Kevin's uncle was coming over to drive Alice, Monique and her baby, and also Alice's case with her wedding outfit and honeymoon clothes in the boot. Alice was to change at his house, and his daughter Ann would be her bridesmaid.

"Breakfast in bed, darling, then a nice relaxing bath," said Aunt Annie, carrying a tray in for her niece. "Monique is keeping an eye on Estelle while she feeds Raymond, so you just take your time, you've a full two hours to get ready."

Alice did as she was told, and for the first time felt truly relaxed and had a wonderful feeling of wellbeing.

Kevin's Uncle Len arrived at half past ten, and after a cup of freshly ground coffee, Alice sat with Monique and baby Raymond on the back seat of his car. Her wedding hat had pride of place on the front seat. With a wave to Daisy, Aunt Doris, Estelle and her aunt and uncle, who were all travelling in Uncle John's car to Harrogate and then in taxis from the Renwicks' to the church, they all set off.

There had been a keen frost the night before, and the hills were iced over where the sun had not yet penetrated. Uncle Len put both his passengers at ease by pointing out places of interest and telling them of ghostly sightings in the moonlight, and jokes he and his friends had played on the girls when he was a lad. The journey was very pleasant and they had ample time on arrival for Monique to feed her baby and change his nappy, while Alice changed from her tweed suit into a pale blue woollen dress. Auntie Betty, Kevin's aunt, had been a hairdresser before her marriage and took great care and delight in brushing the bride's hair into a fashionable pageboy style. When Alice was ready, she made her final check.

"Something old?" Betty asked.

"Yes, look," Alice said, lifting her skirt to show a very faded blue lace-trimmed garter. "Kevin's grandmother wore it at her wedding in 1894."

"Something new – yes, I know, almost everything. Something borrowed?"

"Aunt Annie has lent me her pearls."

"And your blue dress and hat. You look lovely, my dear; I know you will make Kevin a very happy man," said Auntie Betty as she leant forward and kissed Alice on the cheek.

The taxis arrived, bringing Michael and Raoul to take them to church. After a brief good-morning to all, Raoul took his wife in his arms and embraced her. No one would believe they had only been apart for under twenty hours, given the long separations they had endured during their marriage. Monique was helped into the back of the first taxi, and Raoul handed their son to her and got in beside her. Auntie Betty and Ann sat on the tip-up seats facing them, and Uncle Len sat next to the driver. Michael waved them off; then joined his sister where she stood in the hall, waiting.

"Come on Ally, you look beautiful."

"Michael, will you hold me in your arms, just for a minute?"

He took her bouquet, carefully laying it on the hall table, then held his sister close, not saying anything. Words weren't needed. He had often comforted her in this way when she was nervous or upset.

"OK now?"

She nodded and smiled.

"Be happy – Kevin and you are meant for each other and I know he loves you very much. With luck this war will be over before he is fit for active service, so let's hope we all manage to keep out of real danger. I'm so happy for you both; you're marrying into a wonderful family."

"Yes, I am, aren't I?"

As they entered the church porch, Auntie Betty positioned her daughter Ann behind Michael and Alice; then went to her pew as the priest came to lead them down the aisle to the altar. The congregation rose and began to sing *Lead Us, Heavenly Father, Lead Us*, and the timing was such that Michael and Alice drew level with Kevin and Lawrence at the end of the second verse. The priest bid everyone be seated; then proceeded with the marriage ceremony. After Kevin and Alice had exchanged their vows, and each placed a ring on the other's finger, the congregation and choir sang the hymn *O Perfect Love, All Human Thought Transcending*, during which the newlyweds were led into the vestry. Lawrence, Michael, Uncle John, Aunt Annie and Kevin's parents followed, and the certificate of marriage was witnessed.

"Now, may I kiss my honourable wife?" asked Kevin as he drew Alice into his arms.

The sun came out as the cameras clicked, first Kevin and Alice on their own; then with Michael, Lawrence and Ann the bridesmaid. The final photograph included the whole family; then a fleet of taxis whisked them away to the hotel for the reception. The reception room was on the first floor of the hotel, with a view of the Stray; at one time it must have been a very large bedroom. A long table across the wall facing the windows was laid out with a magnificent buffet, and an iced wedding cake took pride of place in the centre. On a smaller table to one side of the room, the wedding presents were on show, and it was surprising what lovely gifts friends had found after three years of shortage caused by the war.

Alice stood in line with Kevin, his mam and dad, Michael, Lawrence and Aunt Annie and Uncle John to welcome their guests. There was a preponderance of Air Force blue, with only Michael in the navy blue of the Senior Service, so as guests mingled it was easy to keep track of him. At one time when he was with Lawrence and his fiancée Helen, he was introduced to Helen's sister Nancy. Groups dispersed and reformed; there was much laughter and Monique and Raoul had a lovely time – everyone thought their son was adorable. Estelle was carried around the room by her uncles, both of whom doted on her, and when Michael brought her back to her parents Alice asked him if he was enjoying the party.

"I should say so – I have just been introduced to my future wife! I told you that when I found her you would be the first to know, and I haven't told her yet but I'm sure you'll welcome Nancy as your future sister-in-law!"

"Well, you always did have clear-cut ideas and were quick to make up your mind. She is a lovely girl and I'm sure you'll be as happy as we are."

It was time to cut the cake. A sword had been procured, and more photographs were taken as Kevin's hand guided Alice's through the first slice. Waitresses circulated with glasses of champagne and cake for everyone, then Lawrence called for silence.

"Ladies and gentlemen, before we raise our glasses to the happy pair, I would just like to say a few words. We have all been through a very trying time, not least of all my parents. When they got the telegram notifying them that Kevin had been shot down, and when there was no confirmation of him being taken prisoner, we did indeed think he was dead. I watched my parents age overnight; then a few weeks later, or was it months, a young man came looking for Dad and Mam. He told them they were to become grandparents, and as Mam said at the time, it was like a silver lining to a very dark cloud. Kevin had promised our mother he would find someone very special to be a real daughter to her, and when Mam met Alice she knew this was the girl she would love. Miracles do happen. Thanks to Raoul who found Kevin, and to Monique his wife, who as his doctor nursed Kevin back to health, we now have my brother restored to us. So please let us raise our glasses to the happy couple who have at last come out of limbo: Kevin and Alice, cheers and God bless!"